WHAT COMES AROUND

A LOU THORNE THRILLER

KORY M. SHRUM

All rights reserved.
ISBN: 978-1-949577-51-8
Copyright © 2021 by Kory M. Shrum
Cover design by Christian Bentulan
Editing by Toby Selwyn

TIMBERLANE
PRESS

WHAT COMES AROUND

AN EXCLUSIVE OFFER FOR YOU

Connecting with my readers is the best part of my job as a writer. One way that I like to connect is by sending 2-3 newsletters a month with a subscribers-only giveaway, free stories from your favorite series, and personal updates (read: pictures of my dog).

When you first sign up for the mailing list, I send you at least three free stories right away. If free stories and exclusive giveaways sound like something you're interested in, please look for the special offer in the back of this book.

Happy reading,

Kory M. Shrum

For my mother, Leitha.
For my aunt, Angela.
For my grandmother, Frances.

1

I t was November in Paris. Lou Thorne, in her leather jacket and mirrored sunglasses, strolled alone from one end of the manicured garden to the other, taking in the burnt orange and soft golds of the changing trees. The cool air was a welcome change from the blistering summer heat that had lingered well into fall.

The garden path ended, opening on a little café with a glass front and economical black door. The handle and its hinges were gold, giving it an elegant face.

Lou took a seat at a wrought-iron table outside the café, the legs of the chair scraping along the gravel, and waited for the waitress to appear.

She watched the people in their warm wool coats cross the cobblestone paths, each urgently bent toward their own destinations, and picked at the flaking table with her thumbnail.

The waitress burst through the door a moment later, her long black apron slapping against her thighs as she called out, "Bonjour."

"Bonjour," Lou returned. And then using the little French

she knew, added, "*Un café et le journal du jour s'il est disponible. En anglais, s'il vous plaît.*"

"*C'est tout?*"

"*Non.*"

When the waitress waited for more, Louie realized this must've been the wrong response. With a disarming smile, she said, "*Oui?*"

The girl laughed and in heavily accented English said, "That's all you want. A coffee and the newspaper?"

"Yes. Thank you."

"*Très bien.*" The girl disappeared into the glass café again.

As Lou sat at the table, waiting for her order to arrive, she considered the cramped street again. Even though tourist season was over, it was thick with passersby.

An old woman walked a black terrier. Her flannel shawl was draped dramatically over her shoulders. A little black hat on her head. It was as if owner and pet were dressed to match.

Two men on bikes passed her carefully, their long hair pulled back in buns at the base of their necks. A slim girl wearing earbuds pulled a pack of cigarettes from her purse, searching for a lighter with a frown on her face.

Why am I here? Lou wondered, not for the first time.

True, Paris had been the first big and beautiful city she'd ever seen, brought here by her aunt Lucy not long after the deaths of her parents. The trip was meant to console her, inspire her to all the possibilities her strange gift had to offer her. And now Lucy was dead, leaving Lou more than a little sentimental toward Paris. No wonder she wandered its streets.

Sometimes she went to the Le Bobillot bistro in the thirteenth arrondissement and the quaint patisserie across from it, both being her first taste of Paris. But if she had been missing Lucy, she would've been drawn to that bistro.

This was different. Something else drew her to the city these days. Some pull that turned her inner compass toward this place again and again.

For nearly two weeks she'd woken to feel a strong pull toward Paris coursing through her, but when she'd followed it, her target was never clear.

Who was she looking for?

No one stood out. It was always too crowded and she'd been unable to fixate on an exact person. Once she'd found herself in a strange room. Its walls were seemingly made of glass but it had been too dark to see out of it. And there had been no one there. No one in trouble. No killer with an axe or gun.

Just an empty room.

It was unlike her compass to have such difficulty locking onto a target, and Lou wasn't sure what it meant. In the past it meant the person she was looking for was dead.

So why did the feeling linger? Why did the undeniable pull remain insistent?

She'd visited Paris four times this week alone, three the week before. Yet her inner compass, that unknowable force that seemed to guide her dark gift, didn't let up.

It wanted her to be here. She only wished she knew why.

Lou hoped her plan to gather more information would help to narrow down her search.

"*Voilà*," the waitress said, placing a small white cup in front of Lou, the saucer clinking delicately against the table. "*Et le journal en anglais.*"

"*Merci.*" Lou accepted the newspaper, opening it up to find the articles in English as she'd hoped.

Despite her thick American accent and the fact that she'd never made a formal study of a language as Lucy had encouraged her to do, she'd still managed to pick up bits and pieces here and there as she'd traveled. Enough for small functional exchanges at least.

French. Spanish. Japanese. Italian. More Italian than anything, since that's what the Martinelli clan, the murdering mafia whom she'd tracked for years, had spoken.

But for something as complex as reading in another language, the translate feature on her phone could only take her so far.

Who am I looking for? she asked her compass again. She wondered if her questions were too vague.

Give me something, anything to work with here.

Eyes closed, she turned the pages of the newspaper until her hands hesitated. The muscles in her abdomen tightened.

She opened her eyes and read the article title.

Mme. Delphine du Maurier's Death Ruled Suicide

Beloved feminist art historian Delphine du Maurier was found dead in her home on Saturday, October 20, at the young age of 47.

Her body was discovered in the bathtub.

Acclaimed art critic Etienne Martin, her longtime partner, was the one who discovered her in the home they shared. Due to the nature of Mme. du Maurier's injuries, M. Martin was questioned as a suspect but released after more than one hundred eyewitnesses, mainly guests at the FIAC event which he'd attended that night, had placed M. Martin at the Grand Palais during the hours of Mme. du Maurier's death.

"A wound to the stomach is not a common form of suicide," Detective Dulac told reporters. "However, it is also known that du Maurier adored the subject of suicide in art and it is possible that this is some misplaced form of artistic expression."

The couple's townhouse in the fifteenth arrondissement is renowned for its tight security and lack of staff despite the size of the home. No others were home at the time of Mme. du Maurier's death, and no other leads are known at this time.

Lou's compass tugged inside her as she looked at the printed photo of Delphine.

Black hair in a sleek bob and severe bangs cutting across her face. Black glasses framing fierce blue eyes. She wasn't smiling, and the mole to the left of her nose stood out prominently in the photo.

Was she killed? Who killed her?

Lou let her compass spin, reaching out, searching, feeling for a connection on the other end.

But there was nothing. No fixed point. Maybe there was no murderer.

A rich woman kills herself, calls it art. Probably not what I'm looking for, Lou thought, wondering why her compass kept whirling inside her. Like a telephone that rang and rang but no one picked up.

When Lou finished her coffee, she ordered another, which the waitress brought along with Lou's bill.

As Lou flipped toward the back of the newspaper, intent on searching the obituaries, her compass tugged again. She paused, finding a headline halfway down the fifth page:

Algerian Student Remains Unfound

Assia Toumi, 23, has been missing since October 16.

Her roommate, the last person to see her alive, asserts that it must be foul play.

"This isn't like her at all," claims Nada Gaood, University of Paris student and roommate to Mademoiselle Toumi. "Assia was a good girl. A very good girl. She studied night and day and always checked in with me. She told me she was going to the library and never came back. Something must have happened to her. She would have called me if she could."

Ms. Toumi's parents, who remain in Algeria, and a brother who resides in New York City have also not heard from Ms. Toumi.

Both Mlle. Toumi and Mlle. Gaood share an apartment in the

Saint-Lambert neighborhood. Toumi is one semester from completing her Master Aire in Life Sciences.

The police remain diligent in their search.

October 16.

Lou looked up from the paper. Wasn't that about when her compass began tugging her toward Paris? If not that day exactly, soon after.

There was no picture of Assia Toumi as there had been for the beloved art historian.

Lou didn't need it.

She folded the newspaper and laid it on the table beside her empty coffee cup. From her pocket, she pulled out the euros needed to pay her bill and tucked them under the saucer to protect them from the light wind cutting across the garden's path.

Then she rose and strode west toward the approaching night.

Slipping easily into the flow of foot traffic and the smell of cigarette smoke and car exhaust, Lou walked until she found a pocket of shadow, folded between two trees at the edge of the path. A woman bent down to pick up her whimpering toddler, but otherwise, there were no eyes.

Take me to Assia, she thought, and stepped into the patch of shadow.

The world shifted, falling away.

The din of voices, the screech of the Métro, and the rumble of incessant traffic were all replaced by cold, dark silence.

Am I in a grave?

She froze in place, unable to see even the hand in front of her face.

Reaching into her pocket, she grabbed a lighter and flicked it twice. On the third strike, orange flame sprang to life.

No. Not a grave.

She was in the world of the dead.

The Paris catacombs.

The tunnels spreading in both directions were lined with bones instead of bricks and stone.

The world above had smelled alive. Food, perfume, and lilacs on the breeze.

This world reeked like a tomb. That cold, damp scent of crumbling bones, the dust of a decaying world.

Yet there was something much *fresher* than old bones down here, and even the momentary smell of lighter fluid couldn't overpower the acrid stench of something chemical.

She took a few tentative steps forward, her boots scraping across the dirt floor. She supposed those bits beneath her feet were either crushed stone or disintegrating bones. Perhaps both.

The powder caked her boots, and as something rumbled overhead, more dust rained down onto Lou's leather jacket. Something with too many legs scurried across her hair, but she hardly noticed. She was too glad that it was at least twenty degrees cooler beneath the city than it had been above.

Lou stopped.

The smell was overpowering now. It clogged her nose like a soaked rag.

She angled the flames toward the wall of bone closest to her, trying to bring it into focus.

Bingo.

These weren't old bones picked clean and half ground to dust by time's patient hand.

These were slick.

Wet. Fresh.

Lou frowned. She was disappointed. She'd hoped to find

the girl alive, and hadn't. She always regretted when she wasn't fast enough.

She reached out and placed her finger on the knobbed edge of a joint, the synovial joint maybe.

Assia.

"Found you."

2

———

P aolo Konstantine opened and closed his fist, watching the blood fill his split knuckles. At his feet was a bare-chested man, his face purple and swelling.

"*Mi dispiace*," he said, over and over again. "*Non lo faccio piu.*" *I won't do it again.*

"*Di questo sono sicuro.*"

Konstantine was glad that he wore the sunglasses today. It hid the discomfort in his eyes. He didn't like doing this. He'd done his best to delegate all corrections, any cause for violence, to men who enjoyed it. And weren't there plenty of such men around him?

Unfortunately, there were times when it could not be avoided. When the message he must send was a strong one.

"We do not hurt those under our protection," Konstantine said calmly, wrapping the cloth Stefano offered around his hand. "It's a cardinal rule."

He pulled his gun and pressed the cold barrel to the man's forehead.

The man began to plead and cry.

"Gianna?" Konstantine said.

"*Sì?*" A woman stepped forward. She'd been lingering by the church's pews. The side of her face was still swollen. She needed to put ice on her left eye.

"Take this," he told her.

She hesitated until Konstantine turned his gaze on her.

Licking her lips, she stepped forward, her thick hair hanging loose over her shoulders. Her eyes wide and panicked.

When the gun was in her hand, it shook.

"Aldo hurt you," Konstantine said plainly. "Didn't he?"

"Yes," she said.

"Do you want to take his life for what he did to you?"

She looked to Konstantine as if she didn't understand. "I..."

"If you want his life, take it," Konstantine said. "His life is yours."

She looked at the man on his knees as if she'd never seen him before. As if there were possibilities before her she'd never considered.

Her spine straightened. Her hands steadied.

Konstantine thought of Padre Leo. Of all the times he'd been forced to make an example of someone, just as Konstantine was forced to do now. Padre never warned him how hard it would be.

Padre in his black clothes and thin, severe face, more bones than skin. His gray, thinning hair and dark, sunken eyes, which even when very sick had always looked on Konstantine with kindness.

I will name you as my successor, Konstantine, Padre had said. As he'd coughed blood into his handkerchief.

Why in God's name? I am no one, Konstantine had replied.

You are my choice. You are the only one strong enough to protect them when I am gone.

Konstantine remained haunted by his words. Plagued by

a belief that he was failing in every conceivable way, to do as Padre had asked. To keep his gang unified, to keep everyone in line. To elevate them above the poverty into which they'd been born, without bringing more pain into the world.

It was a fine and difficult line to walk.

"Please," Aldo begged, crying into his hands. "Please, Gianna. I'm so sorry."

Konstantine braced himself for the whipcrack of the gunshot.

It didn't come.

With a calm face, Gianna lowered the gun and exhaled. "He isn't worth it."

She handed Konstantine his gun and he nodded, dismissing her. Her hands clasped behind her neck, she started up the aisle of the church, heading toward the outer door and the sunlit streets of Florence.

Konstantine bent, placed his lips beside Aldo's ear. "She spared your life, *amico mio*. Remember that. If you touch her, or any woman again, I will do what she did not. *Capisce?*"

Aldo wiped his ruined face on his shirt. "Okay. Okay."

"Stay away from her."

"I will, I will," he stammered as two men helped him stand on quaking legs. "I promise I will."

Konstantine watched Aldo stumble toward the exit. The placid Mother Mary statue watched him go.

Somewhere in the dark cathedral, clapping began.

He turned. Vittoria, in a long, overflowing red dress, came up the center aisle. Her eyes were painted dark, her lips as red as her dress. Stefano was close on her heels.

"*Fratello!* What a show!" She pretended to fan herself. "You really are the son of Fernando Martinelli, aren't you? *So dramatic!*"

She slid into the first pew and patted the seat beside her.

"When did you get to town?" he asked, putting more distance between them than she'd suggested.

"Just now. I came to see you, of course. I hear you're in trouble, little brother."

"I'm honored, but you're mistaken. There's no trouble here."

Her presence made him uneasy. It was true that they were both born of Fernando Martinelli's wanton indiscretions, but their temperaments were quite different.

He heard from her only when she wanted something, and her requests had yet to be *pleasant*.

"I'm so impressed by what you did there." She crossed her legs and leaned toward him. "Is that conflict resolution as Padre Leo taught you?"

"You do it differently in Venice?" he asked.

"Oh yes. I never ask anyone what they want. I simply kill them. I like to do it when no one is expecting it. At dinner. Teatime. A party. Better if there's an audience. Just pull out a gun and *bang bang*."

"They must think you're mad." He softened the words with a smile.

She returned it. "Oh, I hope so. It is easier to rule when people think you're crazy. Then everyone is too busy trying not to provoke you. They don't have time to plan a revolt."

"Still," he said, "I know you're not insane. If you're here, you must have business with me. Tell me what you need."

She laced her fingers and tilted her head. "I've heard that you're having trouble with Erjon Hysa."

The hair on the back of Konstantine's neck prickled. "Where did you hear that?"

Because she wasn't wrong.

"It doesn't matter. Did you know that I am good friends with Erjon? I introduced him to his wife."

"Your good friend seized two of my ships and killed fourteen of my men."

"Yes, I heard." Vittoria affected a pout. "But I've spoken to Erjon and he's willing to broker peace."

"With me?" Konstantine asked, disbelieving.

"No, with *me*. Since we're allies, I can get him to leave you alone. But in order for me to do this, I'd like you to do something for me."

Konstantine tilted his head to mimic her coquettish demeanor. "And what can I do for you?"

"I want your *strega* to kill someone for me. Someone who is giving me a lot of trouble."

Lou's face flashed in Konstantine's mind.

Vittoria mistook his hesitation. "He is a bad, troublesome man that no one will miss. I swear it. And I hear she loves murdering men like that."

"You assume that she's my pet. That she will obey my command," he said.

"Isn't she? She comes when you call her, right?"

When I beg for her mercy, he thought. Pleading to be saved was hardly the same as a command.

And Lou Thorne was many things to him. His lover. His obsession. Part demon, part angel. The first thing he thought of in the morning and the last before he went to sleep. A face that filled his dreams, his thoughts. He ached for her the way addicts ached for the heroin on his ships.

Yes, she was many things, but certainly not a pet.

"I cannot give you what you ask for," he said.

"Fine." Vittoria's anger flashed, but was quickly concealed by another exaggerated pout.

"Is there something else I can give you?" he asked.

She regarded the illuminated statue of Mary behind the altar, with her palms turned out in offering as if she would embrace them, if only they'd run into her arms.

"Because we're family and because you're in a difficult

position, I'll make another offer. You can give me one of your boys."

"I'm sure any of my men would be happy to serve you."

"No," she said, ice entering her voice. "One of your *boys*. One of the ones I saw playing out in the courtyard. You have so many and it makes me jealous. I need an heir too, you know."

Konstantine's heart dropped. "Which one?"

The truth was he felt deeply protective of all the boys in his care. He had been such a boy once, relying on Padre to keep him and his mother safe. He saw himself in those young, trusting faces.

"I only heard a few names, but perhaps Nario?"

When Konstantine was about to agree, she shook her head. "No, not that one. Matteo?"

His cheek muscle twitched and her smile deepened.

"Yes, Matteo. If you cannot cure me of my little problem, then give me some comfort. Give me Matteo and I will broker peace with Erjon for you. One phone call from me and he won't bother you anymore."

She wants him only to hurt me, he knew. *This is a test.*

Though what outcome Vittoria wanted, he couldn't be sure. To see if he could command Lou? Or at the very least, if Louie would listen to him? Or to simply see how much power Vittoria could wield over Konstantine? He might not know the point of this game, but Konstantine still understood it *was* a game nonetheless.

"What's wrong? Why do you hesitate?" she asked with false concern. "I won't hurt him!"

"Matteo has a life here."

"I'm very good to my people. He will be like my beloved child. Perhaps I'll groom him to rule Venice, assuming he is a bright boy. Or perhaps that is the problem. Perhaps Matteo already is your chosen one?"

Konstantine didn't justify this with an answer.

"Well, then I don't see the problem."

"And if I refuse both offers?"

Vittoria shrugged. "Then you can go to war with the entire Albanian mafia and watch how many of your men they kill. They are much better at war than you are. Far more practiced. Perhaps even little Matteo will be killed. War is what it will come to, and you know it."

He did. How many times had it spilled over into his home in just the two years since he'd come to rule this clan? But transitions were always tumultuous. He had hoped the fighting would level out with time.

Konstantine's eyes fixed on the statue of Mary and her sympathetic stone face. "Give me time to think about it."

When Vittoria opened her mouth to object, he pushed his sunglasses up onto his head and leveled her with a glare. It was a trick he'd learned from Lou.

It worked splendidly.

Her brows arched and her mouth snapped shut.

"All right, but my offer stands only for a week. After that, you must deal with the Albanians on your own. Good luck to you."

She stood from the pew and fluffed the skirt of her glamorous dress, brushing imaginary dust from it.

"Now, give me that tour that you promised me."

"Matilda?" Konstantine called, and a cute girl with freckles and a gap in her teeth stopped before him.

"Yes, sir?"

"Please show Madame Rossi around and end your tour at Toni's gelateria, will you?"

"Yes, sir."

Vittoria preferred the company of women, Konstantine knew. He would oblige her, hoping her good mood would buy him time to think.

Matteo. Dear, sweet Matteo. How had she known how to hurt him? No doubt someone had said something, unknowingly arming her.

A bright, kind boy. A good-natured and playful boy. His favorite.

If he could come up with no better plan, wouldn't Matteo be safer in Venice if war with the Albanians were on the horizon?

No, his mind rebelled. *She will not keep him safe. She will be as careless with his life as she is with all the others. I'll think of a better plan. I only need time to think.*

Only he wasn't left alone as he hoped.

Stefano slid onto the pew beside him as soon as Vittoria's birdlike chatter and staccato steps faded into the shadows.

"What are you doing?" Stefano demanded. "You cannot agree to this. She's crazy."

"I'll do what's necessary." He regarded his good friend. Dark hair, hazel eyes. A thick mouth with a non-existent smile. Even as children, Stefano had been a serious boy. As an adult, it seemed his face had only one job, to convey his constant state of displeasure to the world.

And yet he was handsome.

"Just ask *La Strega* to kill the bastard. She'll enjoy it."

Of that Konstantine had no doubt. Lou often enjoyed the kill. But that wasn't the point.

"How many times must I tell you that I do not *own* her? She does not obey me."

Or anyone, for that matter.

"But—"

Konstantine interrupted him. "Padre left *me* this empire. He expected me to make these hard decisions and I will make them. Just as he did. I will solve our problems. That is my duty."

I don't know how, but I will find a way.

3

Robert King scraped his heel against the curb outside 777 Royal Street. Through the glass window that read *Crescent City Detective Agency*, he could see Piper behind her desk. The top of the desk was covered with its usual mess of papers, and her open laptop. Sleeping in the patch of sun just beyond her door was Lady, the Belgian Malinois King had gotten them over a year ago for protection.

Piper and Lady weren't alone.

King pushed open the front door. "What are you doing here?"

Melandra looked up at the sound of his voice and smiled. "Good afternoon, Mr. King."

Mr. King. Despite his urging to call him Robbie, or even Robert, Mel had persisted in calling him only Mr. King.

"Good afternoon, *Ms. Durand*."

Mel harrumphed.

"We're doing the schedule. Do you have any say where I go next week? If you do, speak now or forever hold your peace." Piper twirled a blue ink pen between her fingers. The silver rings on her fingers caught the fading light and sparkled. He caught a glimpse of the crow-in-flight tattoo on her inner wrist.

King gave Melandra's shoulder an affectionate squeeze as he leaned over the desk and regarded the calendar. He noted the hours, running the math in his head against the cases he knew needed his attention in the coming days.

Then he shook his head. "Looks good to me. Though don't you think you're working too much? That's forty-five hours."

Piper scowled. "I like having money, man. Shoot me."

Melandra made the sign of the cross. "Don't say that. Don't even joke about getting shot."

Mel had been superstitious on this subject since accidentally shooting Lou in the shoulder and nearly killing her.

Piper wrinkled her nose. "My bad."

"You know your limitations better than I do." King slid behind his desk and opened his own computer.

"Damn right I do."

The bell above the door rang. A bike messenger stood at the entrance with a large bouquet in her hand. Piper visibly straightened.

King assumed the flowers were for her, given that Piper was the only one around here with the semblance of a love life. But then the messenger said, "Robert King?"

King regarded the red lilies in clear plastic. "That's me."

The girl handed the flowers over. "I need you to sign here."

While he signed the document, she pushed her bicycle helmet back on her head. Then she left, the bell signaling her departure.

King had two pairs of eyes on him.

"Is it your birthday or something?" Piper asked, now visibly deflated.

"His birthday is in September."

"September!"

"The thirtieth," Mel added.

"Why didn't you tell me! We missed it."

"It's not a big deal when you're old," King said. But the truth was, Lucy had died close to his birthday. Now, the entire month had soured on him. He didn't think he'd ever be able to enjoy a birthday again.

"Let's not get off subject," Mel said, her own grin wicked. "Who sent the flowers?"

King rummaged through the foliage until he found the card. "Beth Miller, the DA."

Mel and Piper exchanged a look.

Piper clapped her hands together. "Yeah, buck those gender norms. Men deserve to receive flowers, too."

"It's not like that." With the lilies in King's arms, he felt dizzy from their heady floral scent. "She sends them to everyone when they close a case."

Piper snorted. "I doubt that. Have you seen her send anyone else flowers?"

King admitted that he had not.

"Next thing you know she'll ask you to dinner," Melandra said.

King wanted to wipe that grin off her face. "Joke's on you, because she already asked me to dinner. We're meeting tonight, actually. Seven p.m. at Jim's."

Piper and Mel exchanged another look, their amusement barely contained.

"She sent you flowers and asked you to dinner? Man, come on. She's not even trying to hide it."

"You two are ridiculous."

"Is she married?" Mel asked.

"No," King replied. "Divorced."

"Likes men?" Piper asked.

"I don't know. I've never asked!"

"Children?" Mel asked.

"One, but he's grown. Lives in Orlando."

Piper shook her head. "Sometimes the gays breed too, so that doesn't give us much." To King she said, "Ever seen her date anyone?"

"Yes, she was dating Phil Roper last year. But now he's engaged to someone else."

Piper slapped the desktop. "Bingo. Interest in male species confirmed."

"You're both wrong. We only talk about work." King closed down his laptop, packing up for the day. He couldn't work in these conditions.

"Where you going?"

"I need to shower before dinner." And he didn't have a vase for the flowers here. They would wilt if he didn't get them into water.

"Yeah," Piper said, leaning back in her chair. "I like to smell good for my bros, too."

The storage closet opened and Lou Thorne emerged. Mirrored shades hid her eyes and her dark brown hair grazed the top of her shoulders. Her leather jacket was tight across her shoulders.

She saw the flowers and hesitated. "Did someone die?"

"They were a gift," King said.

"Is it your birthday?"

King exhaled slowly through his teeth. "No. They're just a gift—why are you here?"

"There's a murderer in Paris."

Now all eyes were on her.

"How do you know?" King asked.

"I found fresh bones in the catacombs. Not in the public part. It must be a section not included in the museum."

King had to admit it was a good place to hide bodies. "There are a lot of those tunnels. It's possible that someone found a separate entrance. Though how they're getting a body in and out without anyone noticing is the question."

"It was only the bones," she said. "Cleaned."

"Easier to transport clean bones in a backpack, I suppose."

King couldn't tell if Lou was looking at the flowers or not. But that slight tilt to her lips made him suspect so.

"I don't have contacts in Paris." He adjusted the flowers in his arms. "If you think there's a killer, you should just take them out."

"I would if I could find them."

"What do you mean?" Melandra asked. Her bangles clanked against the desktop as she sat up straighter.

Piper had forgotten the flowers too and was now straining forward. "You always find them."

"I can't get a lock. Maybe I'm asking the wrong questions."

"Explain, please." Piper waved a hand impatiently.

"I go to Paris whenever I get the urge, but no one stands out. I kept slipping to parks, squares, places with a lot of people. So I went through the paper and searched for missing people. Deaths. I found a story about an Algerian student. When I asked the compass to take me to her, it took me to the catacombs, which is where I found her." Lou cut her eyes to King. "But when I said, 'Take me to her killer,' I got nothing."

"Nothing." Mel touched her throat.

"It's happened before, when I was trying to find someone who was dead."

Piper frowned. "So the killer is dead?"

Lou shrugged. "Maybe *Assia's* killer is. Her bones are the first concrete thing I've found. I'm going to follow that and see where it gets me."

"Her name was Assia? Pretty name," Piper said, her face crestfallen. "How old was she?"

"Twenty-three."

"Oh man." Piper pressed her fingers into her forehead. "I hate it when they're our age. Or younger. Younger is even worse."

"I also wondered if there were two killers," Lou said. She turned to King. "I had a problem getting a lock with the two Winters, remember?"

King nodded. "But you don't think there are two killers now?"

"Nothing is coming up."

King considered Lou's predicament. "I can't imagine the police will ever go down there. The paperwork and red tape that would have to be cut in order to get permission to search the entire tunnel system based on a tip alone."

He whistled.

"You could move the remains to a central place and see if that kickstarts an investigation, though if they're cleaned like you said, they won't get much forensic evidence from the bones. Examining the original site would be better, but if you've already been there, it's polluted."

"At least if you give her back, her family will get closure," Piper offered. "It might be worth moving her just for that."

King tapped his pen against the desk. "It's possible they can't even get to the section she's in. I don't know if all the tunnels are accessible. Were there entry points of any kind? Anything to suggest how the killer got down there?"

"No," she said. "It was pitch black and the walls are mostly bones. I think it's a very old section of the catacombs."

He shrugged. "I'm sorry. I don't know what to tell you. Maybe Konstantine knows someone. Europeans are a bit more friendly with their neighbors than with us."

King saw the time. "I have to go."

Piper snorted. "King has a *date*."

King felt Lou's ice-cold eyes slide over him.

"It's *not* a date," he said too quickly.

Lou said nothing.

"It's not," he insisted.

"Come on," Melandra said, rising from her chair. Her bangles clinked together as she moved toward the door. She pulled the shawl tighter around her shoulders. "After you, Mr. King."

When they were gone, Piper looked to Lou and snorted. "It's *totally* a date."

"Is it?"

"Oh yeah. But good on him. He hasn't even looked at a girl since Lucy died. And that was over two years ago."

"Right," Lou said, her eyes still on the door. "Two years."

It was 6:54 when King crossed the threshold of Jim's Jambalaya, a Cajun restaurant positioned on the edge of Jackson Square, adjacent to the stoic white cathedral serving as the centerpiece to the square. King had been to this restaurant a few times since moving to the city, both for the food and for the Thursday night poker. Tonight, he was looking forward to enjoying a delicious New York strip with a side of red beans and rice and garlic mashed potatoes.

A bright-eyed hostess greeted him and asked if he was a party of one.

"Robert!" a voice called out.

King looked up and saw Beth at a table halfway back.

She looked amazing in a maroon pantsuit that hugged her

curvy frame. Her long braids hung over one shoulder, the strands adorned in beautiful gold beads. The hair near her scalp was gray, matching the silver she'd painted on her long nails.

"No," King said to the hostess. "I'm with her."

The hostess gestured to the path stretching between the tables. "After you then."

King reached the table, pulled out the chair as the hostess put a menu down on the table in front of him. "Enjoy your meal."

"Thank you."

Beth smiled, settling back into her own chair. "I'm glad you could make it."

"Thanks for inviting me. I love this place."

She laced her fingers on the tablecloth. "Do you? It's got great food."

"It does," he agreed.

She leaned forward conspiratorially. "I always feel bad for people who have to eat at *chain* restaurants. I'd rather *die* than eat like that. Where did you like to eat when you were in St. Louis?"

He rattled off a few restaurants.

Beth wrinkled her nose. "Now you know better."

He laughed. "I do."

"What do you plan to get?" She gave the menu a cursory glance. "It's the blackened catfish for me."

King told her of his plans for the New York strip.

She lightly touched his hand. "Good choice."

King hesitated at the touch. He supposed southern women were far more touchy than their northern counterparts. Reaching out and squeezing a hand or an arm was as common as a smile down here, and Mel had told him as much.

"Thank you for the flowers," he said cautiously, folding

the menu and returning it to the tabletop. "They were beautiful."

"I'm glad you liked them. I saw them and thought of you."

Thought of me.

Immediately King saw Melandra's and Piper's mischievous grins in his mind. He shoved them down.

They're wrong, he thought. *They're absolutely wrong about this.*

And yet the seeds of doubt had been planted.

Before he could test his theory, the waitress came, took their orders, and delivered their drinks.

A full ten minutes had passed before King was able to say, "You must have a hell of a flower budget."

She looked up from her menu. "What's that?"

"You've closed a lot of cases lately. It must be hell on your office budget."

She laughed. "Nah. I only buy flowers for the cute ones."

King's face flushed, and when his steak arrived, he cut it with a little more vigor than necessary.

A commotion at the door made King turn in time to see Piper walk through the entrance and say something to the hostess. Then she spotted King and waved.

Don't come over don't come over don't come—

"Hey!" Piper bounded to a stop beside their table. "Good evening, Ms. Miller. You guys look *cozy*."

Beth turned her wine glass in the light. "What's the point in working hard if you can't play hard too?"

Piper's smile stretched wider. "I hear you there."

"I hope you're having fun, or does your boss work you too hard?"

"Oh no," Piper said. "He's a great boss."

Piper patted him on the shoulder. "That steak looks great. Good choice." Then, for his ears alone, she said, "But the potatoes have *a lot* of garlic. Better grab one of the mints on your way out."

King plastered on a smile. "Aren't you late for something?"

"Yes!" Piper said. "Yes, I am. But I didn't want to be *rude* and not say hello to y'all. Okay then! Bye."

With a little wave, she was off. Beth watched her go with a relaxed smile.

"She seems like a good girl."

"She is. Very good," King choked out, though he was feeling less than generous with his praise at this very moment.

The sentiment only deepened as their meal progressed. After Piper's appearance, it became impossible for King to miss even the smallest of flirtations. Beth's glances over her wine glass. The brush of her feet against his under the table.

As they were exiting the restaurant, King saw the little basket of mints on the podium. Defiantly, he marched past it without grabbing one.

Outside, Beth's eyes were a rich, deep brown in the streetlight.

"Thanks for a lovely meal," King said.

"My pleasure. Though I have to say..." She reached up and tucked one of her braids behind her ear. "Robert, I'm worried you might not be getting the message, and while I prefer a more nuanced and natural approach to these things, it seems I'm simply going to have to state the evidence for you."

His heart kicked.

"I find you very handsome and I'm interested in seeing if there's more here between us. Romantically."

"Beth, I'm...I'm very flattered by your attention."

"But? Am I not your type?" she asked. Her smile had faltered, but only slightly.

"Of course you are," he said, and immediately wanted to

kick himself for the adamance in his voice. "My wife just died."

Beth put a hand over her heart. "Oh my Lord. I'm sorry. I had no idea. How did she pass?"

"Bone cancer."

"I'm so sorry to hear that. Were you married a long time?"

"No." He shifted his weight. "No, actually we married just before she died. A sort of send-off, but she was in my life for a long time."

This wasn't *exactly* true. When Lucy had left him to raise Lou after Jack died, they hadn't so much as spoken for twelve years. But Lucy had never been far from King's mind, before or since.

"It's been two years since she passed," he added. "I don't know if I'm ready to..."

"Right. I see." Beth considered this, fingering the necklaces at her throat and nodding. "I understand. Well, I want you to know two things."

King recognized this attorney voice, the unmistakable final-remarks-before-a-ruling tone.

"First, I want you to know that this will in no way affect our working relationship."

King relaxed. "I'm glad to hear it."

"I am a professional and so are you. Regardless of what may or may not transpire, I think we can both agree to separate these aspects of our lives, can't we?"

"Sure we can," he said.

"Well then." She rolled her lamplit eyes up to meet his. "Should you prefer a no-strings-attached sexual relationship instead of something so *severe* as dating, I want you to know that I am amicable to that idea as well."

King must've looked as dumbfounded as he felt.

"Sex." She smiled. "Robert, I'm suggesting we just have sex."

A suppressed snicker drew King's attention.

There, twenty paces away, was Piper at her card table, with a half-finished tarot reading spread between her and an emo kid, his skateboard propped against his knee, black eyeliner thick around his bright blue eyes. They were both looking at him, but it was Piper's grin that made his face burn.

4
———

Lou pulled a can of cat food from the cabinet and set it on the counter. Before she even removed the can opener from the drawer, four soft feet landed on the stool beside the kitchen island. A pair of golden eyes watched her over the lip of the counter.

Lou peeled back the lid on the metal can.

Meow.

"Yes, this is yours." She pulled a fork from the drawer and scraped the meat into the little dish Dani had given her, the word *Octavia* written in an embellished script across the white porcelain.

Lou pushed the dish toward the cat, who made the last jump between stool and island countertop to eat it. When she was finished, she pressed her head into Lou's hand, purring.

"You're welcome." She scratched her ears, enjoying the feel of the British Blue's soft fur against her fingertips. Lou had to indulge in these moments, considering that after feedings were the only times Tavi showed genuine affection.

The cat reminded her of another golden-eyed beast. One

who required far less maintenance than this princess. At least Dani had kept to her promise of keeping the litterbox clean so that Lou didn't have to touch it.

Once the cat grew bored of Lou's attention—which was quickly, Lou noted—she hopped down and returned to Lou's bed. She curled herself into a ball at the end of the mattress, soaking up the last of the fading sunlight.

It would already be night in Paris.

Lou grabbed her leather jacket off the arm of her sofa and slipped it on. She put the two Browning Hi-Power pistols, gifts from Konstantine, into her holster.

"I'll be back later," she said to the cat. This was a strange and nonsensical exchange that had developed since Lou had agreed to take Octavia when Dani lost her apartment.

But she hadn't been able to stop herself from declaring her arrivals and departures.

Lou stepped into the linen closet.

It was pitch black in the small space. Only a strip of light shone from under the closed door. Lou adjusted her weight against the bare wall, taking in the scent of the lavender sachet she'd hung from the ceiling. The wall notches, which used to hold shelves, scraped against her jacket as her mind searched the dark.

Take me to Assia's killer, Lou asked her compass again.

Nothing.

Well, almost nothing. Lou felt the cold north wind of a barren wasteland blow through her. It was a sensation she always felt when trying to locate the dead.

Take me to the one responsible for her death, Lou tried again.

Here the compass moved. It warmed, whirling to life inside her. As it sifted through all the possible coordinates in time and space, Lou breathed.

This pull was stronger, but still not an exact match.

Take me to someone who knows something about her death.

Delphine crossed Lou's mind and the pull clicked into place. A tug through Lou's navel drew her forward. The closet fell away. The scent of lavender and the compressed air of an enclosed space were replaced by the light breeze of open air. Lou stepped out of the shadow of an enormous tree and into the twilight of a manicured park.

She recognized it as the Jardin du Luxembourg because of the iconic Medici fountain stretching before her. The dark pool shimmered in the moonlight. At the far end of the pool, the outline of the lovers entwined, the moment before they're ambushed by Polyphemus.

Ten paces east brought her out into the open, a yard from the stone benches lining the path. A man had his face in his hands, sobbing softly.

Is he the one I'm looking for?

She was still trying to decide how she would initiate a conversation when a shadow moved in the corner of her eyes and her compass seemed to redirect its attention.

She turned and found a girl, no more than sixteen or seventeen, with a dustbin, sweeping cigarette butts off the gravel path.

She wasn't alone. Five yards away was a second shadow, tracing the edge of the hedges. As the girl moved, the shadow moved. More than that, it was *closing* the distance. Getting nearer and nearer, the deeper into the park that she went.

Lou stepped through one patch of darkness and emerged through another, so close to the pair that she could smell the cologne wafting off the hidden man.

Now that she was closer, Lou realized the girl wore earbuds, humming to a tune under her breath.

Lou waited. If he made a move, so would she.

She wanted to make sure she wasn't about to kill a friend who only wanted to jump out and scare someone in jest. Yet Lou got her answer when the girl propped the dustbin against the trash and reached into her pocket for her phone.

The man leapt from the bush and grabbed her arms.

But instead of laughter, instead of a hand across the chest in the universal *oh god you scared me* gesture, the girl cried out. It was cut short when a large hand was clasped over her mouth. Her arms went up to shield her, the forearms crossing one another in defense.

As soon as the woman's back hit the ground, the man was on top of her. Whether he wanted to rob her, beat her, or rape her, Lou would never know. She was already yanking him up by his hair before any real progress could be made.

Hauling him between the trees, Lou felt the gravel of the Jardin du Luxembourg shift into the wet, marshy land of her private lake. In exchange for the manicured foliage, miles of Nova Scotian wilderness sprang up around her. The toads, which had been indulging in song a moment before, paused in their rehearsing. Geese resting on the lake after a long day of migration took sudden flight.

It was beautiful, this wilderness, saturated in the late afternoon sun.

But Lou's true sanctuary, her Alaskan stronghold, wouldn't be available for a couple more weeks, when darkness would descend over the arctic.

Lou would settle for this for now, sunlight and all.

The man lost his balance and was pitched forward. His arms went out to break his fall, hitting the water's surface and sinking. On all fours, his knees remained on the muddy shore. His arms were submerged in water up to his chest.

Lou could only guess that the stream of words pouring from the man's mouth were the typical mixture of disbelief, anger, and indignation. Conveyed by generous use of profanity.

When he saw Lou, he definitely swore.

"I don't speak French," she said calmly. "If you want to insult me, you'll have to do it in English."

"Who the *fuck* are *you*?" He managed to pull his hands out of the muck with a defined sucking sound. He tried to right himself, shake the mud off, but his arms went out to balance himself on shaking knees.

Lou didn't answer his question. Why should she? In two minutes, he would be dead.

"Why did you hurt Assia?" she asked.

"Who?" he spat.

"Assia," she said again. "The missing Algerian student. Do you know anything about her death? Did you hurt her?"

"I haven't hurt anyone. I would never hurt anyone."

"The woman in the garden would say otherwise."

"We were just talking. We were friends." He was looking around, taking measure of the trees. The terrain. If he was looking for help, he was out of luck.

The nearest town was at least thirty miles away. There was nowhere he could go that Lou couldn't follow, and no one to hear him except the coyotes and deer.

"She didn't look happy to see you. Your *friend*," Lou said.

"What do you want from me? Why did you bring me here? *How* did you bring me here?"

She chose to answer the first question. "I'm looking for Assia's killer."

"I don't know who that is, but I swear, I haven't killed anyone."

His eyes were wide and shimmering in the dark. When Lou pulled her Browning and pointed it at his forehead, those eyes only widened.

She didn't understand the stream of French that followed, but she suspected that he was praying, maybe begging. The way he pressed his palms together and turned his face to the sky suggested as much.

If this man really is innocent, if he's never hurt anyone, tell me where to take him, Lou thought.

She inched forward, closing the distance between them.

Except her compass didn't respond to the request. No home coordinates were sent.

Not so innocent then.

The man rose suddenly, throwing all his weight against her, knocking her back.

As she was falling she folded her arm so that he came down on her bent elbow.

On impact he cried out. He rolled onto his side, winded. Before he could regain his breath, she had him by the legs, pulling him into the water.

"You fucking bitch," he said.

She yanked hard, pulling him under at the same time that she sank herself.

He began to writhe, trying to untangle himself from the anaconda-like limbs holding him beneath the surface. But the water was already changing from pale blue to deep red. The temperature change was palpable, the cold Nova Scotian lake fading to a memory. When Lou broke the surface she was in La Loon once again.

The nightmare landscape of her childhood.

Its strange purple sky, twin moons, and smoky yellow mountains greeted her. As she climbed the embankment to the oil-black shore, she stared out over the red waters she hadn't seen in weeks.

The air smelled like sulfur and the taste of ash was on her lips.

A screech ricocheted through the eternal twilight, and Lou smiled.

The branches of the waterside forest bent and twisted as a beast cut through the undergrowth, barreling toward Lou at a speed that had always astonished her, no matter how many times she saw it.

As Jabbers broke through the trees, the beast barked twice in what Lou could only guess was unrestrained glee. The black, muscular body contracted as it circled Lou twice. Serpentine skin the color of tar and six legs with scaly feet that cut deep rivets in the earth. Her yellow, forward-facing eyes dilated at the sight of Lou, as her nose was shoved into Lou's belly, pushing her back.

Again, she thought of the little cat in her apartment and wondered how two creatures—infinitely different in their physical traits—could remind her so much of each other.

Lou placed her hands on the large, cool head. "I haven't been gone *that* long."

The creature cooed another frightening sound, temporarily revealing the inside of its cotton-white mouth and rows of sharp teeth.

The man spoke from the water, a surprised, choking sound.

"Your mistake," Lou said. "If you'd remained quiet, maybe she would've overlooked you a bit longer."

The plates that ran down Jabbers's back rose, erecting in a line of tension from the base of her long neck to the tip of her tail.

"Too late," Lou said as the beast leapt into the water.

Lou was still wet when she stepped out of Konstantine's closet. He was on his bed, his ankles crossed and a book open in his lap. She turned her wrist until the GPS watch lit. It was almost eleven p.m. in Florence.

He lifted a mug to his lips. "Good evening, *amore mio*."

"Bedtime?" she asked.

"I would ask you to join me, but not in that condition." He regarded her dripping body and his wooden floor.

She followed his gaze down to her soggy boots. "I'll clean this up."

She stepped into his bathroom, stripped, knowing full well his eyes were on her back. She didn't mind. There wasn't anything he hadn't seen in their time together. And if she was being honest with herself, she liked his eyes on her. Liked how clearly his hunger mirrored her own.

She made quick work in washing the otherworld out of her hair and off her skin.

When she stepped into the bedroom again, a pair of Konstantine's black sweats and a white t-shirt lay across the foot of the bed. And a comb lay beside them.

He remained in the same reading position, as if he hadn't moved at all. As if these items had simply appeared for her.

The moment she reached out for the clothes, he pounced, trapping her face down on the bed, his body braced above hers.

"*Must* you wear clothes to bed?" he purred into her ear.

She felt the warmth of him through the towel. "Then why did you put them out?"

He kissed her ear, her neck. Slowly, she rolled onto her back so she could look up into his face.

He remained above her, bracing his weight so that she could position herself as she liked.

Keeping her eyes locked on his, she opened the front of the towel.

"Is this a game?" he asked. "To see how long I can stop myself from looking down?"

She grinned and wrapped her naked legs around his waist.

His eyes slid from her face to her chest, trailed between her breasts and over her abdomen.

"You lose."

He gripped her hips and grinned. "Do I?"

He placed a kiss on her throat, her collarbone. Electricity skittered across her skin. She slid one hand into his hair, felt his dark locks curl around her fingers.

When he looked up and met her eyes, he said, "A successful hunt tonight?"

"How did you know?"

"There is still the hint of sulfur on your skin. You only have that if you cross over. You only cross over if there was a body to bring."

"You want me to shower again?"

"No. I want you to stay right here." He grazed her ribs with his teeth. "But am I right?"

"I took a man from Paris," she said.

And mentioning the city caused her to recall the park in its twilight splendor. The way the hedgerows had stood in tight formation like soldiers holding a line. The way it had been quiet, nearly deserted, with the smell of the city pressing through the thinning branches, which were quickly losing their leaves.

"Hello. Where did you go, *amore mio*? Back to Paris?" Konstantine purred, biting her ribs a little harder.

"Yes."

"If it was a successful hunt, why do you look so displeased?"

"My compass isn't working," she whispered.

He stopped teasing her with his teeth. "Really?"

She frowned harder. "Or it might be working but my questions aren't getting me anywhere."

He seemed to consider this, and when Lou fell back into her thoughts, he came to lie down beside her on the bed, putting his head in his hand.

"What have you asked?"

It was true that no one—not King, nor Piper, or even

Konstantine—would understand what it was like to use the compass inside her, but Lou thought that Konstantine might understand this much.

She repeated the questions she'd asked thus far. Who killed Assia? Take me to her killer. Who hurt her? Take me to Assia. Where was she before she died? Who is responsible for her death? Who knows what happened?

She took him through the last two weeks of her searching, ending with her night in the Jardin du Luxembourg.

"I'm sure the man I took was going to hurt the custodian," Lou finished. "But I don't think he was the one I'm looking for."

"Maybe it was the man who was crying, or even the young woman herself."

"Or someone I didn't see," Lou said. "As soon as I saw the man stalking her, I homed in on him. It's possible that I didn't look around well enough."

"Is there anything I can do to help you?" he asked.

"Do you have contacts in Paris? Official ones. Police? Detectives?"

"Yes."

"Find out if they will go into the catacombs and get Assia's body."

He considered this. "Anything else?"

"Yes," she said, and hooked her thumbs into the waistband of his sweats and tugged, sliding them easily down, exposing his backside. She loved the feel of her hand sliding over those muscles. "Help me fall asleep."

He was *more* than happy to oblige her.

5

___

The anxiety coursing through Piper's body made her feel like she was covered in ants. She checked herself in the bathroom mirror for the third time, adjusting her suit jacket on her shoulders, brushing at her lapel. Did she need to take her makeup off? She'd skipped the eyeliner and had gone for fresh-faced, but was it too much?

She couldn't remember the last time she'd fretted over her appearance like this.

Calm down. You're sweating, she chided herself. *You'll be a mess before you even get across the river if you don't get ahold of yourself.*

Dani appeared in the hallway, a tight blue dress hugging her curves. It was the color of the sea at night and it suited her.

She brushed her long dark hair over a shoulder and pushed a small diamond earring through her right earlobe. "Wow. You look great."

Piper exhaled the air from her puffed cheeks. "Why am I meeting your parents again?"

Parents were not Piper's forte. Nor were rich people. And apparently she was about to lunch with both.

"Because they want to meet the woman who saved my life. And you generously agreed to that," Dani said.

"They should be meeting Lou then, right? If I recall correctly, I was unconscious by the dumpster when Diana kidnapped you."

It was Lou who saved Dani's life, not Piper. When Diana Dennard had kidnapped Dani from her apartment and had blown it apart, it was Lou who had chased Dennard down, fought her and her minions, and even jumped off the side of a building after her.

Piper, on the other hand, had been knocked out with one punch.

Of course, they hadn't been able to tell any of that to the authorities.

The official story was that there had been a gas leak from an unattended stove in the adjacent apartment, causing the explosion. Piper had come over for a late dinner, had smelled the gas and forced her way into Dani's apartment. As far as they knew, it had been Piper who had dragged the unconscious Dani to safety.

No mention of Lou or murderous psychopaths was made. No one even asked why Piper's nose was twice its usual size.

Dani snorted. "Can you imagine Lou meeting my parents? They'd die of fright at the sight of her."

I'm going to die of fright, she thought.

Dani must've seen something in Piper's face, because she reached out and squeezed her shoulders. "Hey, it'll be fine. I mean, they're boring snobs, but they don't bite. It'll be a quick lunch, an hour or two tops, and we'll head back. The whole thing won't take us more than four hours."

Piper took a big breath. "Okay. Fine. Let's do this."

Dani drove. It was easier since of the two of them, she was the one who actually knew where her parents lived. Piper tried not to squirm and feel out of place, which she already felt every time she was in Dani's luxury SUV. It was the leather seats, the automatic buttons, and the fact that this was also the first car she'd ever ridden in where the car *talked back* to you.

It didn't help that Dani looked like a million bucks in the driver's seat. All calm reassurance and the perfect poise of good breeding.

By the time they arrived in Mandeville forty-five minutes later, Piper had chewed both her thumbnails down to their quicks.

"Oh my *god*," Piper groaned as Dani's SUV slowed to a stop in the circular drive. "You're *kidding* me."

"I know. It's a bit ostentatious."

Ostentatious didn't begin to cover it.

The two-story plantation house stood surrounded by old live oaks and acres of perfectly manicured lawn. The windows shone, gleaming as if they had just been washed that morning. Black lanterns hung from the ceiling of the balcony, with what Piper hoped were flameless candles flickering in their glass casings.

As the SUV rolled to a stop outside the front door, a man stepped off the porch. Dani let him open the door for her, and she climbed out, all smiles, placing a kiss on each of his cheeks.

He was short, only a few inches taller than Dani, with dark eyes like hers. Gray hair encircled his bald crown. He spoke beautiful, fluid Spanish, which Dani returned with equal ease.

In a natural pause in the conversation, Piper reached her hand toward the man. "Hi. I'm Piper. It's so nice to meet you, Mr. Allendale."

Dani and the man froze, exchanged looks, and burst into laughter.

But the man shook her hand. "It is very nice to meet you, Ms. Piper, but I'm not Señor Allendale."

Laughing, Dani said, "This is Juan. Our butler."

"Oh god, sorry. Right." With the Spanish and the kissing, and the door opening, Piper had just assumed this must be Dani's father.

"He just wants to park the car," Dani added.

Her face was burning. "Valet parking. Of course there's valet parking."

Dani's smile faltered as she handed the keys over to Juan.

The front door opened and a woman stepped out into the bright afternoon sun. As soon as Piper saw her, she knew it was Beverly Allendale, Dani's mother. They looked nearly identical except in the shape of their bodies. Dani was curvier from the waist down, and Beverly more slender.

But looking at the older woman's face was a wonderful preview of what Dani might look like in thirty years, and Piper wasn't a bit disappointed.

"Piper," Mrs. Allendale said with a bright smile. The jewelry on her wrists and fingers caught the sunlight and sparkled as she reached her hand out to take Piper's. "It is so nice to finally meet you."

"You too," Piper managed, trying to recover from her blunder. Fortunately, Juan was driving the SUV away. "Thank you for inviting me."

"Of course!" She touched her throat and laughed. "How could we not invite the hero of the hour?"

Piper flashed a shy smile.

"Daniella, why don't you show Piper around while I check on lunch. I think Margot is almost ready."

"Where's Papa?"

"Where he *always* is. In his office."

Dani took Piper's hand and pulled her into the house. "Come on."

The inside of the house was even more breathtaking than the outside. High ceilings with large windows, white marble floors that echoed as if they were walking through a museum rather than someone's actual home.

Dani rattled off the names of opulent rooms as they passed. Names for rooms that Piper had never considered. The *salon*, which was somehow different than the *lounge* and the *parlor*. The *family room*, which was different than the *den* and the *sitting room*. Though in Piper's opinion, all six of these rooms looked like a living room.

These people had *six* living rooms.

The bathrooms, at least, were all called bathrooms, though Piper had seen seven and counting. One for every day of the week.

When they were halfway up the grand staircase, Piper's hand tightened on Dani's arm.

"Is this a joke? Did you really grow up here?"

Dani wrinkled her nose. "Yeah. It's weird, right?"

"I feel like I should be in a maid uniform." She affected a fake British accent. "Will the miss have her tea in the *salon* or the *sitting room* today?"

Dani elbowed her. "Be serious."

Except that Piper was being serious. The deeper into the house they went, the smaller and more insignificant she felt.

I could never compete with this.

They stopped in front of a carved white door, Dani resting her hand on the golden handle.

"Are you ready for this?" she asked with a nervous grin.

"Probably not," Piper returned, pulling on the collar of her shirt as if she could undo it. "But here we go. Is it another living room? Because I don't think I can handle any more settees."

"No settees. I promise." Dani pushed open the door and revealed a bedroom. It was soft pinks with a creamy white border and trim. In the center was a four-poster bed with hibiscus flowers on the comforter. Three large teddy bears rested against a heap of pillows.

One wall held a mound of ribbons and medals. There were so many that they were pinned overlapping one another, four layers deep.

There was a bookcase full of books arranged by color, and a gleaming white desk with photos.

"This is my room," Dani said. "*Was* my room."

"That's a huge violin." Piper looked through the glass window of the display case. "You played the violin?"

"It's a viola. And yes, I did, for nine years. I wasn't very good at it."

On the opposite wall Piper peeled back the ribbons, inspecting each.

"First place in barrel racing. What the heck is barrel racing?"

"Horses," a voice called from the door.

They turned and found Beverly in the doorway, one hand gently resting on the doorframe. "You should take Piper out to see Buttercup. She'd be so happy to see you."

"No wonder Dani has such great posture." Piper backed away from the wall of achievement as if it might bite her.

"Yes, between that and the orchestra, Daniella should! Play something for us, *mi querida*."

"Oh no." Dani waved her off. "No one wants to hear me play. I haven't picked that thing up in over a year."

"*Daniella Vivienne.* I didn't buy you a Cecilio just for it to rot in a case. Play us a song."

"Mother, it isn't even tuned."

When Beverly only stood in the doorway, one hand on her hip, making it clear no one was going to leave this room until

Dani played that instrument, Dani sighed and pulled it out of the case.

"Don't blame me when your ears start bleeding," she muttered.

She twisted the end of the bow until the hairs tightened. When she ran the bow across the strings it released a horrible screech. "I told you."

But after a moment of turning the pegs, she tried again, and the sound that came out was a beautiful swell of music. The notes were lower and richer than the violin music Piper so often heard from buskers in the French Quarter, but still very beautiful.

"Play something elegant." Her mother clasped her hands under her chin. "Play that sonata I love."

Piper didn't know classical music, but what followed was a very serious and somber piece that she could imagine echoing through the *parlor*.

Watching Dani sway gently to the music, her eyes closed, Piper's heart sank.

Look at her. Just look at her.

She'd never felt farther apart from another human in her life. Worlds apart. Galaxies apart.

Dani's dark eyes fluttered open, met Piper's, and she smiled.

The song folded from its aristocratic tenor into a robust Irish folk tune. Which Dani began tap dancing along to.

The sudden shift made Piper burst into laughter despite herself.

This only seemed to encourage Dani more, and she threw herself into the folk dance with her whole heart.

Piper felt like clapping along and began to until Mrs. Allendale's eyes fell on her. She clasped her hands together instead.

Dani finished with a defiant arms-out *ta-da* pose. And let out breathless laughter.

"Incorrigible," her mother said. "If that's how you're going to treat such a beautiful instrument, you might as well put it back. I hear Regina's daughter wants to learn to play. Maybe I'll give it to her."

"Oh, Mother, don't be so serious. We're just having fun."

Piper saw the wrinkled nose and half-formed sneer on Beverly's face, and had a pretty good idea of what Beverly's opinion of *fun* was.

"Have I missed the party?" a man asked from the doorway. Unlike Beverly and Dani, he had an accent.

Dani went to him and kissed his cheeks. "Hi, Papa."

"What's that wonderful tune you were just playing? It was fun."

Beverly scowled at him. "Don't encourage her."

"It's an Irish folk song," Dani said, her face still flushed from the excitement. "Papa, this is Piper. The one I told you about."

Mr. Allendale came into the room and reached out both hands for Piper's. Before she knew what was happening, he was placing kisses on her cheeks.

"I thank God every night that you were there," he said kindly into her ear. "And now I thank you."

He kissed Piper's hands before patting them affection- ately. "Such a blessing."

Guilt filled her. *I didn't do anything. I don't deserve this.*

This guilt only multiplied under the soft gaze of his dark eyes.

A voice called up from downstairs and Beverly replied in Spanish. To their little party of four she said, "If everyone is done being *silly* up here, Margot says lunch is on the table."

The table couldn't be more grand if the king and queen had shown up for lunch. The place settings were fine china, with cloth napkins beside them. The water glasses were crystal.

When a woman appeared with a little basket, Piper was expecting bread. Instead it was a steaming towel.

It wasn't until Piper searched the table and saw Mr. Allendale wiping his hands that she understood what she was supposed to do with it.

"Thank you," she said, and cupped her hands to receive it.

The entire meal was like this. Watching Dani's every move so she could understand what fork went with which course. How to ask for more water. Where the napkin went after it went to her mouth. She thought she was doing a pretty good job, but given the eagle-eye glare from Mrs. Allendale, Piper was sure that she was falling short by the woman's measure.

"I read your piece on the city council corruption," Dani's father said across the table as he lifted his water glass to his lips. "Very good. *Very*, very good."

Dani was obviously pleased to hear this, sitting up taller in her seat. "Thank you, Papa."

"Yes, we're all very proud of your accomplishments," her mother said, forking a bit of salad from her plate. "But I think it's time you stop experimenting with this hobby and come home. If you intend to be the CEO of a Fortune 500 company by the time you're forty, you really need to get going."

Dani's face pinched. "I don't want to be the CEO of a Fortune 500 company, *Mother*. We've talked about this."

"You're wasting a wonderful opportunity. Both your father and I could offer you executive positions in either of our companies. And with a bit of experience you could—"

"Mom, *please*. I don't want to run a business. I want to tell stories."

"Stories!" she harrumphed. "Be serious. You have to think about your future."

"I do think about my future. My future in *journalism*."

Piper took another drink of water, and over the rim locked eyes with Dani's father.

Aloud, he said, "My loves. We're here to celebrate our good fortune."

"If Dani hadn't *been* in that ridiculous apartment when it *exploded*, there would be nothing to celebrate."

"She wasn't in it when it exploded," Piper said, and one look from Mrs. Allendale made her regret opening her mouth. "Technically."

Dani put her silverware down. "There was nothing wrong with that apartment. It was very nice."

Beverly arched both of her brows, as if this was retort enough.

"I don't see why you left the one I picked out for you. It was in a much nicer location."

Dani's face began to turn red, her jaw working.

Hoping to spare her, Piper said, "Actually, there were several break-ins and *two* armed robberies in that neighborhood. One just next door."

This was a lie, of course. But it was the kind of lying that Piper could do well, lying that defended and protected her friends or soothed hurt feelings.

And Piper was more than certain Dani didn't want her mother to know the real reason she'd moved out of that apartment. That it was because Dmitri Petrov, a ruthless Russian mob boss, had attacked her there. Had tortured her and hurt her there. That even though she'd survived, and had her severed finger reattached, Dani hadn't been able to sleep in that place without having panic attacks.

Beverly reached up and touched her throat. "How would you know that?"

"I work as an assistant to a private detective. We track crime in the area very closely. That neighborhood was a target because it was so nice."

"You work with a detective?" Beverly asked. Her eyebrows stayed up this time. "And Daniella too, I'm assuming, helps with these cases. How many criminals do you come into contact with when you do this work? *Dangerous* criminals, I'm sure."

She sneered these words as if they left a bitter taste in her mouth.

"Actually—"

Dani kicked her foot under the table and Piper swallowed her response.

"No," Piper said instead. "Though she would be a great resource if she ever chose to help us solve a case. She's an awesome journalist."

Mr. Allendale smiled. Beverly, however, looked ready to choke.

To her husband she said, "I told you. I told you it was too dangerous."

There was a rapid exchange between them in Spanish which Piper didn't follow. And then Dani was in it, all three of them speaking louder and louder over each other until Mr. Allendale held up his hands in surrender. He fell silent, but Dani and Beverly charged on.

This must've gone on for five full minutes, a long time to silently bear witness to an argument.

Finally, Daniella switched to English again. "Father, if you don't end this we'll never make it through dessert."

"Beverly," he said. "*Por favor, mi amor. Te lo ruego. Como tu marido.*"

Her mother sighed and lifted her wine glass to her lips. She drank deeply but said nothing.

To Dani, he said, "What will you two do after this?"

Dani took a moment to compose herself and then replied, "I want to take Piper out to meet Buttercup. Then we'll head back. We both have to work tomorrow."

Her mother huffed as if no one at this table but *her* knew what the notion of *work* was.

Everyone ignored this, including Mr. Allendale, who reached out to pluck a toothpick from a little metal dish on the table.

After a tense and silent dessert featuring lemon meringue pie and coffee, Piper followed Dani out into the back garden.

The manicured space with its splash of color and topiary was just as impressive as the rest of the estate. A light breeze rolled through the trees and the windchimes played a soft, melodic tune.

Juan waved as he passed them with a shovel in one hand.

"So this was your backyard, huh?" *Of course it was.* "Did you ever climb that elephant?"

Dani's body was still rife with tension. She only threw a cursory glance at the elephant-shaped shrub to the right of the pool. "No, I didn't."

"Are you okay? That was pretty intense back there."

"I just need some air. Come on." They took five steps toward the stable in the distance. "Wait. Let me grab a snack for Buttercup. She'll be disappointed if I don't show up with at least a carrot. Do you want to try feeding her?"

"Sure?"

"Okay. Be right back." Dani disappeared back into the house, leaving Piper alone in the garden. The light from the pool hurt her eyes, and she wished she'd grabbed her sunglasses from the car.

I don't even know where the hell the car is, she lamented. She collapsed on the last step between the house and grass and put her face in her hand.

Piper closed her eyes, listening to the windchime music.

"Are you sleeping with her?"

Piper started, turning to find Beverly on the top step, looking down on Piper in the grass.

"I...I'm sorry?"

"Are the two of you together like a couple?"

Piper wasn't sure what to say. She and Dani weren't exclusive, and Piper had never asked if she was out to her parents. What was she supposed to say?

"We're..." She searched for a word that didn't sound so vulgar as *hooking up*. "We're taking it slow."

Oh my god, why the hell did I say that?

"I'm sure you, like my *husband*, think my expectations for Daniella are too high. But I love her. Do you understand?"

"Of course." She was sure there was no other acceptable response to such a question.

"I want what's best for her. Can you look me in the eye and tell me that living in the French Quarter, surrounded by *criminals* and *vagrants*, is the best thing for her?"

Did she just call me a vagrant? What the hell is a vagrant? Isn't that like a hobo?

"Tell me that you really think that's the life my Daniella deserves."

"She deserves to be happy."

"Happy? What's happy? Getting attacked? Getting hurt? Getting her *finger* cut off?"

Piper stilled.

"Oh yes, I know about the attack. I have eyes and ears everywhere," she said, pointing in all directions around them as if these eyes and ears were going to pop out at any moment.

"It's true that I don't know exactly what happened to her, if it was a mugging or—heaven forbid—*rape*, but I know she was hurt. The nurses told me what condition she was in, and when she came home, to be honest, I thought, *Good. Thank*

God! Thank God all this insanity with the little newspaper is over—
and yet here we are. Now she's right back in that shithole,
living with *you*, and I'm supposed to be happy about it?"

Piper felt as if she'd been socked in the gut.

"And I'm supposed to believe *you* or this detective of
yours is going to keep her safe? That you can make sure the
other nine fingers stay attached to her beautiful hands? *Please.*
Look me in the eye and tell me nothing bad is going to ever
happen to her again."

Piper looked her in the eyes and said nothing.

She thought of how many times bullets had ripped
through Lou's arms or shoulders. How many times she'd been
stabbed. How closely they stood on the heels of killers and
deranged lunatics. After Dmitri, there had been Diana. And
who next? She supposed eventually, if they were in this long
enough, another Dmitri or Diana was going to cross their
paths. And what, exactly, was Piper going to do about it?

"Well then." Beverly looked triumphant, as if she'd gotten
the answer she'd wanted. "If you care about her, if you *love* my
daughter, tell her to come home."

6

—————

Konstantine woke first. He marveled at the naked woman stretched long beside him, her breathing rising and falling in a calm rhythm.

How far they'd come in just two short years. Two years since she'd pointed her gun at him and wanted to end his life, and now...

He longed to touch her, to reach out and count the freckles spread across the bridge of her nose. Freckles he could only see because of the morning light spilling through the crack around the shuttered window.

He didn't dare. He knew she was a light sleeper and that she slept as poorly as he did. Instead he lay in the glow of his happiness, his good fortune, afraid that should he make the wrong move, he would shatter the illusion and his dream come true would end.

So he slipped from the room quietly and went downstairs.

As he moved around the apartment, he played two messages from Stefano. Both were bad news. The Albanian mafia had found three of their mules in Athens and had slit their throats, leaving their bodies on the steps of the safe-house Konstantine owned there.

Another had been hit by a car and left to die on the roadside. The car accident could be a coincidence and not a symptom of the war brewing between their rival gangs, but Konstantine didn't think so.

Stefano was asking how he would like to respond.

I could ask Lou to end it. I could ask her to send a message to the Albanians and all our problems would stop, as it had with all the other gangs that had crossed her.

Not one of the gangs she'd hunted had crossed him since. But she'd hunted those men for herself, never for him.

As he pulled the coffee beans from the counter and plugged in the grinder, he considered asking her.

He couldn't imagine himself doing so.

On some days their alliance felt tentative at best. Had they really crossed so much distance that now he could ask such things of her? To *protect* the men that she would rather kill?

Padre's men. His men.

They had crossed an ocean of differences in their short time together, but he didn't believe her so loyal—yet—to do his killing for him. To ask her to do it might only push her away, break their bond irreparably.

The last time he'd pushed her to question her position, asked her to question who she really served, he hadn't seen her for months.

He didn't want her to leave him now. Or ever.

You can broker a deal with Vittoria, he thought. *You need only give her Matteo.*

He exhaled, trying to push these thoughts to the back of his mind.

As the coffee brewed, Konstantine arranged bread rolls and cut fruit on a breakfast tray. He would take it up to the bedroom and leave it on the foot of the bed for Lou before heading to the church to begin his day.

Except before his coffee had finished brewing, he felt a presence over his shoulder and turned to find Lou crossing his living room toward him.

His heart skipped a beat at the sight of her in his clothes, her hair mussed from their love-making. A dark hickey visible on her bare shoulder where his oversized shirt had slipped down.

"I stayed," she said.

He wasn't sure what to make of this statement, given his thoughts the moment before.

She must've seen the confusion on his face. "My mattress is against the window so that I don't sleep in the dark. I always slip if I sleep in the dark, but when I'm here, I don't."

Dare he hope it was because she *wanted* to be with him? He didn't dare suggest it.

"I must really like your bed," she said with the hint of a smile.

"You're welcome to it anytime." He wanted to devour those lips. "Are you hungry?"

She reached across his arm and grabbed the coffee. "I came for this."

He laughed. "Of course you did. Now that you are awake, tell me, where will you take your breakfast, *amore mio?*"

"Where do you eat it usually?"

He nodded at the desk.

She settled into his desk chair, and he put the tray down in front of her. She already had the coffee in her hand.

He was going to be late, but he didn't care. Stefano would have to forgive him.

"How did you sleep?" Konstantine leaned one hip against the desk.

"I already told you I like the bed." She brought the coffee to her lips. "Aren't you going to eat?"

Sensing more than a little threat in her question, he laughed. "Yes, I will."

He poured himself a cup of coffee from what was left in the moka, added cream, no sugar, and plucked a frittole from the pastry bag. They'd been a gift from Vittoria, and seeing it there on his plate made him think of Matteo all over again.

"What's wrong?" Lou asked.

"Nothing."

"You're a terrible liar."

"Am I? I would say I'm better than most."

Perhaps I don't want to pretend with you.

He pulled a chair up to the desk and joined her.

She didn't humor this with a response. She only watched him over the rim of her coffee cup, waiting for an answer.

"It will be a difficult day," he said. "That's all."

Her eyes sparked. "Do you have to kill someone?"

"I hope it won't come to that."

She looked disappointed by this answer, and the urge to ask for her help rose up in him again.

Just ask. It's only a question, he thought.

No. It's too soon, a second voice countered. *You must build your alliance brick by brick if you want it to hold for the long haul.*

And even a third voice, the most indignant of all. *You don't need her to solve your problems for you. Who's in charge here? Can you run Padre's empire or should he have chosen someone else?*

"What will you do today?" he asked.

"Go to Paris."

"Ah, yes. To solve your mystery. I haven't forgotten your request. I'll see who we have in the city, though it will be difficult to get anyone into the catacombs, especially if you believe it's outside the bounds of the museum."

The voices began again. *You help her. Why shouldn't she help you?*

Lou spoke, unaware of this intense silent exchange. "I'll move the bones so that her family can get her back. It'll be better than not knowing."

"If they have been cleaned as you mentioned, it is unlikely there will be helpful forensic information."

"Is there more coffee?"

"Shortly." He rose to make more.

"Don't bother if you need to go."

He ignored this and reloaded the moka. "The girl disappeared on the sixteenth of October? And the art woman died shortly after?"

"Yes."

"So you believe the deaths are connected? Why?"

Lou was at the window, looking down at the courtyard below. "My compass keeps putting them together. Half the time I'm asking questions about one, I'm sent somewhere connected to the other. It could be coincidence, but—"

A rough knock on Konstantine's front door came the moment before it burst open. For a moment, Konstantine thought, *This is it. It's the Albanian assholes and Lou will kill them and all my problems will be solved.*

Only it wasn't the Albanians. It was Stefano. "*Konstantine! Dove sei? Sei morto?*"

He saw Lou at the desk, half of a bread roll in her mouth, and sputtered to a stop in the middle of the living room. Maybe it was seeing her in the light.

Seeing her in the light of day always startled Konstantine as well. At night she seemed ephemeral, more creature than woman. The way she moved with the darkness made him question if she was even real.

But in the sunlight, it was impossible to deny that she was

flesh and blood. From her small wet lips, her dark eyes, and the spray of freckles across her nose. The color in her cheeks.

All of these things made her seem *very* real.

Stefano's eyes fell on Lou's bare shoulder.

She made no move to cover herself, eyeing him defiantly over the rim of her mug.

"*Sei un vampiro, Konstantine? È così che ottieni il tuo potere?*" he asked.

"What do you want, Stefano?"

"*Ho capito, ho capito,*" he said. Then, switching to English, added, "I thought you were dead. I see now you were just being lazy this morning."

Konstantine looked to Lou, waiting to see how she would react to this intrusion, but she remained the perfect image of composure that she'd been when he'd turned to make more coffee.

Only one thing had changed. Her Browning pistol now lay on the desktop.

When had she pulled the gun? How had she pulled it *and* put it down before he'd even turned around?

Stefano crossed his arms over his chest. "I hope this is a *work* breakfast, as the Americans say. Have you asked her—"

"*Sta zitto. O ti chiudo la bocca io.*" Konstantine sneered. "*Non ti voglio far male.*"

Stefano only stared at him. "*Chiedo scusa.*"

"I'll be in soon. You are in charge until then," Konstantine said.

Stefano looked ready to say more. The color had risen in his cheeks and he was getting angry—Konstantine could see that clearly. But instead of an outburst, he turned toward Lou.

"*Vi auguro una splendida giornata.*" He gave a dramatic flourish of a bow in Lou's direction. Then he walked out the door, slamming it behind him.

There was a long moment of silence.

"Did he just tell me to go fuck myself?" Lou asked, with a hint of a smile.

"He told you to have a great day."

"Yeah." She cocked her head and squinted her eyes. "But was it code for 'Go fuck yourself?'"

"Ignore him. He loves to push the buttons."

"Push your buttons. He couldn't find mine with a flashlight."

"Yes, push my buttons."

"Why do you let him?" she asked, leaning back in his chair.

God, he loved to see her in his clothes, his place, so at ease with him.

"I trust no one more." He thought she might be incensed by that. That perhaps, as most women would, she would take this as an insult. But her face revealed nothing.

"Why?" She held her mug out for more coffee. He poured it into her cup.

Konstantine shrugged. "We joined the Ravengers around the same time. He is one year younger, so he is like a little brother to me. He would give his life for me. And I for him."

She didn't laugh. She didn't mock him for his sentimentality. She drank her coffee and said nothing.

When Konstantine had collected the tray, taken it into the kitchen, and was preparing to excuse himself, she said, "What does he want you to ask me?"

His heart skipped a beat.

Just ask her.

Ask her and lose everything.

"It isn't important," he said.

"It seems important. What does he want me to do?"

You could tell her. You could just try it out and see how it goes.

But as he looked at those soft brown eyes, saw her

standing there in his clothes in his apartment, the smell of him all over her, he couldn't do it. He couldn't risk everything he'd worked so hard to build.

"Don't worry about it," he said, pushing his hands through her hair, and to his surprise, she let him. He placed a kiss on her cheek by her ear. "This isn't anything I can't handle."

The Mississippi River burned orange with the sunset. The water shimmered pink and gold as a riverboat made its slow approach upstream toward the downtown drop-off point. As she changed out of Konstantine's clothes into her own for the day, Lou pondered how she preferred winter sunsets to summer ones.

This particular sunset still had a bit of autumn left in it, seen in the lingering golds that had not yet been replaced by the frosty blue and lavender of the winter sun.

As she laced on her leather boots and cleaned her mirrored sunglasses, she considered Stefano's face, the way it had looked when he'd told her to have a good day.

Trouble in paradise, Lou thought with a smirk. Konstantine was having a spat with his little wife.

Why should it matter to her if there was more in-fighting within the Ravengers? All of that was drama she had no interest in. She had her own work to do.

Then again, hunting serial killers was slow work. She couldn't kill as quickly or efficiently as she was used to when hunting mafia and their mules. On those nights she'd had as many as twenty bodies to drag onto the shore of La Loon.

If he's in danger, he'll tell you, she thought.

"Like hell he will," she muttered to herself.

But it didn't matter. If he was in danger she would know either way. That drop-kicked feeling would ricochet through her guts as it always did when someone needed her.

As she pulled her leather jacket onto her shoulders, she marveled at how easy it was to dress these days when her shoulder wasn't a torn, ruined mess. It had taken seven months to fully heal, and while it was true that serial killers might be slower hunts than the extravagant bar burners she preferred, they were also less strenuous on the body.

Lou gave Octavia a pat on the belly and was rewarded with a swift, sharp bite on her fingers. Lou tolerated this, enduring the furious kicks of her paws against her palm. To Octavia's disappointment, Lou withdrew her hand and stepped into the dark closet.

It would be almost two in the morning in Paris when she arrived.

Perfect.

She leaned her back against the rough wood and listened to the dark. She had a new question to try tonight, since her others had proved unfruitful.

Who am I supposed to find in Paris? Take me to who I'm supposed to find.

Lou's compass whirled inside her. Then with a definitive *snap* it locked into place and jerked her forward through the dark.

A bedroom materialized around her. In the dim room, a man was sitting up in his bed, his head in his hands. He was crying.

She must've made a small sound or cast a shadow against the wall, because he looked up suddenly.

"*Delphine,*" he whimpered. "*C'est vraiment toi?*"

"I'm not Delphine," Lou said, recognizing the man at once. It was Etienne, Delphine's partner. He looked like Steve Jobs, with his thinning hair and the gray in his beard. At this late hour, with the deep bags under his eyes, he also looked utterly broken.

"No," he said. "Of course not. I see her ghost everywhere."

She moved to leave but his hand shot out.

"Please, stay. It's so difficult at night. It is when I miss her the most."

Lou lingered in the shadows, unsure of how she must look to him. Like the ghost of his dead lover? She'd been called a ghost before. A witch. A vampire. Even an angel.

People saw what they wanted to see. Lou knew this.

His lip shook. "Where did you come from?"

"The darkness," she said. Something about bedrooms at night, the intimacy of it, demanded truth.

He laughed, a small, sad sound. "I pray for an angel and dream of an angel of darkness. *Bien évidemment*. But you speak English. What a strange little dream this is."

Finally the crying quieted. He wiped at his eyes.

"I miss her," he said again.

"Delphine?" she asked. She remembered the photograph of the art historian in the paper. Her severe black bob and fierce eyes. The unsmiling portrait.

"*Oui*. The love of my life. My muse. My artist. She's gone, and all I have now is her art. Her beautiful *boîtes de lumières*. But there will be no more of them and these will not last. Nothing lasts." He looked up and locked eyes with Lou. "How can I go on without her?"

"Why did she kill herself?"

"She didn't! She would *never*!"

"She was murdered."

"Of course!" he snarled. "My Delphine could never hurt herself. Not when she had so much work left to do. *We* had so much to do. Together."

After she'd read those newspaper articles, Lou'd asked her compass to take her to Assia, but perhaps that was a false trail. Assia might not have been the reason why Lou had been drawn to Paris over and over again in the passing weeks.

Perhaps Delphine was the one she was meant to avenge.

Would finding her killer give this man peace?

"I can't believe she's gone. Why? Why would God take her from me?"

"I'll help you," Lou promised.

He looked up, eyes wet and red-rimmed. "Really? Will you?"

"Yes," she told him. "I will."

7

———

Dani slipped into bed and wrapped her arms around Piper's waist. Piper tensed.

Dani pulled back, frowning. "What's wrong?"

"I'm just tired. It's been a long day." And now there was a *viola* in the corner of her bedroom.

"Hey." Dani pressed on Piper's shoulder until she turned over and faced her. "What's going on?"

Piper kept thinking of the horrible conversation she'd had with Beverly Allendale in that ridiculous garden. "Your mom knows about Dmitri Petrov."

Dani's eyes widened. "What?"

"Maybe she doesn't know *exactly* what happened, but she knows you got your finger cut off. Probably why she insisted you play the viola, to see if you could."

"I told them I was in a really bad car accident." Dani searched her face. "Did *you* say something else?"

"What? No." Mostly because Beverly hadn't given her a chance to say anything. "She's the one that said, 'Yes, I know about the attack. I have eyes everywhere, yadda yadda.' She said she spoke to someone at the hospital."

Dani swore in Spanish. "No wonder she wouldn't shut up about the CEO stuff. She always brings it up, but usually it doesn't devolve into an actual argument."

Look me in the eye and tell me nothing bad is going to ever happen to her again?

Piper licked her lips. "Do you think—"

"No," Dani said. "Don't even say it. If you and Lou get to run around and chase bad guys and get beat up, I have every right to chase my dream of being a Pulitzer Prize–winning journalist. So whatever the hell she told you in the garden, forget it. It's not happening."

If you care about her, if you love her, tell her to come home.

Did Piper love her? She didn't know. She had feelings, that was for sure.

Despite the flash fire that had flamed through her eyes, Dani relaxed. "Is that what's been bothering you? Ever since lunch you've been quiet, and I thought maybe you hated my parents."

"Lunch was fine. I liked the pie."

"Oh wow. You only say 'fine' when you're trying to be nice. Was it really that bad?"

Piper thought of the wall of ribbons and the way Dani had looked playing the sonata in the middle of her monstrously large childhood bedroom.

Now that Piper knew where Dani had come from, what she was used to and expected in life, she felt an uncrossable ocean spreading between them, a gulf that couldn't be bridged no matter how hard Piper worked to close it. There wasn't enough overtime in the world to give Dani a life like that.

"Earth to Piper." Dani's eyebrows were arched, her gaze laser-focused.

Piper knew that look. Dani wasn't going to let it go until she understood what Piper was thinking. Because she was stubborn and insistent, she wouldn't table the conversation until whatever needed to be said was said.

"I just..." Piper searched for the words. "I just wish you would've better prepared me for today, that's all."

"Prepared you for what? My mother?"

"*Everything.* That house. Your *mother*. For a lunch served on lace *doilies* or whatever the hell those things were."

"Mulberry silk placemats."

"Ugh, *god*." Piper grimaced and sat up in bed.

"What?"

"The fact you even know what it's called."

"Of course I know what it's called. My mother mentions it every time we have company."

"She didn't say it to me. Probably would've been bad taste to bring it up in front of Little Orphan Annie."

Dani's lips parted. "What? No."

"Maybe just a street rat then. What does that make you? Jasmine?"

"Stop it." Dani's face burned. "My mother was perfectly civil."

"The hell she was. She made sure I knew I'm not good enough for you. Between the ribbons and the horses and the *viola*."

"I thought you liked music!" Dani looked on the verge of tears.

Piper's cell phone went off. She slipped out of the bed and grabbed it off the charger even as Dani reached out to her, but Piper stepped away.

"Hello?"

"Is this Piper Genereux?" a man asked, his voice gruff.

"Yeah."

"Can I have your mother's name, please?"

"What?"

"I need to verify you're next of kin. Please tell me your mother's name."

Piper's heart plunged into her chest. *Next of kin. Oh god.*

"My mother's name is Nadine Crenshaw."

"Thank you. Ms. Genereux, we have your mother here at New Orleans General. Can you please come down as soon as possible? Just enter through the emergency room reception area and give your name at the check-in desk. We'll be waiting."

"Now?" A pounding headache was forming behind Piper's eyes, and it was already after midnight. "You want me to come now."

"Yes, as soon as you can."

"Okay, I'm on my way."

Piper pressed the phone to her forehead and released a slow, tight breath through her clenched teeth.

I need you, she thought, hoping that despite time and space Lou would hear her. *Please come get me. I need you.*

"What happened to your mom?" Dani asked in a quiet voice. The tears had pooled in the corners of her eyes but hadn't spilled over her cheeks.

"I don't know. They told me to come down to New Orleans General. She's probably..."

Dead.

"I'll take you." Dani pushed back the covers.

"No," Piper said.

"What? Why? Piper, why are you so mad at me?"

"I'm not mad, I'm just..." *I can't spend another minute in your luxury SUV or I'm going to kill myself.*

"I can get there by myself."

Dani threw up her hands. "Don't be ridiculous. It'll be faster if—"

"No! I don't want to ride with you, okay? Just...just don't..."

Lou stepped from the shadows. Her leather jacket was open over a white-t-shirt and green flannel, her eyes hidden behind mirrored shades.

Lou's face was already hard-set. "What happened?"

"I need you to take me to the hospital."

"Are you hurt?" Lou asked.

Piper checked her coat pocket for her wallet and keys. "No, I just need you to take me there. Now. Please."

Lou reached out a hand for Dani but Piper snatched her arm, stopping her. "Just me."

Without another word, Lou hooked an arm around Piper's waist.

Then they were gone.

GIVEN THE UNNATURALLY BRIGHT CONDITION OF MOST hospitals, Lou delivered them to the shadowed walkway around the corner from the entrance. They walked in together, Lou making sure her jacket remained closed to hide the two Browning pistols she wore.

Piper exhaled slowly before speaking to the receptionist. "My name is Piper Genereux. You asked me to come down here to see my mom."

"Please take a seat over there and I'll let them know you're here."

Piper chose an empty chair in the middle of the waiting area. Lou took the red plastic chair beside hers.

"You don't have to stay," Piper said, fidgeting in her seat. "I know you hate hospitals."

Lou didn't deny it. "I'll stay."

"You don't—"

Lou lifted her shades and leveled Piper with a look. "I'm staying."

Piper nodded, her eyes on her lap, her shoulders collapsing.

Lou watched a man hold his wrapped arm with a bloody rag. He made a kiss face in Lou's direction and she opened her jacket enough for him to see her guns.

His eyes widened and he shrank back from her. Then she returned his kissy face, and he looked like he was going to be sick.

"It's finally happened," Piper murmured.

"What's happened?" Lou closed her jacket, already bored with the man.

"She's dead."

"They told you she's dead?"

"No. Not yet. But they're going to. It's not like I didn't know this would happen. I just thought—"

Lou pressed a steady hand into her back. "Breathe."

Except that when the doctor came to the reception desk and spoke to the nurse, Lou saw his face. And her suspicions were confirmed as he took a moment to adjust the lab coat on his shoulders before approaching them.

Piper's mother was definitely dead.

"Miss Genereux?" he asked, stopping in front of them.

Piper lifted her head from her hands. "Yeah. That's me."

Lou could feel her muscles tightening under her hand. *She's preparing herself for the blow.*

"I'm sorry to tell you that your mother passed at eleven forty-eight this evening."

Piper was nodding, but her lower lip quaked.

The doctor continued in a low, practiced tone. "She was unresponsive when she arrived, and we tried to clear her airway and administer Naloxone, but she was too far gone, I'm afraid. We won't know until we get the toxicology report back which narcotic it was, but given the track marks on her arms and the results of the preliminary tests, we suspect it was heroin. When we have the official results we will let you know."

Piper was still nodding, pressing a fist against her mouth.

"We can release her body to you whenever you're ready."

Piper lifted her head. "Her body?"

"Typically the body is released to a funeral home, where they will prepare the remains for burial or cremation. Just let us know which funeral home you will be using and we will take care of everything on our end."

"Do I need to identify her? You're sure it's her?"

"There was identification on her body when it was found. Her face matches the ID."

"Where was she found?"

"Outside."

"God." Piper made a choking sound. "Oh god. He *dumped* her outside?"

"You'd be surprised how often that happens," the doctor said. "Especially in cities as large as ours."

Lou squeezed the back of Piper's neck. The movement drew the doctor's eyes.

"How long before she needs to be moved?" Lou asked.

"There's no rush. She will remain in our cold storage until you make arrangements." When they said nothing, he added, "I'm sorry for your loss."

"Cold storage." Twin streams slid down Piper's cheeks. "She's in *cold storage*."

Lou pulled her up from her seat and walked her out. They made it into the shadows at the edge of the parking lot before Piper began to sob.

"Oh god, oh god, oh god." She had her hands clasped over the back of her head. "He just *dumped* her on the hospital steps to *die*. Oh god, that bastard. That fu-fu...Oh god, get me out of here. But don't take me back to my place, please."

Lou didn't wait. She pulled Piper through the dark, then from the closet into Lou's moonlit living room.

While Piper paced, Lou turned on the lamps, drew the shades.

"Sit here." Lou eased her down on her purple sofa. "Put your head between your knees. Deep breaths."

Piper was dangerously close to hyperventilating.

Lou was trying to decide if she should steal some oxygen when Piper tumbled into her bed and began to cry in earnest.

Lou let her, kicking off her boots and climbing in after her. She pulled her against her body and held her tight, the sobs strong enough to shake the both of them.

This is what Konstantine did, she thought. *When Lucy died, he held me like this.*

Her throat tightened.

For a long time it was only tears. Only the deep release of her grief. Then the words came.

"I knew this was going to happen. I *knew* it. I don't even know why I'm crying when I knew this was going to happen."

"She was your mother." Lou pressed her cheek against Piper's hair.

Lou hadn't had a great relationship with her own mother. The woman had been cold, critical. But Lou had still cried when she died. Still dreamed of her, longed for her.

"It'll get easier," Lou whispered.

She held Piper until she fell asleep. Piper had been still for about thirty minutes when the watch on Lou's wrist buzzed. She turned its face until she found the page. It was Dani's number.

Quietly, she slid from her bed. When she was sure Piper hadn't woken up, she stepped into her dark closet.

"Oh thank God," Dani said as soon as she saw her. "Is Piper okay?"

"Her mom died."

"Oh no. How?"

"A drug overdose."

Dani's eyes widened. "Oh wow. I...I had no idea."

"She'd been an addict for a long time."

"Where is she now?"

"In my apartment, sleeping."

"But Octavia's there. She's super allergic."

"I'll clean the apartment."

"Why? Just bring Piper back here."

"She told me she didn't want to come back here."

"So she'd rather go into anaphylactic shock than be here with me?" Dani clasped the back of her neck. "What did I do? I only asked her to have lunch with my parents."

"Maybe she didn't want you to see her upset."

Dani's anger collapsed in on itself as she pulled the comforter to her chest. "Is she really upset? What am I saying. Of course she's upset."

Dani put her head in her hands.

"Okay. Fine. Maybe it's not personal. Maybe it's just bad timing. Does she need to plan a funeral? Was there a will? Does she know what cemetery her mom wanted to be buried in? Or if she wanted cremation?"

"I don't think she knows."

"Have you planned a funeral before?" she asked. "I haven't."

"I was only twelve when my parents died, and King handled Lucy's death."

"Okay. We'll figure it out. If Piper isn't in a state to handle it, we will. I'll talk to King in the morning and ask him what needs to be done."

Lou, sensing the end of the conversation, stepped toward the darkness.

"Wait," Dani called out.

Lou turned back.

"She...she might not want to see me right now, but she needs someone. Stay close to her, okay? I've never lost a parent, so I don't know what she needs, but I'm sure you do."

Yes, Lou thought. *I know what she needs.*

8

———

Lou found Konstantine in the basement of his church. He sat behind his mahogany desk, a mound of papers spread out in front of him and the blue light of his computer screen illuminating his face. Behind him the fireplace crackled, adding a delicious warmth to the chilly room.

She stepped forward from the dark corner of his office, but he didn't look up.

She made it all the way to the edge of his desk without earning so much as a glance.

"Did you sleep well?" he asked coldly without looking up.

She tried not to smile. *Jealous much?* "I haven't slept."

This earned her a look. He was searching her face, her body, for injuries.

"I brought Piper back to my apartment."

His brows lifted. "Did *she* sleep on the sofa or in your bed?"

"My bed."

Color rose in his face.

Lou pushed her mirrored glasses up on the top of her head. "I didn't sleep with her. Her mother died."

The jealousy evaporated in an instant.

"I'm sorry to hear that. How did she pass?"

"A drug overdose."

His expression darkened. "Have you come to punish me for that?"

Lou understood that Piper's mother had made her choices. Just because Konstantine sold drugs to the four corners of the earth didn't mean he'd injected it into her veins.

More than that, she'd seen Nadine hurt Piper with her own eyes. When Piper had begged her, pleaded with her to leave her abusive boyfriend, she'd shoved Piper away.

Lou didn't need any other reason to dislike the woman than that.

"No." Lou pressed her cold cheek to his warm one. "Unless you're in the mood to be punished."

He laughed, but she still sensed tension in him. In the tight way he held his body. If it wasn't jealousy, then what was bothering him?

She glanced at the paper on his desktop, looking for a clue, but understood none of it.

"Problems at work?" she asked.

"A few." He rubbed his jaw. "Have you always been so efficient at your work? Was it always easy for you?"

She snorted. "No."

She thought of Tito Rubio, the drug mule she'd paid $70,000 to in order to find information on Benito Martinelli, when she could've just popped into Benito's cell and taken him. She'd stolen that money to pay him and had told herself that the family had needed it.

And there had been a hundred other things she'd gotten wrong in her early hunting days. Left trails that others could follow, walked in front of cameras without her glasses on, asked the wrong questions. Her carelessness.

Then there was her first kill—Gus Johnson, the partner who'd betrayed her father. The clumsy way she'd struck him with her father's knife, nearly breaking her back trying to drag him to La Loon.

She told Konstantine these stories, enjoying his laughter.

Finally, when the amusement died away, he said, "Even a deadly lioness must begin as a cub."

She pushed her fingers through his hair. "Why do you want to know about my mistakes?"

He closed his eyes, clearly reveling in her touch.

"I'm struggling with a difficult decision."

"About?"

"I want to avoid death and violence, but in order to do that, I will have to give up something I don't want to lose."

"What don't you want to lose?" she asked.

Instead of answering her, he brought her fingers to his lips and kissed her knuckles.

"I spoke to my contact in Paris. She'll help you and King conduct your interviews the day after tomorrow. I assume you'll be available."

So he isn't going to tell me.

"Assuming Piper can be left alone." She leaned forward, placing a kiss on his neck, once, twice, until he pulled her into his lap. She allowed this, letting him wrap his arms around her and hold her close.

Only when she allowed him to hold her did most of the tension release from his body.

With her lips on his ear, she whispered, "Is this a bad time to ask you to babysit a cat?"

. . .

PIPER WOKE TO SUNLIGHT CUTTING ACROSS HER FACE. FOR a moment, she only looked at the white ceiling and wondered where she was. Her face was puffy and her throat was sore, but she didn't recognize the bed.

She smelled the sheets and immediately knew who they belonged to. *Lou.*

Then she remembered.

The temporary ignorance of her confusion was replaced by the weight of her grief. The closet door opened and Lou stepped into the room.

She'd changed clothes. Now she was wearing black cargo pants, with a black t-shirt under her leather jacket. Her mirrored sunglasses were pushed up on her head.

She offered Piper a cardboard box with two slices of pizza inside. Piper recognized the name from the pie shop in New York that they'd discovered a couple of months ago.

Lou sat down on the bed beside her. "Can you eat?"

"I don't know," she admitted, looking at the pizza. It smelled amazing, but her mouth felt like it was full of ash.

"Take this." Lou pulled allergy medicine out of her pocket and handed it over to Piper along with a can of soda from the plastic bag between her feet.

"Oh shit. Where's Tavi?"

"Konstantine took her for a few days. I'm going to vacuum, but I wanted to wait until you woke up." She shook the box at her again. "Take this until I can get rid of the cat hair."

Piper cracked open the soda can and took two of the allergy pills. "Where's my phone? I need to check my classes. I think I missed a paper."

Lou pointed at the wall where a charger connected to Piper's phone. "Melandra spoke to your professors. She got a note from the hospital and sent it to the school. They're giving you a two-week extension on everything. King said they'll give you more if you press them."

Piper's heart flopped. "Everyone knows what happened to my mom? How she died?"

Lou nodded. "They want you to take a couple of days off. I told them you'd be here."

There was a stack of Piper's clothes and a few toiletries sitting on Lou's couch as well as her laptop and backpack.

Lou followed her gaze and said, "Dani helped me pack that."

The pizza soured in her mouth. "What did she say?"

"About you staying here? She understands."

Does she?

Piper seriously doubted it. God, why did she have to start that fight at the very worst moment?

Lou took a huge bite of her own pizza slice. "She wants to know if your mom had a will."

Piper laughed. A tight, choked sound. "No. She wasn't very *future* oriented."

"Do you know what her wishes were?"

"We never talked about it. My dad is buried in Greenfield. I guess I should put her there."

Lou reached into the bag and cracked open a soda for herself. "Is there anything else you need from your apartment?"

Piper couldn't think of anything. She shook her head. "Thanks for the pizza."

"You've only eaten half of your slice."

"My stomach hurts and my throat hurts. I can't tell if that's from the cat or the crying."

Lou took the food from Piper. "Take a shower and I'll air this place out."

Piper untangled herself from Lou's sheets and padded to the bathroom at the end of the hall. She found a towel and washcloth already laid out for her beside the shower stall. She turned on the water as hot as she could stand it and stepped into the steam.

After she'd got out, dried off, and dressed, she found Lou in the living room, hard at work. The vacuum stood in the middle of the living space with the cord trailing along the floor. One of the windows was cracked, letting in a chilly November wind.

The bed had been stripped, the pillowcases and sheets rolled up into a wad in the corner of the room. The fresh sheets Lou was tugging on were a soft sage green.

Then Lou gathered the old bedding up and shoved it into the laundry basket in her closet.

"How do you feel now?"

"Better," Piper admitted. "But these allergy meds are serious."

She was worried she would fall asleep before she could brush her hair.

"Lie down. I put the food in the fridge for when you want to try again." She turned and saw Piper's face. "What's wrong?"

Tears stood out in Piper's eyes. "I told you I was going to be a great friend, but you're the one who keeps taking care of me."

"You threw me two birthday parties."

"That's not the same and you know it."

Lou considered the river outside the window, letting the silence stretch long between them. Then she said, "Lucy would say friendship isn't about keeping score."

Not about keeping score.

But if Piper wasn't useful to someone, would she even be important to them?

"I have to take King to Paris," Lou said. "But I'll be back tonight."

"You're going to leave me alone here?" It came out needier than she'd meant it to, but almost as soon as she'd said it, she was relieved. Time alone meant she could cry, fall apart, and not embarrass herself in front of Lou.

"I'll be back in a few hours."

"Okay." Piper crawled under the covers with her phone, not failing to notice that the tissue box was already beside the bed, along with two bars of chocolate. "You think of everything. Thank you."

Lou pushed her sunglasses down over her eyes and grabbed her leather jacket off the arm of the couch. "You're going to be out in thirty seconds."

It was true—Piper's eyes were heavy. The allergy meds were working very well.

Piper pulled the clean sheets up over her shoulder. She felt safe and warm in Lou's bed.

She was almost asleep when she heard Lou say, "Call me if you need me."

9

____

King braced against the wall that appeared in front of him as the uneven cobblestones formed beneath his feet. He sucked in a breath and swore.

"I hate traveling with you," he admitted.

Lou stepped forward, separating herself from the shadows. "We wouldn't have made this appointment if you'd booked a flight."

He adjusted the duster jacket on his body and straightened. "Which museum are we going to?"

"Museum of Modern Art. Du Maurier had an office there. Konstantine's contact is supposed to meet us at the entrance so she can flash all the proper credentials."

"Hopefully Delphine's colleagues speak English. My French is shit. Yours?"

Lou shook her head. "I can order things. That's it."

"How far away is the museum?"

Lou pointed up the road. "It's close."

They stepped out of the cramped side alley and into the

flow of foot traffic. King didn't get far before he was pulling gum out of his pocket.

"Paris always makes me wants to smoke," he said. "They really relish it here, don't they?"

"That's gum in your hand."

"It's for the cravings." He unwrapped two thin minty sticks and put them into his mouth. "Hey, we should bring pastries back for Piper. How's she doing?"

"She ate half the pizza I brought her. That's all I've seen her eat."

King's stomach knotted. He knew that feeling. How hard it was to force yourself to eat, shower, *breathe* when someone you loved died.

Lou was watching a small group laughing at a bus stop. When one of them, a young woman, threw her head back, King wanted to snatch the cigarette out of her hand and take a long drag. "We made arrangements with the funeral home to collect Nadine's body. They found Piper's father's grave in Greenfield. They said he'd prepaid to have his wife buried with him, so that's one less thing to worry about."

"Tell me how much money you need. I'll pay it."

King wasn't surprised to hear Lou had money to spare. Lou's living expenses were low, and the principal balance of the money her parents had left in trust when they died had remained largely untouched in the years since. Her monthly payout likely far exceeded her actual needs.

More than that, King suspected Lou wasn't the kind of woman who wanted *things*.

Guns, maybe. But she probably stole those. Paying for them left a paper trail.

Lou rolled her shoulders. "I don't want her to worry about money, on top of everything else."

King couldn't help but smile. It touched him to see how

much Piper had grown on her in the years they'd known each other. *Your wish came true, Lucy*, he thought.

"Me either. I'll go halfsies with you." They passed a boulangerie, and King was hit with the tantalizing smell of warm bread. "I want to stop here on the way back."

Lou barely acknowledged him. She was watching their surroundings. She looked a little out of place in the sunlight. He'd come to think of her as a creature of darkness. Nearly a vampire.

But now, in the sun, he saw she had freckles.

Like Jack.

His heart kicked.

"You need to ask Piper what she wants to do about her mother's estate. Because there's no will, it'll go into probate. There's probably nothing of value except for the house, if there's any value left after back taxes. You can search the place for important documents and see what constitutes the estate. It needs to be done sooner rather than later, but I can't imagine she's feeling up to it."

"I'll take Dani tomorrow," she said. "Watch out."

King had been craning his neck to look through the glass window into the bakery, counting the cakes and breads on display. He turned back just in time to dodge a guy on his skateboard.

"Sorry," he muttered, angling his broad body to let him pass.

"This is the museum." Lou nodded toward the large building coming into view. King let her lead as they walked past the burbling crystalline fountain and lines of tourists trying to get inside.

"Monsieur King!" a woman called, and King turned in time to see a petite blonde with thin lips and narrow eyes waving him down. He returned the wave, changing his trajectory.

When they were closer, King extended his hand. "Bonjour. Are you our contact?"

"Bonjour," she said, returning his handshake. "And yes, I am the one you are looking for. I'm Uma Bernard."

Her eyes cut briefly to Lou, but after a polite smile, she turned her attention back to King.

"Is it just the two of you?" Uma asked.

"Yes."

"Good," she said. "Our appointment with Director Mercier is in seven minutes. Shall we go?"

She didn't really wait for an answer before she pulled open the glass door to the museum and marched inside.

Lou followed her with King on their heels. As workers stopped them at the turnstile, their escort showed her badge and had a short, seemingly fierce exchange in French, before they were allowed to pass.

They walked past patrons and art galleries, King enjoying the high ceiling and sacrosanct feeling he usually got in large museums. On the second floor they came to the administration wing, and after another exchange, were allowed into a locked office, opened only by the guard's keycard.

King found himself in a reception area, a young man with neat, slicked black hair typing away furiously on his keyboard.

"*Bonjour!*" Director Mercier called, doing up the lowest button on his suit jacket and stepping toward them. He was tall, like King, with salt-and-pepper hair and thick black spectacles. He'd shaved that morning and bore a small cut on his right cheek. "*Il est agréable de vous rencontrer.*"

"They would like to speak in English," Uma announced, and the man immediately switched languages.

"Ah, of course," he said. His words were not nearly as accented as King was expecting. "Please come into my office."

When they were seated comfortably in the little office with a large window overlooking the courtyard, they were asked if they would like coffee or tea. Both King and Lou declined. Uma accepted.

"What can I do for you today? I understand that you have questions about Madame du Maurier."

It was clear from Lou's position beside him that she didn't intend to speak unless absolutely necessary. Her posture was alert but relaxed, her gaze carefully hidden behind her sunglasses.

King was fine with taking the lead, though he had only the information that Lou had given him on the historian's death and what he'd been able to find online.

"Yes, did you know Delphine du Maurier well?"

"*Bah, oui*," he said. "She has worked in this museum for over twenty years. Of course I knew her."

"Do you think she committed suicide?"

He leaned back, lacing his hands over his lap in a perfect poise of contemplation.

"Had you asked me a year ago, I would have said it was impossible. Delphine seemed very happy with her life and her work. But all artists are temperamental."

He gave a noncommittal shrug.

King pulled a notepad and pen from his pocket. "When you say 'her work,' are you referring to her articles?"

"No, her art."

"I wasn't aware that she created art as well as studied it."

"But of course," he said with an exaggerated nod. "It is true that she was known for her opinions. If a piece was misogynistic or hyper-masculine in any way..." He pulled at his collar as he released a nervous laugh. "She would... *écarteler?*"

"Tear it apart," Uma offered.

"*Oui*. Tear it apart."

King looked at his notepad and read the title of one of Delphine's articles. "*La beauté des femmes mortes.*"

The director laughed. "Not a good translation, but yes, that was a popular feminist piece. Did you read it?"

"I tried," King said with a friendly smile. In truth, he'd only been able to find the abstract in English. The rest had been in French, and all the translation apps he'd found had failed to render the ideas into something understandable.

If the director thought less of him for this, he didn't say so. "It was an argument that women were more beautiful when dead than men."

Lou shifted beside him. King made a point not to look over.

"She meant this figuratively, I hope," King said. "In some artistic sense, you mean."

"She was talking about how when artists paint men in the arms of Death, it is dramatic, sensationalist. It shows vigor. Courage." He balled his fist and shook it for good measure. "However, when *les artistes* paint women in such ways, it is *sucré*. Beautified. They rob the women of their moment of transformation. Their deaths deserve to be as glorious as a man's."

"I see. Inspector Dulac, in his official interview, also mentioned Delphine had an interest in suicide. I assume she also wrote about this?"

"*Oui, c'est vrai.* She argued that women were rarely depicted as subjects in art about suicide. Suicide is often portrayed as power over oneself, one's destiny. But women are not given such power over their bodies in life or in art. This was Delphine's belief."

King jotted some notes down before asking, "What can you tell me about the art she made?"

"I can do you better," he said.

King arched a brow. "Do me better?"

Not the offer I was expecting today.

Their guide said something in French, quickly under her

breath, and the director lit up. "Ah, yes. Sorry. I can do you *one* better." He rose from behind his desk. "One moment, please."

For an awkward moment, the three of them sat in the silent room saying nothing.

Then the director returned with a handful of small black boxes. He placed them on the desk in a single row.

"Delphine made these," he explained, his hair falling forward into his eyes as he arranged them.

"Black boxes," Lou said skeptically.

The director laughed and pressed a button on one of the boxes. It lit up, illuminating the contents.

In this particular box, it was a beautiful butterfly. It was wing-pinned in place, suspended to give the impression that it was in the throes of dying, transfixed forever, in that moment before complete death. The main part of its body was cut open as if to reveal its inner workings fighting to keep it alive.

"She was trying to dissect the two layers in the wings. But they were too delicate," the director said with a touch of sadness in his voice. "She had better luck with the caterpillar."

He turned on the light and the second box revealed a similar display. A caterpillar, curling in agony, on the brink of death but with one portion of its torso dissected and on display.

The third box contained a mouse, its mouth open in a silent scream, one of its legs cut open to reveal the workings beneath.

"How many of these do you have?" King asked, trying to write a description of the light boxes on his notepad.

"Oh, we have nearly a hundred here. She had been fighting for years to get the work on display, but it was always denied."

"Who refused to show her work?"

"Albert Kavanaugh. They did not get along and he is Head of Collections. He decides what we display. I have final authority on the matter, of course."

"And you never sided with Delphine?"

"*Non.* To be honest, to me this is not *true* art. Not because it is macabre but because it is too scientific. They are very skilled but there is no feeling. No heart. For me, art is about revealing what is inside the artist's heart. I see none of Delphine's heart in this."

King considered the vivisected creatures. There was a coldness to the light boxes, that was true. A clinical style in the way the creatures had been frozen, broken open, and their misery put on garish display.

"Can you think of anyone who might want to hurt Delphine?" King asked.

"Being stabbed in the stomach is a crime of passion, *non?* Perhaps it was an accident."

King waited for his question to be answered.

"I can think of many who would be pleased to know that Delphine du Maurier was no longer in this world. But I can't think of anyone brave enough to confront her. She was...*effrayant?*"

"Terrifying," Uma said.

"Yes," the director said, peering into the light box with a considerable frown on his face. "She was terrifying."

As King went into the boulangerie to order a baguette for Mel and cakes for Piper, Lou stood on the sunlit street outside and replayed the meeting in her mind. There was something about the director's interview that had bothered her.

It wasn't the director, she decided. There had been something about those light boxes.

They had made her think of the room Nico, Konstantine's nemesis, had tried to trap her in. Every inch bathing her in relentless, inescapable light.

And there was something about the dissected creatures that had troubled her. What had the director said? The animals had to have been alive when Delphine had begun her work. In order for those expressions and their fear to be preserved for all time, she'd had to capture them at the right moments.

But those light boxes...

Where did I see something like that before?

Her compass whirled inside her, but before it could click into place, King came out of the bakery carrying two plastic bags. "Do you fancy a coffee? They didn't have any in there."

"I want to check something," Lou said. "Are you ready?"

King was not, as evidenced by his face. "Sure. It's cold out here. The cakes will keep for another pitstop. But hey, before we go, I need to tell you..."

King's sudden blush made Lou stiffen. "What is it? Are you sick?"

Sometimes King got nauseated when he traveled with her.

"What? No." He frowned.

"Is someone dying?"

He puffed out his cheeks. "No one is dying. It's about what Piper said about my date."

"I thought it wasn't a date."

"It wasn't," he insisted. "I just wanted to make sure you *knew* it wasn't a date."

"Piper said she offered you casual sex instead."

King threw back his head and sighed at the sky. When he was ready, he spoke slowly. "All I'm trying to say is that I'm not ready. I loved—*love*—your aunt very much. I don't want you to think I'm in a hurry to replace her."

Aunt Lucy. Lucy with long hair and bright eyes. Her penchant for yoga and vegan food. The fact that she tried every day to be a good person and still swore like a sailor and hated people half of the time. That she'd never wanted nor asked to raise a child, but when Lou's parents had been murdered, Lucy had shown up and taken Lou into her life without hesitation.

More than that, she'd shown Lou the beauty of her gift, the power of it. She helped her to let go of all her fear.

And Lucy and King? What did she think of them?

Lou knew that Lucy and King had something in the past, and that they'd rekindled it in the last few months of her life. Otherwise, she knew nothing about what they'd meant to each other.

And it was none of her business.

Yet here was King, concern filling his face. The way he was waiting for her to say something, anything, as if her opinion on his dating life mattered.

"I don't think Lucy would care," she said finally. "She would say you don't have anything to prove to me, or anyone."

King looked away, up the street toward the river, as if the answer were out there somewhere. Then he said, "Sometimes I have dreams about her. She's always telling me to relax."

Lou snorted. "Sounds like her."

"I'm *not* ready to find anyone else," he said again. "But I'm glad you wouldn't hold it against me if I did."

Lou simply stood there, eyes hidden behind her shades, and let King assume whatever he needed to assume about her thoughts.

"All right, let's get out of here," he said finally, nodding once, sharply, as if they'd agreed upon something.

They walked until Lou found a shadowed alleyway. There was a couple locked in a kiss beneath the awning of a boutique, but they didn't even look up as Lou took King's arm and melded into the darkness.

When the world materialized again, they stood beneath a shady canopy of trees. Tombs rose around them in every direction. Many of the stones were stained black by time and acid rain.

"Where are we?" he asked, looking unsteady on his feet.

"Père Lachaise, by the look of it."

"What were you hoping for?" he asked.

"I wanted to know if Delphine was really dead. I had a thought during the interview that maybe she'd faked it as an art stunt."

King's brows shot up. "Good idea. But we're in a cemetery."

"And there he is."

Lou pointed at a man kneeling in front of a gravestone. The grave marker was large, made larger by a sculpted angel, a weeping angel, her face hidden by her folded arms, wings drooping down her back.

"That's Etienne," she told King. "Her partner."

"She must be dead then. Doubt he'd be crying over an empty grave."

"Unless it's for show," Lou said. But when she asked her compass to take her to Delphine, she was tugged forward toward the grave. She didn't think Delphine had faked her death. She was fairly confident that the woman was in the ground.

"Does he speak English?" King asked, adjusting the sacks in his arms. "I can interview him if he does."

"He spoke it the other night," she said. She didn't elaborate that in his grief, Etienne had also spoken French, calling her Delphine, clearly mistaking Lou's appearance in his dark-ened bedroom for the ghost of his dead love.

Lou took the cakes from King. "Go talk to him."

"Where are you going to be?" he asked.

How to explain that she didn't want Etienne to see her in the daylight?

"I'll be right back," she said.

King didn't seem perturbed by this. He was already pulling his notepad from his pocket and walking toward the crying man.

Lou watched for a moment, sticking close to the thick shadows.

Take me to Delphine's killer, she thought, hoping her compass might work this time.

But it settled on the cold, desolate nothing again.

There was no killer. Could Etienne be wrong? But he'd seemed so certain. Maybe he'd already killed the killer.

Would he tell her if he had?

King's low voice rumbled through the cemetery and the man turned, his eyes bleary from crying. He pulled his glasses off his face and wiped his tears.

Then he looked up suddenly and met her gaze.

Can he see me?

She was deep in the shadows, barely more than an outline beside the crypt resting between two old-growth trees.

Can he even see me?

She thought, by the small smile she saw cross his face, that he could.

10

____

Ten boys sat in a tight circle. Knee to knee, they spoke in low tones beneath the covered table, the statue of the Virgin Mary watching them from above.

Matteo held a flashlight under his chin, illuminating his round face, as the other boys listened raptly to his story.

"*C'era una volta...c'era La Strega*," he whispered. "This witch cursed the Martinelli family."

"Why?" Franco asked. He was the youngest of them, only four years old.

"*Sta 'zitto.* Do you want me to tell the story or not?"

Crestfallen, Franco fell silent.

Matteo liked it when the others listened to him, paid attention to what he said as if it mattered.

Matteo wasn't the oldest. Both Monte and Nario were two years his senior, but they all listened to him the same when he told these stories.

Perhaps that was why he couldn't resist when they asked him to do it, usually at the end of the day, after their schooling and their work, here in their own little hideout.

"There was a curse on the Martinelli family," Matteo began again. "The *capo di capi*, Fernando Martinelli, made a deal with *La Strega*. Martinelli promised to give his soul in exchange for power and money and girls."

"Why would he want girls?" Franco asked.

Nario shushed him with an elbow. "*Idiota. Non sai nulla*."

Matteo continued. "*La Strega* agreed. She would give the *capo di capi* everything he wanted as long as he handed over his soul when she wanted it. But when the day came for Fernando to pay up, he tried to cheat her. He didn't want to lose his soul. So he betrayed her."

"Who? The devil or the witch?"

"Shut up, idiot. They're the same person."

"How did he betray her?" Brando asked. His big ears cast even larger shadows than usual in the flashlight's beam.

"He sent his son Angelo to kill her and her family."

"Did it work?" Monte asked, chewing his thumb mercilessly.

"*Sì*," Matteo said. "Her family died, but the strega didn't. So she cursed them."

All the boys' eyes grew bigger, doubling in size. Many stopped blinking.

"One by one," Matteo said gravely, "she hunted the Martinellis down and killed them. She took back the money, the power, and the girls."

Monte elbowed Nario. "*Chissa' che avra' fatto con le ragazze*."

Matteo ignored this. "All the Martinellis died until there was only one. *Il nostro Konstantine*. And she came for him too."

Several of the younger boys gasped. Nario was leaning forward as if to hear Matteo even better.

"But Konstantine is smarter than any of those guys. He was ready when she came."

"What did he do?" Franco tried to sit up taller, adjusting himself on his knees.

"He knew he couldn't kill her, so he made a new deal. He asked *La Strega* to spare his life. And to make him *even richer* than the Martinellis. And when he dies, she can eat his soul."

"We're going to be richer even than the Martinellis?" Brando asked. "*Voglio un paio di scarpe nuove!*"

Nario nudged him. "Konstantine didn't sell his soul so you could have Air Jordans, you idiot!"

"So now, because of Konstantine's promise, *La Strega* protects him and only kills our enemies."

"Not true—she killed Calzone and Vincente. They were Ravengers."

"They weren't loyal. They sided with Nico!"

Monte said, "I wonder how he got her to make a new deal?"

Monte thrust his hips as much as the tight space would allow before puckering his lips at Franco.

"*Cazzate*," Andre said, rolling his eyes. To Matteo he said, "You're making all this up. You've never seen *La Strega* in your life."

"I have!" Matteo cried, shoving him. "I'm friends with her."

Here the boys laughed.

The fabric lifted suddenly and a head appeared, large and disembodied. The features were distorted and monstrous in the bouncing beam of the flashlight.

"Who's under there?" a voice boomed.

All the boys screamed.

KONSTANTINE HAD HEARD THE HUSHED WHISPERS COMING from the Virgin Mary and had stopped halfway through the cathedral. He'd been heading out for the night, longing for his bed after a long day in the basement office, sorting through his holdings and considering which strategic moves he would make next, before the idea of dinner called to him.

What do we have here? he'd thought, crossing to the statue and bending down until he was sure that the voices were coming from beneath the covered table behind it.

Only he hadn't expected to find hysterical boys screaming into his face when he lifted the cloth.

"*Dio mio.* What are you doing?" Konstantine waved his hand. "*Fuori.*"

The boys filed out one by one.

He spotted Matteo instantly, looking the most shame-faced of the group. His flashlight hung limply by his side. "Matteo, I need to speak with you. The rest of you, it's late. Have you all eaten? Done your homework?"

A chorus of "Sì, sì" resonated through the church.

"Then wash up, get to bed. You'll worry your families. Do you want to make your mothers sick? *Vai, vai.*"

The boys fled in all directions, leaving only Matteo, small and worried beside him.

"If it's about the story I was telling—" the boy began.

"What? No." Konstantine moved to the pew and beckoned Matteo to join him. "I have to ask you about something else."

Matteo reluctantly sat beside him, his legs too short to reach the floor.

He will be a handsome man, Konstantine thought, and the tenderness he felt in his chest was almost too much to bear.

"Have you ever been to Venice?" Konstantine asked.

"Venice? *Sì.* Nonno took me for Carnevale."

"What did you think of it?"

Matteo shrugged. "I like the canals. They have more pigeons than we do."

Konstantine smiled, but he couldn't keep the expression on his face. "Matteo, I must ask you to do something for me."

"Me?"

"Yes. Did you see the woman that visited us the other day? The one in the red dress?"

"*Sì.* Signora Vittoria." His big eyes searched Konstantine's face.

"I want you to go to Venice and live with her."

His face folded. "Did I...did I do something wrong?"

Konstantine's heart clenched. "*No. Certo che no.*"

"Then why do you want me to leave?"

Konstantine considered the lies he'd constructed for this moment. The many stories he'd conceived for why he would have to ask this small boy to leave his home, his friends. But now that he was looking at those large brown eyes and the innocent, trusting expression, he couldn't bring himself to lie.

"The truth, Matteo, is that I need her to do something for me. I want her to make an agreement with a difficult man so that we do not go to war with him."

"War," the boy repeated. "Like what happened with Nico."

"Yes, exactly. We can avoid another fight like that, but she has told me I must give you to her. That was her price."

"Why me?" he asked.

"Because she knows you are my favorite."

He hoped this praise would soften the blow but still expected him to cry. Perhaps beg.

Matteo sat up straighter, his back erect with pride. "I'll go."

"You will?"

"It is like a mission," he said. "I will be undercover for you. I'll learn her secrets and bring them back for you."

"No, don't do anything she might hurt you for." Konstantine kissed the top of his head. "She will be good to you or I will kill her. And you will not be there forever. Only until I can come up with a better plan."

"Don't worry, I will make you proud of me."

Konstantine placed a hand on his head. "I am already proud of you. *Sei un bravo ragazzo*, Matteo."

A shadow moved and Konstantine turned. He'd expected to find Lou there. Anytime something moved in the shadows, he expected Lou now.

But it wasn't Lou. It was Stefano.

He was watching them silently, his eyes dark and unhappy.

11

Piper jolted awake. She couldn't be sure of what she'd been dreaming, but it must've been awful. Her heart rabbited in her chest, beating so hard it hurt. The only fragment she could recall was something about dishes falling out of the cabinets, breaking and cutting her as they piled up, blotting out the world.

She sat up and found the apartment quiet. "Lou?"

Her voice ringing through the sparse apartment was her only answer.

The space buzzed with silence, shadows washing it in swaths of gray. Light through the venetian blinds cut stripes across the sofa, the coffee table, the bed, her exposed arms.

When she'd woken that morning, Lou had been lying beside her, her chest rising and falling in an easy rhythm as sunlight poured through the wall of windows at her back.

Now it was night again, and the shimmering river no longer sparkled like fish scales in sunlight. It was scrunched, black silk reflecting the stars above. The arch was lit, on display for all to see.

I slept the whole day away. Again, she thought, and felt bad about it.

King and Mel were carrying on without her, she was sure, but it must've made their lives harder.

I'm failing them. I'm letting everyone down.

She pressed the heels of her hands into her eyes and breathed. Her body ached. Her head felt fuzzy, unclear.

Piper untangled herself from the warm sheets and stretched. She walked around the apartment, turning on the lamps and getting herself a glass of water from the kitchen sink. She pulled one of her sweaters off of the clothes piles that had overtaken Lou's sofa and tugged it down over her head.

But her hands and feet were still cold.

God, I wish I had a hot drink. Cocoa. Coffee.

More food—a basket of fruit and French pastries on the island's countertop—had been added to the leftovers filling up Lou's fridge.

For the first time, Piper thought she might actually be able to eat something. She found a plate in the cabinet and filled it. Lou didn't have a microwave, and Piper didn't want to go through the trouble of heating up the stove, so she ate the pizza cold. And when, surprisingly, she found she was still hungry, she ate a pear cut in half with a slice of swiss cheese.

When she noticed her lower back hurt, she refilled her water glass and drank it down. She recognized this particular pain. She often felt it if she was drinking too much soda, or went out drinking too many nights in a row.

The kidneys were always the first to tell you they were unhappy.

Once she'd finished eating, she searched the covers for her phone and found that she'd missed three messages from Henry and one from Dani.

She opened the one from Dani first.

Hi. I hope you're okay. I miss you.

Piper's stomach clenched. She didn't want to think about Dani now or the difficult conversation they would have to have the next time she saw her. She was going to ask Dani to move out. She'd decided that almost as soon as she'd seen the viola sitting in the corner of her bedroom.

This was better for everyone, really. Piper had already felt horrible that she was so allergic to cats that Dani had to give up her beloved British Blue, Octavia, just to stay with her. And now that she'd seen her parents' estate, and knew just how much Dani was conceding in order to slum it with her in the Quarter—no. Just *no*.

Piper couldn't bear it. The guilt. The feelings of worthlessness. It would be better for everyone if Dani found a place of her own. A big, luxurious place where she could be comfortable. Happy.

Next time I see her, I'll just tear the bandage off, she thought. *Get it over with and done. It'll be fine. She'll be happier.*

Who was she kidding? It was going to be terrible. It would hurt like hell.

Piper loved living with Dani. She loved waking up beside her, smelling her perfume on her pillows, seeing her socks in the drawer beside hers. She loved it when Dani came through the agency door at the end of the day with takeout in her hand, looking beautiful and windswept from her walk home. The fact that her face always lit up when she saw Piper hard at work.

The way she would flirt with her if King wasn't around.

I'll see you upstairs, hot stuff. How she'd lean over the desk and give her a kiss.

Piper groaned, feeling especially defeated, and opened her texts from Henry.

P! Where the hell are you?

Seriously where are you? Your detective boss and the psychic queen are both giving me the run around.

I swear to God if you don't answer me I'm going to cut a bitch.

Piper responded to the third text with a quick swipe of her thumbs.

Mom died. Overdose. I'm hiding out.

Da hell, P, why didn't you tell me? Where are you? I'm coming over.

I'm out of town, she replied.

You damned liar!!!

Piper went to Lou's window and angled her phone's camera lens until the illuminated arch was clearly framed behind her. She took the picture, holding still so that it could adjust for the low lighting.

She reviewed the selfie and considered deleting it. She looked like shit. Her hair needed to be brushed and the circles under her eyes were as purple as bruises, probably made worse by the long shadows in the apartment.

She sent the photo anyway.

Fine. You're in STL. Do you want to talk? I can call you.

Piper didn't and said so.

Okay. But you better let me know the minute your ass is back in town. I mean it.

She sent the salute emoji, and that was it.

It was easy to fall into an internet spiral after that. She doom-scrolled the news and her social media, and when that led to her hating herself and her life, she signed into her online classes. She had messages from all three of her professors, offering their condolences and promising extensions on her assignments.

She assured them she would complete the work as soon as possible and thanked them for their patience. When there was nothing else to check on, nothing else to distract her mind, she had a choice between showering or streaming a movie through her computer.

Maybe I'll have it in me to bathe later, a voice said.

Gross. Lou is going to think you're disgusting, lying around in her sheets, stinking them up with your BO.

If she loves me, she'll forgive me.

The idea that Lou might be able to smell her and judge her for it was enough to get Piper into the shower. That and the fact that she was still cold.

So into the shower she went. She thought she was doing great until sometime between conditioning her hair and washing her back, she began to cry. And once she'd started, she couldn't seem to stop.

It seemed like an eternity before the tears ended and she was able to get out of the shower.

By the time she'd dressed, she was thoroughly exhausted. She fell back into Lou's bed, her eyes fluttering closed as soon as her head hit the pillow.

The nightmares began again.

What struck Dani first was the sharp, cloying smell of cigarette smoke, followed by stale body odor. On its heel was something acrid. Piss? Rotting food? She couldn't tell.

She covered her nose with her hand reflexively. If Lou was bothered by the smell she didn't show it. Her hands remained in the pockets of her leather jacket as she surveyed the cramped living room, nudging strewn pillows and trash with her boot.

As Dani's eyes adjusted to the dim light, aging furniture riddled with cigarette burn holes, a scuffed coffee table, and windows covered with blankets came into view.

There were unwashed dishes piled on the end tables. The coffee table itself was laden with empty beer cans, and a tray with a dirty spoon and syringe. There was white powder residue all over the table. An empty pizza box had been left open and had served as an ashtray, crumpled butts littered amongst the rock-hard crusts.

"This is where her mom *lived?*" Dani was unable to hide her shock.

"Yeah." Lou was looking for something. She'd pushed her mirrored shades up onto the top of her head and was peeling a painting from the wall.

"God," Dani murmured, and tucked her hair behind her ears. "I had no idea."

"She didn't tell you that her mom was an addict?"

"No. She'd told me her mom was sick, but I assumed it was cancer or something."

Why didn't you tell me?

"Was she always like this? Did Piper grow up here? In this house with..." She wasn't sure how to finish the sentence. *All of this.*

She hoped her open palm sweeping the room delivered the point.

Lou was scowling at something. "I think it was different before her father died."

"How long ago was that?"

"She was fourteen."

Dani ran a hand through her hair. "She's been dealing with this for over a *decade.*"

Now that Dani saw the house, things began to click into place. Why Piper never talked about her family. Why she worked so much and always seemed to worry about money. Why she was so sensitive about how she looked, the cleanliness of her apartment, or how far she'd gotten in school.

Why she would sit up suddenly at night, listening to a sound Dani's ears couldn't even register.

Always on the lookout for trouble.

Why didn't you feel like you could tell me?

Dani wanted to help in the search, but she was terrified of touching anything. She'd done so much research on the opioid epidemic raging across America right now. If any of this was Fentanyl, it could be absorbed through the skin and kill a person.

"Don't touch the white stuff," Dani said as Lou bent toward the coffee table in order to inspect the lower shelf.

Lou's grunt could be taken for agreement, or acknowledgment at least.

"Why did she tell you and not me? You guys aren't even —" *Having sex.*

Lou's eyebrows arched as Dani bit the sentence in half.

Lou was lifting the last painting in the room. "She didn't tell me. I saw it when I was here."

"Oh. Why were you here?"

Lou pulled back the rug, checking the planks beneath. "King asked me to check on her. I did."

So, King suspected too. And probably Melandra. Dani was the last one to know. Why? Because she hadn't asked. She hadn't pressed Piper for answers or even suspected that maybe something worse, something horrible, was lurking in Piper's life.

Dani had assumed the story about the sick mom had been true and had left it at that.

Some freaking journalist I am.

The way Lou wouldn't look at her, the way she turned slightly away, made Dani feel worse.

She knew all this. *She thinks I'm a spoiled idiot because I couldn't even imagine where Piper came from.*

Worse than that, the other issue made sense. Why Piper had freaked out when she'd lunched with her parents. At first Dani had simply thought Piper had been overreacting.

She hadn't understood why she'd been so uncomfortable

and embarrassed in that house. It was a little over the top, Dani knew, but it was hardly a palace.

But it must've seemed like a palace to her.

Her eyes scanned the dark, stench-soaked room again.

Her family's wealth, the extravagances, must've seemed like such a slap in the face after everything she'd been through, after everything she'd been asked to do without.

Dani pinched the bridge of her nose. "At least I know why she got upset about lunch."

"Because you're rich."

"*I'm* not rich," Dani said reflexively, feeling the heat rush to her face. "It's my parents' money. Oh god, that's something rich kids say."

Lou's lips twitched in a would-be smile.

Dani pointed an accusing finger at her. "You're far from poor. Why isn't she mad at you?"

"Do I look rich to you?" Lou asked. "I don't even have a car."

"So I'm supposed to wear thrift store clothes and drive a horse and buggy? *What?*"

Lou looked under the sofa. "You should be asking her, not me."

"Fine. You're right." Dani clasped her hands at the back of her neck. "But I wish she would've talked to me. I'm not a psychic or a mind reader like Mel. How the hell was I supposed to know what the problem was?"

Lou tossed the rug back down.

"I don't think there are any papers down here. I'm going to check upstairs." Lou jerked her chin in the direction of the doorway behind Dani. "Look in the kitchen."

She was halfway up the stairs before Dani could form a rebuttal. With a sigh, Dani found the kitchen. It was just as bad as the living room. Peeling tile and stained countertops.

The fridge was silent and warm, apparently out of order. When Dani flicked the light switch nothing happened.

She used her phone light to search drawers and cabinets. She lifted an ashtray overflowing with cigarette butts to get the stack of mail beneath it. She went through it slowly, meticulously. Most of it was junk mail, political flyers, coupons. Then she found the bills. Most of them had menacing *PAST DUE* stamps on them, including one from the IRS.

Dani gathered these up and put them into the inside pocket of her wool coat.

The photograph on the fridge of a preteen Piper sandwiched between her parents made Dani's throat clench.

But most of Piper's face had been burned out with a cigarette, a black hole with seared edges where it should have been.

"What the hell?" Dani murmured.

"Come up here," Lou called.

Dani took the narrow stairs, which creaked so loudly under her heels that she half expected the wood to give way and cave beneath her. At the top of the stairs she had a choice of three doors, the bathroom straight ahead and bedrooms on either side. Lou poked her head out of the right-side bedroom and waved a piece of paper.

"I think this is what King wanted."

There was a bare mattress on the floor with clothes piled on top of it, more on the floor surrounding it. Lou had a steel lockbox open, papers overflowing from inside.

"I found a copy of Piper's birth certificate, her parents' marriage license, and a note where Nadine refinanced the house."

"Bring the whole thing," Dani said. She lifted a framed photo of Piper off the nightstand. Piper, eight or nine years old in a red-and-gray softball uniform, her smile bright and cheerful. This one, blessedly, had her face intact. "Piper can go through it and decide what she wants to keep. Do you think the room across the hall is hers? *Was* hers?"

"It was."

Another pang shot through Dani's chest.

"Should we see if there's anything important in there? Anything she might want?"

Lou was trying to get the papers into the box and latch it closed. But now that it had been opened, no configuration seemed to get the accordion of documents back into the box. "We took most of it when she moved out. But sure, go look."

Dani wandered across the hall with the framed photo still in her hand and pushed open the door slowly, almost as if she expected someone to jump out at her.

But Lou was right. It was mostly empty.

There was a small twin bed in one corner of the room, a bed barely big enough for a child. Gray light filtered from the single small window in the upper-right corner.

Dani reached out and touched the covers, surprised to find them coarse and pilled. The pillow was flat and stained, without a cover. The closet was empty as well as the drawers. There was a box of toys under the bed, most of them things only a small kid would play with, but Dani pulled the box out anyway, inspecting each one in turn.

A stuffed rhino. Half-full coloring books. A set of markers. A murder mystery board game. A ball that one could shake and get a yes or no answer. A paddle with a ball tied to it. A ukulele with two busted strings.

She made sure I knew I'm not good enough for you. Between the ribbons and the horses and the viola, Piper had said.

Dani's eyes welled up with tears as she looked at the broken ukulele.

No wonder she hates my viola.

A presence loomed behind her, and Dani turned. Lou was

in the doorway, the unruly lockbox tucked under her arm. Her sunglasses were over her eyes again, her face relaxed and unreadable.

"Do you think she would want any of this?" Dani dabbed her eyes with the back of her finger. "Should I bring it back to the apartment?"

Before Lou could answer, the front door creaked open. They both froze, listening to the intruder enter the house, the screen door slamming shut with an angry *thwap*.

The box of toys shifted in Dani's lap and slid to the floor.

"Who's up there?" a man called out. "Piper, is that you, you dumb bitch? Trying to steal shit when I ain't home?"

"Take this." Lou handed Dani the lockbox. "I'll be back."

12

───────

Konstantine took Matteo to Venice himself. As they flew in his private jet, he spoiled the boy with a meal of Fiorentina steak and bolognaise served on fine china. He tucked a cloth napkin into the boy's pressed collar and poured the glass of water himself.

When he asked for a sip of Konstantine's prosecco, he obliged the boy. Then Matteo ate his weight in chocolate truffles, commenting again and again on the niceness of the jet, his leather seat, the view of Italy below.

He thinks this is an adventure.

This alleviated Konstantine of some of the guilt he felt.

Throughout all of this, Stefano remained silent in his seat, careful to keep his hazel eyes averted from them, pretending to look out the jet's window. But Konstantine saw how his fists opened and closed in his lap and his expression remained dark. Even as boys, Stefano had been like this. When something had not gone to plan, he would brood.

Konstantine tried to elevate Matteo's sense of adventure by giving him the window seat in the car as they traveled from the Venice airport to the boats. As they glided over the water, he pointed out the churches he knew, the fountains and monuments. Matteo cried out with laughter when a dolphin leapt up in the distance.

But then all too quickly they'd arrived. The boat rolled to a stop outside of Vittoria's cream-colored villa. Her gleaming windows were shut tight against the chilly November morning, which had just begun to warm.

As soon as the boat docked, the doors opened, and two young women and a man came out. One of the women dashed back inside as soon as she saw Konstantine step onto the ramp and pull Matteo up onto the street.

He had a terrible moment when he imagined Matteo falling into the canal and drowning.

"Do you know how to swim?" he asked the boy suddenly, wrapping a hand around his shoulder and leading him toward the villa.

Matteo frowned, his eyes catching the morning light and brightening. The little lines between his brows knitted. "Of course I know how to swim. What idiot doesn't know how to swim?"

Konstantine made a point not to look back at Stefano, who sank like a rock in deep water.

As they waited on the cobblestones, Konstantine's entourage began to haul Matteo's luggage and trunks onto the road.

"What's all this? Are you going to stay here with me?" Matteo asked hopefully.

Konstantine's heart clenched. "I can't stay. They're gifts from me."

"Gifts?" The boy's eyes widened. "What kind of gifts?"

"You'll find out later when you unpack." Konstantine winked.

I want to give him something to look forward to. Anything to lengthen the magic.

In truth, Konstantine had done this shopping himself and it had taken him days. He'd enlisted the help of some of the other boys, asking about Matteo's tastes and interests, to help fill the gaps in Konstantine's knowledge. By the time day had bled into night, Konstantine had accumulated enough clothes, shoes, treats, books, and trinkets to suit a prince. Not to mention a brand-new gaming system.

He hoped these offerings would make Matteo's separation from home bearable.

Vittoria appeared in the doorway, a flourish of gold today. Her dress billowed and flowed around her, and she stepped into the sun, smiling.

"Arrived already!" Vittoria called out. "My little treasure! Come here."

Matteo stiffened beside him, pressing his weight into the side of Konstantine's leg the way a much smaller child or even a dog would do when afraid.

"It's all right. Go on." Konstantine squeezed his shoulder, pushing him forward.

He watched the boy cross the portico into Vittoria's arms with a sinking feeling in his guts. How would he have felt if Padre Leo had sent him away like this? As if he'd done something wrong. As if he were unwanted. He could only hope the gifts, and their little adventure, would work against whatever voice might whisper such things to him.

It's only for a little while, Konstantine told himself. *Until I find a better solution.*

Vittoria pulled Matteo into her arms and kissed him.

"*Bel ragazzo. Mia piccola bellezza*," she cried. She pinched his cheeks. To Konstantine she said, "Aren't you coming in for lunch?"

"No," Konstantine said. "I have to get back."

In truth, Konstantine was afraid of what might happen if

he lingered. If Matteo's courage might fail him, and Konstantine's too.

"Well, then." Vittoria affected a pout. "Wave goodbye, *il mio piccolo principe*. Who knows when you will see each other again."

Konstantine lifted his hand even as his stomach clenched. "*Ciao, Matteo. Essere intelligento. Stai attento.*"

Be smart. Be safe.

Please don't let him cry, Konstantine thought. He couldn't bear it.

And there was a moment when Matteo's eyes seemed bright, his lips quivering. But then he waved, his upper lip stiff.

"Ciao, Konstantine," he called. "Thank you for my gifts!"

He's putting on a brave face for me.

Good boy.

Then they were gone, closing the door on him and leaving Stefano and Konstantine in the chilly morning. Clouds had moved over the sun. Rain was imminent.

Konstantine turned away, motioning for his entourage to return to the boats and prepare for their departure.

When Stefano and Konstantine were alone in the last boat, Konstantine said, "Your face is so red, I think you will burst, *amico mio*. Say whatever it is before it kills you."

"I can't believe you're doing this. Matteo today and who tomorrow? Will you send me to a Turkish brothel tomorrow?"

Konstantine tried to push the image of Matteo's uncertainty, that silent pleading, out of his mind. He'd made his choice and had done the best he could to soften the blow. "Vittoria won't hurt him." *I hope.* "It's done."

"Is it?" Stefano asked, cursing beside him. The gloomy shadows of the canal suited his stern face, the pale waters churning around them. "I'm not so sure."

. . .

Piper startled awake. She sat up and found herself in the dark, heart hammering so hard that she thought she would die. It had never beat so fast in her life. She didn't know her heart *could* beat so fast. She sat there for a moment, in the tangle of Lou's bedding, unable to draw a full breath. Her throat felt tight and constricted. She was cold again, but this time covered in sweat.

She reached out for Lou and found she wasn't there.

The pillow was unoccupied, the sheets empty.

Maybe she'd gone out for food or to check on King or Mel.

What if she never comes back and I die here and they find my dried-up corpse mummified in this apartment, her mind whispered.

Shut up. This is nothing. I was just having a bad dream.

Once Piper's pulse began to slow, she reached out for the glass of water by the bed. She drank it down, touched her forehead and found it was damp too. Her clothes and the back of her neck as well.

I need another shower, she thought. *That's all I seem capable of lately.* Sleeping. Eating. Showering.

And the nightmares, of course. Piper was getting really good at the nightmares.

Dreams in which her mother was crying somewhere in their house, but no matter where she looked, in what rooms, closets, behind curtains or furniture, the attic, she could never find her. She just heard that unending, relentless crying, which grew more desperate the longer Piper searched.

In other dreams, Willy was beating her. Hitting her mother hard across the face, breaking open the skin, and her mother kept twisting away from him, trying to get away, but couldn't. When Piper would dash forward to stop him, to protect her, she would find that she was in a glass box, trapped on all sides and unable to do anything but beat on the glass and scream her mother's name.

In one particularly horrible dream, she'd heard her mother locked in her bedroom, crying, begging. But no matter how hard Piper slammed her shoulder against the door, she couldn't get it to open.

"Please. I don't want to," her mother had cried behind that door.

And a man would only laugh.

That time, Piper woke sweating with the sound of his laughter in her ears.

She's dead. She's dead and no one is hurting her. No one.

Piper placed her head in her hands and tried to breathe.

Was this what it had been like for Dani? Had every panic attack she'd had after Petrov had tortured her been as intense and unrelenting as this? If so, Piper had a newfound clarity of what she must've gone through each night that she'd wrestled with her own fears.

It wasn't fun. That was for damned sure.

Piper wasn't sure how long she'd stayed like this, her head in her hands, half disgusted with herself, trying to build up the energy to get up and take care of herself.

The closet door creaked open and Piper lifted her head to find Lou stepping into the room, her mirrored sunglasses pushed up on her head, her leather jacket hanging loose from her shoulders.

"Hey," Piper said, hoping she didn't look as bad as she felt.

But if Lou thought she looked like shit, she was amused by it. Why else was she smiling?

"I have something for you."

Piper laughed. "I don't think you're the kind of girl to give flowers. Is it food?"

"No. Get your coat on. It's cold where we're going."

Piper's laugh soured. "I don't think I'm in any state to be in public. Look at me."

"We won't be in public. In fact, this place is the opposite of public."

Piper was more than a little intrigued when she slipped from the warm bed and put on socks, her shoes, and her puffy black coat. She hated how shaky her limbs felt.

She probably just wants to take me somewhere cool to cheer me up, Piper thought. Maybe the top of a tall building for a beautiful view.

Just try not to throw yourself off, that dark voice whispered again.

Of course, Piper should've known what a "Lou gift" might look like.

When they emerged from the closet again, she did find a beautiful view. It was the Nova Scotian wilderness at night. Stars brighter and more beautiful than Piper had ever seen, a river of them twinkling above her, seemingly close enough to touch.

The trees were covered in snow and glowed spectral with moonlight. It was a gorgeous, magical landscape.

Until she saw the man propped against the tree, his head cocked to one side in his unconsciousness.

"Willy?" she asked. She looked to Lou. "You kidnapped *Willy*?"

"I thought you might want to kill him."

"Kill him!" Piper took a step back. "How in the world can I kill him?"

Lou opened her jacket. "I've got a Browning and two blades. If you want me to get a grenade or a flamethrower, they're back in the apartment.

"A *flamethrower*, Louie? *Jesus*."

Piper covered her eyes with her hands, then opened them again. She did this a few times, but the landscape didn't change. She wasn't dreaming. This was real life. Lou had kidnapped her mother's druggie boyfriend and had brought him to the middle of nowhere.

To kill him.

Then again, if that wasn't friendship…

Piper looked around, realizing where they were. "Is this where you bring the people you kill?"

"Yeah." Lou pointed at the placid lake, shimmering with moonlight. "La Loon's through there."

"I can't believe you just offered me a grenade." She burrowed deeper into her puffy coat. "How am I supposed to kill him?"

"Aren't you angry?"

Piper threw her hands up. "Of course I'm angry. Sometimes I'm so pissed I think my head is going to explode."

"Then kill him."

Kill him. It was an idea that Piper hadn't even considered. Had she wanted to beat the hell out of Willy? Yes. Had she wanted to maybe choke him with her bare hands? Absolutely.

Yet, look at him. He was nearly bald on top with graying hair. Slumped against the tree, he looked frail with his pale, track-marked arms and potbelly. He was sick. He was abusive. But ultimately, he was just an old guy with a life barely worth living.

And really, it came down to the fact that Piper didn't think she had it in her to kill someone.

Lou offered her the butt of her gun. Piper took it, looking at it as the strange foreign object that it was. It was heavier in her palm than she'd been expecting. Colder, too.

Piper didn't think she'd ever even held a gun before. Had she?

Willy began to stir, no doubt roused by their voices. When his eyes opened, they fixed on Piper immediately.

"You fucking bitch, I should've known—"

Then his eyes slid to the gun and widened to tea saucers.

For a delicious moment, Piper understood everything. She knew exactly why Lou loved this so much.

Willy tried to get up, shoving himself against the tree as he staggered to his feet. "Oh god. No. *Hey*. I'm sorry. Okay. I'm sorry. I told her not to take so much but she didn't listen. She got into my stash and double-dosed."

"Yeah right." Piper felt something roll through her, something like a winter breeze, and for a moment the gun didn't feel like cold, dead metal. It was warming in her hand.

It was coming alive.

Willy held his hands up in front of her, palms facing them as if this would keep them back. "I swear to God, I tried to save her. I tried CPR. I even took her to the hospital!"

"You dumped her on the curb like some trash," Piper replied.

"That's just because I didn't want to go to jail. It didn't mean I don't care. I do care. I cared about your momma so much. And now she's gone. And I'm...I don't have anybody."

He began to cry, his shoulders shaking with the effort. To Piper it was more than pitiful. It was pathetic. He slid down the tree onto his knees again, covering his face with his hands.

Piper raised the gun. Pointed it at the sobbing man.

On the count of three.

One...

Two...

Three...

Nothing happened.

The crickets chirped. An owl hooted. The breeze caressed Piper's cheeks, chilling them.

But no gunshot sounded.

"I can't," she whispered, and lowered the gun.

Lou's fist slammed into the side of Willy's head and he slumped unconscious against the tree.

Piper covered her mouth. "Why did you hit him like that? That was so hard."

Lou shook out her hand, opening and closing the fingers. "It knocks them out. I hate it when they cry."

"He's going to have a concussion."

Lou only looked at her. "No, he won't."

Piper gave her back the gun. "I'm sorry. I can't kill him."

"Even after everything he did to you and your mom?"

"I know." Piper sighed.

"He *wants* to hurt you."

"I know, but—" Piper searched herself for the anger, for the fury that had made her want to hurt this man a thousand times before. Yet in this moment, she couldn't find it. All she found was her grief. That cold, desolate sadness blowing through her like snow on a winter's night or the river of tears that seemed hell-bent on flowing through her.

"I guess I don't have it in me," she said. "Are you disappointed in me?"

"No. Why?" Lou shifted her weight. "Are you going to be disappointed in me?"

"What? Why?"

Instead of answering, Lou grabbed Willy's leg and dragged him toward the lake. He slid easily over the freshly fallen snow, slipping into the water behind Lou and sinking.

"Are you going to *drown* him?" Piper didn't think she could watch someone be murdered either. "Wait, what is happening right now?"

"I don't want to take the chance he's going to come after you later."

Before Piper could consider whether or not she was okay with...whatever *this* was, Lou was already disappearing beneath the water, tugging Willy down with her.

For a moment, Piper just stood there, regarding the

endless nighttime wilderness, her mind empty for the first time in days.

Her cheeks were cold. Her hands were cold, but mostly, it was that stone inside her stomach that was cold.

She lay down on her back, pulling her coat around her. Snow began to melt through her sweatpants and dampen her legs, but the rest of her was decently warm.

Above, the stars twinkled, reminding her that this world, this existence, began long before she'd arrived on this planet and would continue on long after she was gone.

Her situation had been far from ideal, but it wasn't everything. Piper could move on. She could get past this. She just didn't know what the hell the next step was.

And another thing had occurred to her—the heart of the matter was that her fear and anxiety over her mother's safety had consumed so much of her energy and mind that now she didn't know what to do without it.

What could her life look like when she didn't lie down every night wondering if this was the night the call would come?

The call came. It was done. Now what?

What was Piper going to do next?

Lou appeared above her, her hair and face dripping. She shook out her leather jacket before lying down in the snow beside Piper.

"I don't know how," Piper began, feeling the tears slide out of her eyes as she looked up at the endless stars. They began to freeze almost instantly against her skin. "I don't know how to move past this. It's just—it's just so much and—"

She exhaled a shaky breath.

Lou reached out and grabbed Piper's hand. She held on tight.

13

———

Lou stood in her apartment, her hair freshly washed, watching Piper sleep. She'd managed to get the girl to eat dinner, clean up, and tumble back into her bed before she passed out from exhaustion. She hadn't been sure what would happen at the lake. She'd guessed, accurately, that Piper might not be able to pull the trigger. Her aunt Lucy would have said that some souls are just gentler, kinder. That no matter what happens to them, the darkness will never eclipse their light.

Lou had known that Piper was this way.

Yet it still surprised her sometimes, how generous the girl could be with her forgiveness.

But she hadn't truly realized how tenderhearted she was until she'd seen her expression when regarding Willy. There was none of the hatred Lou'd expected. None of the blind fury that had caused Lou to chase Angelo Martinelli to the ends of the earth.

Piper had looked at him and had felt sorry for him.

Sorry.

She has a good heart, Lucy would've said.

Maybe I'm more like my mother than I thought, Lou mused.

Courtney Thorne had been cold down to her bones.

And Lou had felt nothing when she'd dragged Willy onto the shores of La Loon and watched him stir, awakening to the sound of Jabbers's death screech, having only a few seconds to comprehend what might have been happening before those powerful jaws snapped shut, dealing the killing blow.

She'd felt nothing when the beast had torn him apart, ripping through his abdomen the way children tear through presents on Christmas morning.

And now it was done. The threat eradicated. Piper safe again.

Lou ran the comb through her wet hair one more time before placing it on the kitchen island beside Piper's half-eaten sandwich. She watched the girl's chest rise and fall one more time, no hint of nightmares now, and stepped into the linen closet.

She waited in the dark, listening to it, conjuring it.

When it opened up to her, she stepped through into a church centuries older than she was.

Konstantine was sitting on a pew, his head bowed between clasped hands as if in prayer. Lou might have thought that was an intimate, spiritual moment if not for the blood.

There was a pool of it on the stones ten feet from Konstantine's nice Italian leather shoes, and it had smeared in the direction of the hallway, as if something had been dragged in that direction.

Konstantine, too, had blood on him. It was slicked up his arms, soaking the ends of his sleeve. A splatter across his shoes. A smear across the side of his neck.

She touched his shoulder, half expecting him to collapse or his head to lull.

But he looked up and met her gaze. *"Buona sera."*

"Are you okay?" she asked.

He leaned back in the pew, seeming to take note of the blood on his hands, on his shoes.

"*Sì*. Not my blood."

"Bad day at work?" She could tell from his voice alone that he was in a bad place. Something had been bothering him for days now, and she wondered if he would ever tell her what it was.

"Sometimes it is difficult for me to do what must be done." He opened and closed his fist, the blood cracking along his knuckles. "When the person is not a *complete bastardo*."

Lou regarded him, but said nothing. She wasn't sure he'd finished talking.

He met her gaze. "Do you think less of me, *amore mio*? I am not as—"

She wondered what he would say. Ruthless? Single-minded?

"I'm not as strong as you are."

That was twice tonight that someone Lou cared about was asking her if she thought less of them. And why? Didn't they know she was the broken one? The one so corrupted with darkness that she could become one with it?

Don't say that about yourself, a voice said. It was Lucy's voice. Stern and certain.

Lou stretched her arm across the back of the pew. "Strength has nothing to do with it."

She thought of the way Piper had looked on the banks of her lake, gazing up at the stars with her coat pulled tight around her. Piper was one of the strongest people Lou knew, and she hadn't been able to kill that asshole. Hadn't wanted to.

Lucy, too, had been strong. And her father.

None of them were killers.

Lou sank onto the pew beside him and told him all of this, finishing with the story of capturing Willy Turner from Nadine's house, carrying him to Nova Scotia, and making Piper the offering of his life. How she'd refused.

He considered all of this silently. Then after a stretch of silence said, "I want to be like Padre Leo. But I fear I'm more like my father."

"I considered fucking Angelo once," she said.

Konstantine's face visibly reddened as he turned to her. "Excuse me? Why would you say this to me? And why are you changing the subject?"

"I'm not changing the subject." Lou noted the jealousy and tried not to smile. "I'm saying that I knew I'd rather blow my own brains out before I ever had sex with a Martinelli."

He didn't seem to understand. Fine. She would spell it out for him.

"You're not like your father," she said. "You're nothing like any of them."

His face pinched in confusion until she slid across the pew and put her face quite close to his. Then she kissed him, slow and deep, enjoying the taste of blood on his lips.

"*This* would never have happened if you were."

Lou and Konstantine made love twice before he finally fell asleep beside her. But his dreams were not easy. She could tell by the crease between his brows. Lou noted this, intrigued by the idea that for once, she wasn't the one plagued by nightmares. After Lucy had died, and Lou had found killing impossible, she'd been the one unable to sleep, unable to eat. For that reason alone she could never fault Piper or Konstantine their troubles.

But Piper's pain, Lou understood. Grief and loss, she'd met.

Konstantine—*What's going on with you?*

The Florentine apartment was chilly with the early morning pressing against the wooden shutters. A thin beam of light traced the edge of the window's frame.

The compass inside her whirled, and for an exciting minute she thought was going to get an answer, a clue to the secret he was bearing so poorly. But then the compass locked on its destination and she knew at once it was Paris.

Lou slipped quietly from Konstantine's bed, laced on her boots and still damp jacket—*I need to reproof this soon or get a new one*—and stepped through the welcoming shadows.

She knew at once that she was back in the catacombs. The damp smell of old earth rose around her, reminding her of the Meramec Caverns her father had taken her to when she was a child. Only instead of stalagmites and stalactites collecting the moisture from the air, dripping, it was the bones of the long dead.

Lou wasn't alone down here.

She heard movement ahead, perhaps ten or fifteen feet further down the path. Feet scuffling over the crushed bone fragments.

How can they see anything?

She didn't flick on her lighter, even for a chance to see their face. Instead, she crept quietly forward, seeing if she could close the distance between them.

All she needed to do was get her hands on them. Then a hop and a skip to the lake and all her questions would be answered.

Yet she'd taken only one step before the sound of bones clattering into place on top of one another ceased. There was a sharp intake of breath.

Then someone charged toward her. She felt the forward movement, that rush of shifting air, a heartbeat before she heard it.

Without thinking, she faded through the pitch, collapsing into and through the shadows, only to appear again in the catacombs further down the line.

But she still couldn't see.

Lou couldn't understand the murmured cursing in French either, but she knew it was a man.

Did he think I was a ghost? I must've seemed like one, disappearing in front of him.

Was he wearing night-vision goggles?

She thought he must be.

The bones rattled faster now, and Lou suspected he must be stacking them on top of each other hastily, anything to finish his work and get out of here.

If she could just get close enough to grab him...

Another gasp of surprise, and she expected him to rush at her again, but this time the footsteps fled in the opposite direction, down a dark corridor that Lou knew was there but couldn't see.

She ran after him anyway, stretching her arms out until she thought she was close, only to swipe empty air.

A creak. A slam.

The footsteps stopped as quickly as they'd come.

Lou froze, listening, waiting for an ambush. She itched to pull her lighter and turn on the light, but she knew that her strength and advantage lay in the darkness surrounding her.

That if he did manage to hit her or cut her in the dark, it would only work to her benefit, as she could take them both the moment he put his hands on her.

But there was no ambush.

And while the footsteps were gone, in their place was a muffled noise. Climbing? Digging? She couldn't be sure, except to note that it was definitely moving away from her, growing more distant by the second. Behind the left-side wall, perhaps?

Damn it. She pulled the lighter from her pocket and struck it twice. Orange flame and the smell of lighter fluid sparked into the passage around her.

She stood alone on the earth-packed path. She retraced her steps, running her hand along the walls, trying to look for an exit, a sign of where he'd gone. Then she tried the other wall. Both were mud, caked earth that stuck to her fingertips.

No doors. No hatches.

Then she searched the floor with her boots, shifting the crushed bones and years of dust back and forth but finding nothing. The only thing she couldn't inspect with her hands was the ceiling. She lifted the lighter as high as she could and examined it.

Nothing. No outlines of a hatch or door. No hint of light.

She swore. Retracing her steps, she went back down the corridor.

Just before a bend in the path, bones spilled across the walkway. Some of them were still inside a black canvas bag. The skull had cracked, the jawbone hanging loosely to one side. The other bones lay on top of one another like a fortune teller's palette.

Lou shoved the bones into the bag and zipped it closed.

Where is he now? The one I just saw.

The shadows morphed around Lou, shifting, swelling. They offered her passage through that momentary pause of infinity, in the space outside of time.

Then she was at a park. Large ornamental trees lined a path ahead of her, bearing a strange resemblance to the city of the dead below her feet.

Maybe she really was traveling between the city of the living and the city of the dead.

Lou searched the sea of faces. A crowd had formed despite the hour. She rolled her wrist and checked her GPS watch for the local time. It was just past ten in the evening.

Why were there so many people here?

A fountain splashed and burbled beside her. A woman bumped into her and apologized.

Then the band started up and the cheering began.

As she scanned the grounds she couldn't decide which was her attacker. She hadn't gotten a clear look at him. He could be standing right in front of her, looking at her, and she would have to rely on her compass to tell her who it was.

She scanned the crowd for a second time, widening her search to the houses that surrounded the park, their windows dark and watchful.

No click from her compass. No confirmation that her eyes had lain on the one she was searching for.

With irritation nipping at the back of her neck, she stepped between the trees, through the thick shadows, with the duffel still in her hand, and was gone.

14

———

When Piper's eyes fluttered open the next morning, Lou said, "Do you want to go to the agency with me?"

"Sick of me already?" she asked, her chin still tucked beneath the covers.

"I thought you'd like to help us with the Paris case. I have a bag of bones here."

Piper's eyes, which had been fluttering closed, open wider. "Excuse me, what?"

"My target dropped a sack of bones in the catacombs. Not everything is there—I think he got some of it into the wall before he took off—but I want to take what I've got to King to see if he has any ideas."

"You're going to take King a bag of bones." The sleepiness that had been pressing against Piper's brain dissipated like mist in the noonday sun. She threw back the covers. "Hell yes, I want to see this."

Piper put herself together the best she could, but little could be done about the purple bags under her eyes. Those would likely linger for as long as she continued to cry her eyes out every night. She did manage to get down the bagel that Lou offered, already toasted and spread with thick cream cheese.

Once she'd finished it, Lou offered her a pair of mirrored sunglasses.

"Bless you," she said, and slid the glasses over her eyes. "Oh god, it's so dark. How do you wear these all the time? Do I look nuts?"

Lou opened the closet door. "You look fine."

It was a tight fit, the two of them and a bag of bones.

"What's that weird smell?" Piper wrinkled her nose.

"I think it's the chemical he used to clean the bones."

Piper felt the weight of Lou's hand on her hip and relaxed into it the second before the darkness compressed and the world dropped and reformed around them.

Then she was pushing open the storage room door and stepping into the sunny detective agency.

King had his back to them, humming some classic rock song that Piper thought she recognized as he loaded a coffee filter with several scoops of coffee.

"Please make enough for me!" Piper called out. She'd been seriously yearning for some coffee since she'd eaten the bagel.

"Hey!" Instead of adding coffee to the filter, he stopped what he was doing and reached out a large, steady hand and placed it on Piper's shoulder. "It's good to see you. How are you holding up?"

Piper felt tears threatening to form. *God, I'm not even back two minutes and I can't keep it together.*

King nodded as if he understood what the sunglasses were for. "I'm sorry about your mom, kid. That's a tough break. But you're going to be okay."

Am I okay? Am I okay?

He gave her a quick, firm squeeze before returning to the coffee pot. "What about you, Lou? Do you want any?"

Lou shook her head.

The sight of him relaxed Piper. She'd been afraid he'd be drowning under heaps of work and blaming her for it. But his desk was orderly. The paperwork manageable.

The belt around her chest loosened.

"Where's Lady?" Piper asked.

"With Mel," he said, adding water to the reservoir.

Too bad. Piper could've used a bit of canine therapy.

King looked from her face to Lou's and back again. "What brings you in?"

"I work here," Piper said.

"Not for another week you don't. You need the time off." He pressed the start button on the machine and returned to his seat.

"What about the funeral?" Piper asked, resting her weight against the desk.

King leaned back in his chair, lacing his hands behind his head. "Lou gave us the paperwork about your father's burial and the prepaid invoice for your mother's burial plot. I just spoke to them this morning, actually. I was going to call you after lunch."

Piper scratched her elbow, resisting the urge to wrap her arms around herself. "What did they say?"

"They spoke to the hospital and agreed to pick your mom up on Tuesday. They wanted to know if you wanted to see her or—"

"No," Piper said, her throat closing on itself. "No, I don't want to see her like that. Can't they just do the cremation or a closed casket or whatever?"

"They can. I'll tell them that's what you want. Do you want a visitation? Did she have friends or anyone who might want to come say goodbye?"

Only two minutes into this conversation and Piper felt exhausted and sick.

"No. She didn't have anyone. Willy sort of alienated her from her friends until it was just the two of them. And now he's—"

She looked to Lou.

"Gone." Lou's face gave nothing away, but King's brows still rose.

"Okay. But to be clear, you'd rather just say your goodbyes at the funeral?"

It would be weird to be back in the cemetery. Piper went every year on her father's birthday, but that wasn't for another four months.

"Yeah. If that's okay."

"It's more than fine with me. Since you don't want anything but the burial, they'll take care of it and give us a time and date. I'll pass it along as soon as I have it."

"Thank you," Piper said. "I'm glad you're helping me. If I had to—"

She didn't even know how to finish.

"No problem," he said with a kind smile. "You're too young to be planning a funeral anyway."

An awkward pause bloomed and stretched between them, and Piper wanted the conversation to change but she couldn't figure out how to do it.

Then Lou dropped the duffel onto King's desk.

King immediately frowned. He began unzipping it, talking as he did. "What do we have—*Shit*. A little warning next time."

Lou smiled, and despite her sorrow, Piper laughed.

This only encouraged King more. He pinched his nose, pretended to gag and sputter, even though Piper was one hundred percent certain that he was more than okay with a bag of bones in his face.

"What do you want me to do with these? Dare I ask where you got them?"

Lou pulled two of the red waiting room chairs over, pushing one toward Piper. "What do they tell you?"

"Nothing," he said. "I don't have a forensic background. And if you're looking for a bone reader, she's four blocks east. But she takes long lunches."

Lou wasn't giving up so easy. "What *questions* do they make you think of?"

The coffee pot beeped.

"Wait, I'm going to need coffee for this," King said.

"I'll get it." Piper hadn't even relaxed into the chair before she was up again. She made King's coffee first and put it on his desk before making one for herself, adding the cream, sugar, and vanilla syrup that she liked. Now was hardly the time to think about a diet.

King sipped his coffee and smacked his lips dramatically. "I missed the way you make the coffee."

He's being extra nice to me. I must seem really pathetic right now.

"Well." King considered the bones. "I'd check out the bag. Who made it? See if I can find a serial number or a tag that can tell me where it was purchased, where it came from, how many of them there are. How old is this one? Can I narrow down a purchase date? I would definitely get the bones to a lab, find out what I could about the victim. Age? Sex? Any identifying marks such as old wounds, broken bones, or dental records. I'd cross-reference these against any known missing persons."

King took another sip of coffee.

"Once I knew who they were, I'd try to reconstruct the timeline leading up to their death. Their last known movements before they disappeared. This would tell me who they came into contact with, give me a list of people I should interview, maybe even a time of death, but that's really hard to determine, especially since it seems chemicals were used to strip off the flesh. You smell that?"

He sniffed the air above the opened bag.

"I'd see if they could tell what chemicals were used to clean the bones and see if that gives me any leads. If it's unique in any way then I'd try to trace it the same as the bag."

He considered the sunny street outside before saying, "I'd see if I can make any connection between the victim and someone who had access to the chemicals."

"Damn," Piper said, enjoying the rush of sugar hitting her bloodstream. "That's a lot of work."

"It is. Your way is way easier." King placed his mug of coffee on the desktop and cut his eyes to Lou. "Can't you just pop up and grab the guy instead?"

"He's been sticking to public places," Lou said. "It's hard to pick him out of a crowd."

"And you think the person who killed Delphine is the same one melting down people and putting their bodies in the catacombs?"

"I don't know. Maybe not. She didn't get melted down."

King considered this, flicking the duffel's pull tab. "So we still don't know if we're hunting one killer or two. What about the boyfriend? I didn't have a good feeling when I talked to him."

"Etienne?" Lou arched a brow. "Why?"

"He answered all of my questions fair enough, and I only got the impression that he'd lied once."

"When?"

"When I asked if he had any idea who'd hurt Delphine, he said no. I'm not sure I believe that."

Lou rolled her shoulders inside her leather jacket. "A hundred people put him at an art event at the Grand Palais."

King shrugged, unconvinced. "People fabricate alibis all the time. He could've wandered around just enough to make sure everyone saw him. Left, killed her, and returned as if he'd never escaped at all. The Grand Palais is a big place, right?

We should check and see if there's security footage for the entrances and exits for that whole night to see if he did just that. But even if we find it, it's possible that he knows a secret exit."

"I don't think he killed Delphine." Lou took a letter opener off of King's desk and used it to scrape her nails clean. Piper wondered if that was blood she was cleaning out. "I've specifically asked my compass, 'Did he kill her? Is this Delphine's killer?'—and both times I got nothing."

King arched his eyebrows. "I'd still like to look at that event footage."

"I'll see if I can get—" Lou's words were cut off by the ding of the door as someone stepped across the threshold into the agency.

It was Dani, looking gorgeous in her white wool coat, her long hair sleek and beautiful over her shoulder. Piper's heart took off like a shot.

She wasn't sure why, but she stood up.

What am I going to do? Run away? She's blocking the door. If I go upstairs, she's going to follow me. I can't escape through the closet without Lou. Maybe if I just go in there and hide, Lou will know I want to—

Dani wrapped her arms around Piper and hugged her tight. Against the panicked ranting of her mind, she found herself softening, relaxing into the embrace. It helped that Dani smelled so nice, her hair and skin fragrant. Her cheeks were chilly from the November wind blowing through the Quarter.

"I'm so sorry about your mom," Dani whispered. Her hold tightened. "I can't even imagine."

Piper wanted to say something. Maybe *thank you* or *it's okay*.

But she looked up and saw that both King and Lou were trying not to look at them. King had suddenly taken a deep interest in the bottom of his coffee mug and Lou kept cleaning her nails with the silver blade of the letter opener, but her back had turned slightly, further blocking them from view.

"Sorry." Dani stepped back, releasing her. "I just missed you."

"It's okay." *I missed you too.*

All the warm feelings from their hug evaporated when she remembered what she'd vowed to do the next time she saw Dani.

I should just ask her to move out now. No need to drag this on, make it difficult. It'll just be worse if I wait any longer.

"Um, can I talk to you upstairs for a minute?" Piper asked. Dani nodded. To Lou, "Are you good down here?"

Lou looked like she had all the time in the world. "Yeah."

King, suddenly jolted back to action, said, "We can talk about our next steps for the case."

Dani already had her key out and was opening the door that would lead up to the apartment.

Piper took a deep breath and followed her.

15

Matteo lay on his bed, his stomach churning. He was homesick.

His room in Venice was nice, especially once he'd begun to unpack all of the lovely gifts from his luggage. Inside, he'd found brand-new shoes with clean soles. Pristine clothes that still had the tags on them. Packages of sweets, comic books, and movies.

And Venice was interesting. The gentle lapping from the canal outside his window lulled him to sleep each night and cheerful sunlight woke him each morning.

But it was colder here and he didn't know anyone. Despite his forced cheer and determination to make Konstantine proud, he found himself longing for his friends. For the sight of Konstantine crossing the piazza and lifting his hand in greeting before stealing their soccer ball with a few swift kicks then returning it with a smile. For stories and rumors shared in whispers each night beneath the Blessed Virgin.

Konstantine and the other boys who hung around the church were Matteo's first feeling of family after his nonno died, the last family he had in the world.

So he wanted to help Konstantine.

But Matteo had the distinct impression that no matter what he did to please her, Vittoria didn't like him. After the warm greeting, she'd largely ignored him. When she caught sight of him in passing in one of the villa's many hallways, she regarded him not only with a cold eye but with a certain irritation. As if his very presence annoyed her.

Then why had she asked for him? *If she doesn't want me here, why ask me to come?*

To distract himself, Matteo focused on his mission. He'd listened to the adults talking at mealtimes. He'd picked up rumors on the street when traveling with the house maid to complete errands, carrying packages and shopping bags for her. He'd pretended to get lost in rooms and stairwells so he could eavesdrop on phone calls and whispered conversations in the corners of hallways.

There had been much internal debate about whether or not he should record the information in his Bible or in his comic books. If it was the Bible, Vittoria might read it. Or perhaps, under the guise of piety, she might ask him to read her a passage or page some night after dinner or before bed. The comic books, he reasoned, she'd have no interest in at all.

So there, in the white spaces between panels, he etched the secrets he learned, placing only one or two on a page to make them far less noticeable at a glance.

It had become a ritual for him. Each evening after dinner, when he was excused to his room for the night, he would spend the hours before bed recording the secrets he'd collected that day by lamplight.

He had been writing in a Deadpool comic when someone knocked at his bedroom door.

Quickly, he closed the comic book, shoved it into the middle of a stack of others just like it, and sat up.

Vittoria appeared in the doorway, not waiting for permission to enter. That was fine, Matteo thought, if a little rude. It was her house, after all.

Tonight, she wore a black silk jumpsuit cinched at her waist by a thin leather belt. Her hair was pinned up off her shoulders, with only a few ringlets framing her face. Her lips had been painted bright red to match her long fingernails.

She'd changed since dinner. Standing in the lamplight of his little room, she looked smaller, her eyes darker.

"What have we here, little prince?"

She closed the door behind her, shutting them up in the room together.

"I'm just reading," he said. Matteo kept his body still, his eyes on her face.

He didn't fidget or look at the stack of books.

"*Just* reading?" she asked with a hungry smile. "Because a little bird told me that you've been writing things down as well. Letters to your friends, perhaps? Maybe to Konstantine?"

His heart beat faster as he considered what lie he might tell, which one she would believe.

"Won't you tell me what you've been writing?" she asked.

Her face was menacing, painted half in the lamplight and half in shadows. And the dark flowing around her seemed to dance and move.

"*Niente di importante*," he said. "Just stories."

"I want to see them." She opened her hand and extended it toward him.

He shifted on the bed and it creaked. "I'm a little bit shy."

She tilted her head at that, but her hand remained opened, waiting.

Matteo pulled the first book from the pile of comics and handed it to her. Now he did fidget in place, the bed creaking as she opened the cover and regarded the first page. Then a second.

His fidgeting was for show, of course. There was nothing dangerous in this comic. It was what Konstantine would call a diversion. In this one and several others he *had* written stories. Sometimes he changed the character's dialogue or drew on their faces.

"I like to imagine the stories differently," he said, looking up at her through long lashes, hoping he seemed embarrassed. "It's fun."

"Clever boy." She closed the comic book. "I can see why he favors you."

Matteo smiled.

Vittoria didn't return it. "Unfortunately, this means I must hurt you for no reason. I'd really hoped you'd give me a reason, but you've been such a good boy. Too good, really."

The nervous sputter of Matteo's heart slid into true panic. "You're going to hurt me?"

Vittoria sighed. "Yes. I'm sorry, but it can't be helped. I see no other way."

"What—" Matteo searched for the words. "What did I do wrong?"

Because if it wasn't the eavesdropping, what had been his sin?

She looked at him then, searching his face. "You like to get what you want, don't you, Matteo? It feels good when you get something that you want?"

"*Sì.*"

"Well, you see, I asked Konstantine for what I want, and he *didn't* give it to me. He gave me you instead. You can understand how that's made me very unhappy, can't you?"

His heart was pounding so loudly in his ears he could barely hear her. He was measuring the dimensions of his room with his eyes. The distance from where he sat on the edge of the bed to the door.

It wasn't a big room, but he definitely couldn't reach the

handle without passing her. And she would certainly grab him before he ever escaped the room. This close to her, he could smell her perfume. Something sweet. Too sweet. It made him nauseous.

She tossed the comic onto the bed. She began undoing the leather belt around her waist.

No, he thought. *No, please.*

"This is what's going to happen," she said, wrapping one end of the belt around her hand. "I'm going to whip you. Hard. And when I believe you've cried enough, I will have you call Konstantine. Perhaps a video call would be best. When he sees your beautiful little face stained with tears, how absolutely *pitiful* you look, he will feel terrible for sending you here. Then he will give me what I *really* want."

"I can call him crying now," Matteo said. "I'm very good at pretending."

Vittoria tilted her head, smiling. "He's no fool, Matteo. I want this to be *real*. Now, take off your shirt and kneel."

"Please," he said. "Maybe tell me what you want and I can get it for you."

She clucked her tongue. "Such a good boy. But no, you cannot give me what I want."

"But—"

Her hand struck him before he'd even seen her move. It was a sharp slap that caught his ear, making it ring. His jaw throbbed from the impact of it and his mind blanked with the shock.

She hit me. She actually hit me.

No one had ever hit him before.

His friends, especially Nario, got a little rough and shoved him sometimes, but that had been play.

Tears welled up in Matteo's eyes.

Vittoria's smile spread. "Yes, that's a good start. Now kneel down in front of me. Look at the wall."

Please, he thought. *Please don't let her hurt me.*

He thought of the strega. With her cool leather jacket and guns, and sunglasses. The way she moved through the dark as if she was made out of it.

He slid off the bed until his feet hit the cold tile floor. Slowly, he grabbed the bottom of his shirt, his brand-new white polo shirt from Konstantine, and pulled it up over his head.

Please come. Please.

He balled up his nice new shirt and held it against his chest, offering Vittoria his bowed, bare back.

"Yes, like that," she said. "We will hurt your back and spare that pretty face of yours."

The leather belt hit the floor in the ready position with a soft *thwap*.

Matteo drew a breath, bracing himself for the pain.

16

Piper felt like an idiot. She was standing in the middle of her living room with the most beautiful girl alive and she was about to ask her to move out.

If only my heart doesn't explode first, she lamented. She placed a hand over her chest and felt the knocking.

"Are you okay?" Dani reached down to slip off her heels one by one and threw her coat over the back of the island's stool. Then she rolled her eyes. "Of course you're not okay. Your mother just died. I just meant, what's wrong? You look upset."

"I think—" Piper searched those big brown eyes. Her beautiful full lips. *Just say it, you idiot.* "I think you need to move out."

Her stomach clenched so hard she thought she might puke.

Dani, on the other hand, looked as if she didn't understand. "What?"

God, don't make me say it again. It's so hard already.

"I think you might be happier if you didn't live here." Piper rubbed her sweaty hands against her pants. "You could get Octavia back and find somewhere with more space. I bet you could find a nice place closer to your work."

Dani's brow furrowed. "It's a twenty-minute walk from here to *The Herald*."

"I just think it would be easier for you if you found a different apartment."

Dani eased herself down onto the sofa and pressed her palms together in front of her face. "If you need more space because your mom died, I can—"

"No, that's not it," Piper said, coming around to join her on the sofa. "I just think you'd be more comfortable if you lived somewhere else."

"What are you talking about?" Her eyes rapidly searched Piper's face. "I want to be here with you."

"You can't mean that."

Dani's eyebrows shot up. For a long pause she said nothing, clearly trying to calm herself. "It's true that we moved in together very quickly. Had my apartment not blown up, I probably would've waited for at least another year, possibly two."

Piper's hand shot up. "See! You wouldn't have moved in with me if you'd had any other choice."

"What are you talking about? That's not what I just said."

"But it's true that you moved in with me because you didn't have another option."

Dani frowned. "Of course I had choices. I could've lived with my parents or gotten another apartment. It's not like I had to be here or on the street."

Piper considered this. Piper wouldn't have been able to find another apartment in the area because she didn't have as much money as Dani did. But with Dani's resources, it was true—she could've gone somewhere else. She could've rented any of the hundred furnished vacation rentals in the city until she found a more permanent arrangement. Hell, she could've gotten a hotel room.

Dani licked her lips. "If this is about the viola—"

"It's not about the viola," Piper said quickly.

"Then what is this? I know your mom died, but this conversation started before that. I'd ask if you were trying to break up with me, but you never actually asked me out, so it can't be that." And here Piper heard the first notes of bitterness in her voice, and Dani must have caught her own tonal shift too, because she added, "Not that I blame you. You had plenty of reasons for not trusting me and taking it slow. I get it. But this whole move-out-because-you'll-be-more-comfortable thing is bullshit. Tell me what's really going on."

Piper could barely think over the thunderous pulse in her ears. How in the world was she going to explain that Dani was too rich to live here? It sounded stupid in her head, so she could only imagine what it would sound like if she said it aloud. *Rich people can do whatever they want.* Hadn't she just been reading about a Silicon Valley billionaire who lived in an airstream trailer or something?

"Do you want me to pay more rent?" Dani asked.

"What? God, no." Piper pressed her fingers into her forehead. She was getting a headache.

"Then what is it? Explain it to me. If it's not the viola, it's not what I pay in rent, what is it?"

"I just—I just don't think this is going to work out."

Dani pulled back as if slapped. After a moment she managed to ask, "To be clear, *what* isn't going to work out? Us living together or *us period*?"

Piper took a breath. "Both. Neither. We're too different."

"Says who?"

Piper's blood pressure hit the roof. "Your mother! The world! *Me!*"

"Wow. Okay." Dani looked away, turning toward the opposite wall and regarding it with a distant stare. It seemed like an hour before she said, "So you want me to move out."

"I think it would be best for you."

Dani stood and glared down at Piper, her hands fisting in her own hair. "Don't tell me what's best for *me*, Piper. Not you, or anybody else, gets to make that decision for me. If you want your space, *fine*, but don't pretend that you're doing it for *me*. I want to be here. I gave up my *cat* so I could be here. I'm happy here. In this apartment. And with you."

Piper threw up her hands. "You shouldn't have to give up your cat to be with someone. I feel *horrible* about that!"

"Octavia is fine! She doesn't even like people. It's hardly like she's attached to me. My mother got her and then didn't want to take care of her. Now Tavi only wants someone to keep her bowl full. And it's not like I gave her to strangers! I can see her whenever I want."

"You kind of did," Piper countered. "She's in Italy right now, and you don't even know Konstantine."

Now they were both standing only inches apart, their faces red, their chests heaving.

Piper thought maybe they would kiss, and she wanted to kiss those lips. *Badly.*

But Dani had begun to cry, bright tears standing out in her eyes.

Oh god. Are these anger tears? Anger tears were dangerous.

"I'm sure she's fine," Piper was quick to add. "I don't think Lou would let Konstantine watch her if he didn't know how to take care of a cat. She just did it because I couldn't breathe."

"This isn't about the cat." Dani clasped her hands behind her neck and groaned. "Are you really this dense?"

What was going so wrong here? Whenever Piper had had to distance herself from girls in the past, they might've cried or been bummed out, but they'd never told her that she was *wrong*. They would talk it out, Piper would present her evidence, and then they were able to move into the friend zone.

This conversation didn't feel like it was moving in that direction at all. In fact, it felt like Dani was going to refuse to move out.

Dani blinked and the tears began to dry. In their place was a hard determination. "I want to ask you a couple of questions."

Oh god, Piper thought. *I've activated journalist mode.*

"Okay," she said reflexively.

"Question number one: Do you like me?"

"Of course."

"Romantically?"

Piper didn't think she could convince her otherwise, as hot and heavy as they'd been in the bedroom. "Obviously."

Dani took a menacing step toward her. "You think I'm beautiful? Smart? Attractive? Long-term partner material?"

What game was this? "...Yes?"

"Which one?"

"All of the above."

"Do you have a good time with me?"

"Of course I have a good time with you." The truth was Piper hadn't laughed with anyone so much in her life—not even Henry.

"So there is no problem with me or our chemistry?"

"No."

Dani threw her hair over her shoulders. "Question two."

"We are way past question two. That was like ten questions."

"Fine, *part* two. Do you like *living* with me?"

Piper thought of their lazy mornings, smiles shared over warm mugs and kisses as soon as her eyes were open. Walking into the bathroom and finding Dani in the shower, the beautiful curve of her body framed by the opaque glass.

"Yeah, I like living with you."

Dani's brow furrowed again. "So when did that change? At lunch with my parents?"

Yes. "No."

"You're lying."

"I'm not lying, I just—" *I just what?* Piper's resolve was deteriorating. The more questions Dani asked, the more confused she felt. She *did* like Dani. She *did* like living with her. But she still couldn't stay here because—because—

"Listen." Dani ran a hand through her hair. "I think I get it. When I went to your house—"

Piper's blood iced in her veins. "When you *what?*"

"When Lou and I went to your mother's house."

"Lou!" Piper screamed. "Lou, get up here right now!"

Oh god, oh god, oh god. She must think—Oh god, oh god.

"Why? What's wrong?" Dani's eyes widened. "We were just looking for the papers we needed for the burial and to work out what needs to happen with her estate."

Oh my god, oh my god, oh my god. Piper collapsed onto the couch, her head in her hands.

"Lou!"

"Why are you so upset?" Dani tried to sit down beside her, but Piper flinched away. "It's just a house. It doesn't mean anything."

"Except that I'm hella poor and you're like a freaking duchess."

"You're not poor."

Piper looked up from her lap only long enough to yell again. "Lou! I swear to god, if you don't show up right now I'm going to—"

"What?" Lou pushed open the apartment door, her free hand resting loosely in the pocket of her leather jacket.

"Get me out of here," Piper demanded. The blood in her face was throbbing.

Dani's mouth fell open. "Piper, wait. We need to talk about this."

"No. I can't. *Lou.*"

"Piper!"

Lou's hand was cold on her arm as she pulled her toward the darkness.

Lou had no choice but to stand in her living room and listen to Piper rant for thirteen minutes. As the girl paced and whined and expelled more energy in this one moment than she had in days. Just when she thought Piper might run out of things to say, she would fix on a new tangent and begin again, rehashing the argument from a fresh angle.

At its essence, it boiled down to, *Why didn't you tell me you'd taken her there? How could you take her to my house? God, now she must think the worst things about me.*

Lou knew better than to interrupt this before it ran its course.

Finally Piper fell back onto Lou's bed and covered her face with the bend of her elbow.

When one silent moment had stretched into three, Lou said, "You're embarrassed."

Piper lifted her arm. "Hell yeah, I'm embarrassed. How could I not be? Why didn't you go to my mom's place alone? At least you've already seen it, and hell, drug dens are nothing new to you anyway."

"King asked me to bring her."

"I'm going to kill him."

Lou watched Piper fold in on herself, the energy that had overtaken her moments before quickly draining away. She wasn't sure what to say to her, to reassure her that Dani didn't see her the way Piper thought she did. That no one cared about this the way Piper herself did.

She hadn't finished considering her options when a sudden jerk through Lou's navel tugged her forward.

Someone was calling for her. Someone needed her *now*.

Someone...small?

"I have to go," she said, moving toward the linen closet.

"Fine, abandon me," Piper called out from under her arm. "If you're gone, at least I can cry in peace."

17

———

Vittoria's heels tapped on the cold tile behind Matteo. "I'm thinking twenty or thirty lashes to start, and we will see how you are then, all right?"

Her voice was far too happy for the topic at hand.

Before Matteo could answer, the belt came down. It whistled through the air before one swift snap licked his skin.

He cried out. The pain and surprise scraped along the inside of Matteo's mind, heightening his fear.

"*Per favore. Mi dispiace!*" he shouted.

But the belt came down for a second time.

He bowed further forward, trying to tighten himself into a ball.

It will end, he told himself. *She cannot hurt me forever.*

He braced himself for the third strike. He waited. And waited.

He was worried that he would turn and she would hit him in his face, but a choked gurgling piqued his curiosity.

Slowly, he turned, and gasped.

There she was. *La Strega*.

La Strega had Vittoria against the wall by her throat. Her feet kicked and scraped along the floor as a pale hand held her suspended. The belt tumbled from her grip as she tried to claw at the hand holding her, but there was nothing to grab. The jacket's leather sleeve was impenetrable.

Then someone was beating at the door, pushing it open.

La Strega pulled her gun with her free hand and shot the man opening the door. He fell back as if punched, crumbling onto the floor outside the room.

With this new space, *La Strega* turned and shoved Vittoria out of the room, slamming the door shut after her.

Then it was just the two of them in his little room.

Matteo's heart raced like a rabbit's.

"Do you want to get out of here?" *La Strega* asked, her eyes invisible behind her sunglasses. "*Vieni con me?*"

"*Sì, sì!*" Matteo scrambled to his feet, tugging his shirt down over his head.

She reached out for him.

"Wait!" he cried, and leaned across the bed to grab his stack of comic books. Then in his unsure English he said, "Okay. I is ready."

She extended her hand and he took it, noting the size difference between hers and his own. Then, and he wasn't sure why, but she reached out and clicked off the lamp.

ONE OF THE CUTS ON THE BOY'S BACK WAS BLEEDING, AND IT filled Lou with rage. She wanted to put a bullet—maybe three—between Vittoria's eyes. Instead, she focused on getting him out of there. Once he was safe, Louie would come back for the bitch.

The only problem was she wasn't sure where to take him. Lou had a feeling that this was connected to the situation Konstantine hadn't wanted to talk to her about, and if he still wasn't ready to talk to her, who would?

As the boy scrambled across the bed to grab a stack of comic books, gathering them clumsily into his arms, she thought of Stefano.

Stefano would be all too happy to tell her what the hell was going on.

And while it was easy to find Stefano with her compass, it was harder to tell if he was alone. It'd be quite awkward if Konstantine was with him, and she had to explain that he wasn't the Italian man she was looking for at that particular moment.

But when the light clicked off and the darkness softened around them, she stepped through without hesitation.

In place of the villa's small bedroom was a shadowed courtyard. At the edges, lush trees grew, obscuring the stucco wall encompassing it. At its center, a lit fountain burbled softly. Stefano was at a little wooden table, one knee crossed over the other in the picture of ease. His face momentarily lit as he struck a match to light the cigarette between his lips. Then he was taking his first long drag and exhaling up toward the sky.

Konstantine was nowhere to be seen.

When he saw her, Stefano's ease evaporated. He sat up, shaking out the match.

He crossed the courtyard in three strides, dropping down in front of the boy. *"Matteo! Che ti è successo? Stai bene?"*

"Sto bene, sto bene! Mi ha salvato!"

When he saw the blood on the boy's shirt, he pulled it off, and swore.

In English he said, "That bitch. Did you kill her?"

"No," Lou said. "Should I?"

Stefano stood, motioning toward a door at the edge of the courtyard.

"If you did, it would cause more problems than solutions."

When the boy objected he said, "*Non discutere con me! Entra dentro.*"

He pushed the boy forward and thrust him into the room despite his protests.

It was Konstantine's office, Lou realized. She'd never walked into the room using the door, so she hadn't realized where it was located in the space. She thought it had been like Padre's office, in the basement of the old church, rather than a one-room annex surrounded by a lush courtyard.

Yet there was the large desk in front of the fireplace. The high-back leather chairs and adjacent bathroom.

"Where is Konstantine?" she asked.

"He went home an hour ago. Were you looking for him?"

"No. I was looking for you."

Stefano arched a brow. "For me? Why?"

"Because he won't tell me what's going on, but I think you will. At least you want to."

Stefano laughed, a high, bitter sound. He opened two drawers before finding a small first aid kit and throwing it onto the desktop.

He asked the boy to turn but he refused.

"Come on," Stefano said. "Do you want it to get infected?"

The boy jerked his chin at Lou and slammed his comic books down on Konstantine's desk.

She didn't follow the rapid exchange that followed. Italian was harder to understand when the speakers spoke quickly and the voices rose as the emotions escalated, but after a short tussle, Stefano threw up his hand and handed the boy the kit.

"Matteo won't let me help him. He wants you to do it."

Matteo. So that's his name.

Matteo crossed to her with the kit in front of him, his smile suddenly shy. He held it out to her.

"Please," he said in English.

Stefano rolled his eyes.

Lou tried not to smile. "Turn around then."

When he didn't seem to understand, she made a spinning motion with her finger.

"*Sì, sì.*" He offered her his back.

Lou sat down in the leather chair and regarded the broken skin carefully. Stefano turned on a separate lamp.

"Thank you," she said without looking up.

"*Di niente!*"

There were two stripes crossing the narrow plane of his back. One was red and raised. The other had broken the skin.

"Are you going to tell me what's going on?" she asked Stefano as she opened the kit and found an alcohol wipe.

She tore the corner off with her teeth and fished the soaked towelette out of its tight wrapping.

"Yes," he said. But then added no more. Lou took this to mean they would talk once the boy had been sent away. "Tell me what happened with Vittoria."

"I found him kneeling on the floor and she was hitting him with a belt. I stopped her."

"How?"

"I choked her. Threw her out of the room."

"Did you kill anyone?" he asked, his eyes remaining dark.

"There was a man who came to stop me. He's dead."

Stefano exhaled. "How did you know she was whipping him?"

"*L'ho pregata! Come la Madonna* ," Matteo said.

Stefano's brows arched. "So you can hear prayers?"

Lou's hand stilled above the cuts. Was that what had happened? The boy had prayed to her. She wasn't surprised. Praying wasn't so different than what Piper or King did when they needed her, basically demanding her attention with their minds.

Actually, now that she thought about it, this wasn't the first time. It had been the same when she'd saved Shai, a little boy trapped in a child pornography ring. Hadn't he said she'd answered his prayers?

Still, it made her wonder. Was that what was happening in Paris? In those weeks when she'd kept getting pulled to the city, had someone been praying for help? Maybe not to her specifically, but a desperate plea for anyone, anywhere, to intervene? Assia, maybe?

A lot of good it had done her. Lou had been too slow.

"Matteo," Stefano said gently. "What did Vittoria say to you before she hit you?"

Matteo spoke in soft, flowing Italian, of which Lou understood nothing.

Halfway through, Matteo hissed. Then he muttered, "*Freddo.*"

"Liar," Stefano said. "Go on."

He finished his story while Lou worked.

Once she'd wiped each line and left them wet and gleaming, she searched the kit for bandages. She found a roll of gauze and tape and covered each wound.

Then she pulled the shirt back down and placed a hand on his head. "All done."

"*Grazie.*" Matteo leaned forward and kissed her cheek before she could react.

Stefano swore again. "*Esci di qui bastardo, prima che dica a Konstantine che hai baciato la sua donna!*"

Lou was smiling as the boy fled the office.

Stefano slammed the door behind him and ran a hand through his hair. "To answer your question, we are on the brink of war with the Albanian mafia."

Lou settled back into the chair, lacing her fingers over her lap.

"Vittoria is on good terms with them, but the price she

wanted for helping us was you."

He clearly wasn't as confident in his English as Konstantine was, but his words were perfectly clear, if thickly accented.

"Me?"

Stefano nodded once. "Konstantine refused. So she asked for Matteo instead. But Matteo just told me that it was a trick."

Lou frowned. "What was a trick?"

"Before she hit him, she told Matteo that she was only hurting him so that Konstantine would feel guilty and bring him home. Then she could get what she really wanted. I can only assume that meant you."

"What did she want with me?"

"To kill for her. She has a, uh, what is it called in the American movies? A list of people she wants to die?"

"A hit list."

"Yes, she has a *hit list*," he said. "You kill for her. She makes peace with Erjon and we don't go to war with the Albanians."

Lou considered this, opening and closing her hand as the cooling alcohol dried on her fingers.

"Why didn't he ask me?"

Stefano sneered.

"Because you make him weak. He will cross an ocean for you, spend a fortune on you, risk his life for you, but he can't bear to ask you to do the same. *Why?* Because he *loves* you?" Stefano's anger was immediate and explosive. He slammed his open palm on the desk. Matteo's comic books bounced. "It's stupid. No. It will get him *killed*."

Stefano's anger didn't bother Lou. But his words had struck a chord because they were true.

Konstantine *had* crossed an ocean for her. He'd protected her anonymity from the cameras of the world, including, most recently, those in Paris, where she'd wanted to put Assia's bones.

He had stepped in to save her friends when Petrov had taken them hostage. When it came to cases and information, he'd helped her more times than she could count.

In truth, she owed him far more than he'd owed her.

So why had he not asked for her help?

Stefano rolled a matchstick between his fingers. He was composed again, pushing his dark hair off his face. "When Padre Leo named Konstantine as his successor, I knew he would do well. He was the best of all of us. The smartest, surely. The bravest. But he has one terrible problem. When it comes to you, he does not make good decisions. He doesn't do what needs to be done, do you understand? *L'amore è cieco.*"

And was it true? Did she make him blind? Would he avoid an easier solution if it meant inconveniencing her?

She had to laugh at the irony of it.

King not wanting her to kill if there was another way. Konstantine wanting her to kill but refusing to ask.

"He hates it when I smoke in this office. But sometimes I like to piss him off. A little."

Stefano struck the match on the desk and relit the cigarette he'd extinguished.

You really are like brothers, then, she thought.

"So tell me." Through the thin blue smoke, he asked, "Are you *La Strega*? Are you the witch of our nightmares or no?"

"I'm not a witch."

"You certainly don't die easily. If I thought I could kill you without breaking Konstantine's heart, I would have already done it."

She smiled even though she knew he wasn't joking.

"If you don't really care about him, tell me."

"Because you do," she said.

"*Sì*," he said without pause. "*Sì*, I care for him. I swore to

Padre that I would keep him safe, and I will die for him. I know this. I don't know the day or the hour, but I will die for him."

Lou had no need to question this. She saw the devotion in his eyes.

Stefano pointed at her with the cigarette. "But will *you* protect him? I need to know if I am fighting alone."

It was hard to overlook the earnestness in his face. For a moment it reminded her of Piper, of the night when she'd said, *I'm going to be your best friend, Lou-blue. Just you wait.* And how much she'd meant it when she'd said it.

"I'll take care of the Albanians," Lou said. And just the idea of it set her skin alight with energy. She wanted to do it. She ached for it. It had been a long time since she'd been able to use her gifts in such a way. Serial killers and pedophiles were a pleasant challenge, true enough. But they couldn't compare to the delicious mayhem of a twenty-or-thirty-against-one fight to the death.

And the truth remained. If someone had threatened her with war, or had threatened Piper, King, Melandra, or even Dani, Konstantine would help without even being asked.

He would do what needed to be done without question or hesitation.

Now Lou had a chance to do the same.

"What of Vittoria?" Stefano asked. "Will you kill her for her little manipulations?"

"I want to. But his enemies will have a reason to unite against him."

Stefano nodded once. "*Sì.*"

"Then I guess she and I will *talk*." The way she smiled made Stefano shift nervously in his seat.

Lou stood. "Anything else I need to know before I go?"

"Matteo is waiting for you in the courtyard. I've seen him look into the window three times already."

"I won't keep him waiting." Lou turned to go.

"Strega?" Stefano said, standing and running a hand down the front of his suit jacket.

"*Sì?*" she said mockingly.

"Should I need you in the future, only on behalf of Konstantine, of course, should I...*pray* to you as well? Does it really work?"

Lou smiled. "It couldn't hurt to try."

"*Strega?*" Matteo stepped forward timidly, his head bowed slightly in a picture of humility.

Lou couldn't suppress her smile. "What do you want?"

Stefano stepped out of the office behind her and closed the door, locking it with a key from his pocket.

Matteo spoke in rapid-fire Italian, looking to Stefano for interpretation.

"She already knows *that*," Stefano said. To Lou, "He doesn't want you to tell Konstantine that he was whipped. He's worried Konstantine will be upset."

"Not bad," Matteo said in shy English. "It's okay."

But this didn't seem to be all. As the boy lingered, his eyes searched her face.

Stefano groaned. "Spit it out."

Another rapid stream of Italian, this time punctuated with a flourish of hand gestures. But whatever the request was, Stefano clearly disapproved.

"*No.* No, Matteo."

Matteo took this to mean he should ask again, and again, louder and louder until he received the answer he wanted.

After Stefano refused for the tenth time, Matteo turned to Lou. In exasperation, he cried out, "I want to go! I want to *go*. Back. With you."

Lou laughed. "I already have a pet."

And yet the little boy searched her face, waiting, begging for an answer.

Stefano pinched his brow. "He wants you to take him to the church where all the boys are. He thinks if they see you deliver him, it will be *cool*. I told him not to be silly."

It *was* silly. Yet Lou understood.

Once she'd lost consciousness in a confessional. The priest got her to a hospital before she bled out on the cathedral's floor, but he'd kept her guns and her bulletproof vest. So she'd had to go back and retrieve them. When she did, he'd rambled about God, and angels, asking Lou to explain what she was. Why she had the power to do what she did.

She didn't have an answer for him. Yet that hadn't stopped her from melding with the shadows of his office, performing a rather dramatic exit for no reason except to feed the old man's superstitions.

It had been fun. Sometimes you just wanted to *look* cool.

She reached out to the boy. "Okay."

He ran into her arms nearly squealing.

Stefano huffed behind them. But when Lou turned and he saw the boy in her arms, something in his face softened.

Or she thought it did. It was hard to tell. His grumpy, perpetually inconvenienced expression had returned already.

Lou didn't care. With a knowing grin, she slid her shades down over her eyes and stepped into a pocket of shadow cast by the low-slung roof of the dark office.

Matteo's heart fluttered in his chest as he clasped his arms around *La Strega's* neck. He felt something hard press into his ribs, and knew at once that she held a gun under her leather jacket. If she emerged through the darkness holding him in one hand, a gun in the other, Nario and Monte would never doubt his stories again.

He only wished he knew better English.

Konstantine had insisted they all learn and take their studies of the language seriously, but Matteo hadn't felt the deficit of his education as keenly as in this moment.

"Gun!" he said. "Gun!"

"It's okay," *La Strega* replied. "The safety is on."

He sighed. She hadn't understood, and now they were stepping into that strange nowhere again. It was a breathless place, and though the transfer lasted only a moment, it felt longer.

When they emerged they were in the church, near the pews.

Please let this work, he thought. Every lash on his back would be worth it just to see Nario's and Monte's faces when he arrived with *La Strega*.

The boys were standing behind the Blessed Virgin. This was their meeting place. The last check-in of the day before they went home. Tonight, they were talking loudly over one another. Nario and Monte shoved each other, and Matteo's heart leapt.

They're here!

Lou stepped forward and all eyes pivoted toward her.

The chatter died immediately, their eyes doubling then tripling in size as *La Strega* carefully set Matteo on his feet and urged him toward his friends.

"Thank you, my friend," he said with all the grand pomp and circumstance he could muster. It was difficult with the barely contained hysterical laughter building in his throat.

"Until next time, Matteo," *La Strega* said, and with a slight flourish became one again with the dark.

The slack-jawed boys began screaming, grabbing him, shaking him, demanding to understand what they had just seen.

And for a long time, they didn't stop.

18

———————

Piper exhaled one last shaky breath. There were no more tears to wring from her eyes and her abdomen was sore from its convulsing. She'd cried her heart out. It was done.

"Get up," Lou said.

Piper pulled the comforter off her face and found Lou beside the bed, hands in her leather jacket, a small, smug smile on her face.

"Why do you look so amused? Did you just choke a bunch of guys or something?"

"Get up."

Piper moaned. "Why do you hate me? What have I done to you?"

Lou ignored these questions.

Piper burrowed deeper into the covers. "But I'm not done feeling sorry for myself."

"Too bad." With one hard yank, Lou pulled the covers away. Carried on a draft, they slid across the hardwood floor out of reach. "I have something to show you."

Piper didn't think she could put quite enough disdain in

her eyes to properly reflect her blanket-less feelings, but she tried.

Nothing. Lou's smile only deepened. "If you don't get up I'll bring Dani here."

"I can't talk to her. I'm peopled out for the day."

"Then you should choose option one. No talking to people."

There was really only so much resistance Piper could manage when she was the guest in someone else's apartment, so reluctantly she reached out her hand and let Lou pull her to standing.

"What do I need to wear? A coat?"

Lou thought about this. "Yeah. Just in case."

Piper slipped her feet into her sneakers. "Where are we going?"

"It's a surprise."

"I hate surprises! And my birthday isn't until March."

Lou opened the linen closet.

"*Fine.* But I hope this ends in a delicious sugar-laden coffee." Piper stepped into the closet and pressed her back against the far wall. "Or a burger. I'm in the mood for a burger."

Lou stepped in after her and shut the door tight.

"Is this about your Paris murderer?" she asked. Hearing her voice in the compressed dark was intimate, cloying.

"No." Lou's hand was gentle but firm on her upper arm. The closet disappeared instantly, replaced by that flash of nothingness before a new world formed around them.

Piper's weight shifted and she was pitched forward, her feet trying to find steady ground.

Lou held her upright until she did.

When the world disappeared and rematerialized again, Piper found herself on a busy street corner. The night was punctuated by streetlights and neon signs running up and down the boulevard. The streets looked wet, though no droplets fell from the sky. Maybe there had been a hard rain shower earlier and that had left this portion of the world iridescent.

At first Piper wasn't sure what she was supposed to be looking at. Her searching eyes must've said as much.

"Her," Lou said, nodding toward a girl on the opposite corner. "In the pink skirt."

Piper knew at once why Lou had chosen her. Not because they dressed anything alike. Piper liked baggy pants and crop tops and this girl was in a neon skirt and a see-through fishnet top. Her black bra was visible even from where Piper stood. Her nails and lips were painted bright pink, and it was probably good that they matched because she kept chewing on her nails nervously as she looked up and down the busy street.

They were about the same age and had a certain similarity in their appearance.

"What about her?" Piper asked.

"Her parents didn't have much money. Her father died when she was young. Her mother is an addict. She started college but couldn't finish because life got in the way. She's like you."

"How can you possibly know all that?" Piper asked.

"We crossed paths when I was hunting Angelo. Her name is Adrienne."

Adrienne.

A man walked up to her, said something, and Adrienne plastered on a reflexive smile. But when the man turned, the smile was waning at the corners, even as she took his arm and began up the street.

"Do you think she's worthless?" Lou asked.

"God no!" Piper cried. "Of course not."

"She's had every opportunity that you've had, but this is

her life," Lou said. "She lives in an apartment with a few other girls, and if we went there now, I bet she'd be just as embarrassed as you were."

"Why? She's doing the best she can. It's not her fault."

"But it's *your* fault that you're not a millionaire and your mother died of an overdose."

"That's different." Piper felt like she'd been socked in the guts.

"So I can go put a bullet in her head and throw her in a ditch because it's different? Her life is her own fault."

"*No.*" Piper covered her face with her hands as if this would block out the world. "Ugh. I get it. No more. Get me out of here."

She thought she would be taken back to Lou's apartment then, but instead they appeared outside one of Piper's favorite burger joints in Chicago, a little place that she and Lou had discovered a few months before. She knew it at once by the smell and the sound of fifties music coming through the speakers.

Lou opened the door and held it for her. "Come on."

They chose a table by the window. Lou put her back to the wall, her eyes on the doors.

Piper slid into the opposite seat. For a long time she said nothing. She didn't know what to say.

It was Lou who broke the silence.

"Money is just something that happens. Some people have a lot of it. Others barely any at all. It's not fair how it moves around. People like the Martinellis shouldn't be sitting on piles of it while girls like Adrienne have to choose between giving a blow job or going hungry that night."

"I hear what you're saying." *I don't like it, but I hear it.*

Piper pulled a menu from the carousel at the table's edge even though she knew what she was going to order. The waitress motioned to them, giving the universal sign for *I'll be right with you*.

Lou didn't seem to care about any of this as she draped one arm over the back of a chair. "More money doesn't mean you're worth more. Fish had more money than you and he also tortured, raped, and murdered women before masturbating into their graves."

Not the image Piper wanted front and center of her mind as she searched the list of burger toppings, but Lou was right.

"You're feeling very philosophical tonight," Piper mumbled.

Lou shrugged. "I had a good night."

"If this is a sex thing, don't tell me."

"No sex," she said, the mirrored sunglasses rising as she smiled. "But you need to get over this money thing."

Piper understood this intellectually. Her mind could comprehend the words, see their meaning, but it didn't eradicate that horrible feeling of worthlessness still alive and well inside her. Maybe nothing would ever make that feeling go completely away.

"Okay, fine." Piper sighed. "I'm not worthless because I don't have a degree or a car or a house."

"And Dani isn't worth more just because she comes from money."

Piper groaned. "Okay, but she can speak like three or four languages and play bougie instruments and it's hard to not feel like an underachiever around her."

The waitress came and took their drink orders before disappearing again.

When she was gone, Lou said, "I can't play an instrument and my Italian is shit."

Piper threw her hands up. "Yeah, but you can do the shadow thing and the water thing and you're a freaking warrior badass with guns. Come on! I just have a Netflix account, man."

"I love Netflix," Lou said with a grin.

"Look, I get it. Okay? I really do. Those people who have to live in the trash heaps, or people who lose all their stuff in earthquakes and mudslides and hurricanes, they're still worthy. Most people on the planet can't play sonatas or buy a car and they're still worthy. *Everyone* is still *worthy*. I hear you. And I even agree with you up here." Piper touched her head. Then she touched her heart. "But somewhere in here I feel like everything that happened to me is my fault. That I'm where I am today because of the mistakes I've made, and I'm never going to be better than this."

Lou's good humor was gone. "It's not your fault."

Once the drinks came and they'd ordered the burgers and fries, Lou said, "Besides, you are rich."

Piper blew her straw wrapper at Lou, hitting her in the cheek before shoving the straw down into her water. "If you hit me with some platitude about how the gods created everyone equal and I'm just as precious as a malamute or something, I'm going to choke you."

Lou ignored this threat. "You're rich because your friends are rich."

Piper pressed her hands into the tabletop. "Excuse me? I thought you were trying to make me feel better about myself. Because if so, you just took a wrong turn."

Lou pushed her sunglasses up on top of her head, and the song changed from a slow love song to a trumpet-filled bop. "You've got King and Melandra, and you've got me. We aren't going to let you starve or live in a box. We aren't like your mother."

A fist clenched around Piper's heart.

Lou must've seen the pain cross her face.

"I'm dead serious. You might get threatened by murderers, criminals, or even the mafia, but not one of us is going to let you miss a meal or sleep under a bridge. You know that, right?"

Piper held up a hand, silently begging her not to say more. It hurt. It hurt to hear it. "I know, I just—"

It was the shame, wasn't it? The shame hurt. Because she would absolutely go lie down under a bridge before she could bring herself to ask someone for help. Before she'd let anyone see the ways in which she was utterly and totally failing.

Letting other people look out for her made her feel...*bad*. It had never occurred to her—*ever*—that the people around her might look out for her simply because they loved her.

Piper tried to swallow the lump forming in her throat. "I hear you, so please stop talking. You are literally killing me."

Lou stopped talking.

Piper dabbed at the tears in the corners of her eyes. "But seriously, what the hell happened tonight? Why are you in this wise-woman-on-the-mountain mood? Are you channeling Lucy or what?"

They remained silent as the waitress put their burgers and fries on the table, informing them the ketchup was in the carousel.

By the time she'd stepped away, Lou was grinning. "I'm going to kill some Albanians."

"Of course you are. With that much *glee* on your face, it's probably a lot of them. Is it a gang thing? Your Italian stallion ask for your help in settling a turf war or something?"

"He needs my help, but he didn't ask for it."

"Oh, he has a problem asking for help too, huh?" Piper snorted. "Who does that remind you of?"

19

After the fourth phone call in a row, King was getting a headache. He wondered if this was what getting old was like. He remembered a time when he could spend a whole day updating case files, working on the computer and doing back-to-back calls like the ones he'd just completed without so much as a dip in energy. Now that he was in his sixties, he felt like his battery was perpetually in need of a recharge.

"Maybe I'm just hungry," he said to the dog whose tail thumped against the floor. "Should we quit for dinner?"

King reached down and gave Lady's ears a good scratch. The dog continued wagging her tail. Overcome by the cuteness, King fished a treat from his pocket and fed it to her.

He gave his to-do list one more look and realized he was at a good stopping point for the day, but he needed to give Lou an update on everything he'd learned before heading out. It was moments like this he wished the woman would just get a cell phone.

"How can someone so young be such a luddite?" he lamented to the dog.

Then King remembered that Piper was with her. Or hiding out in her apartment, anyway. At first he'd assumed this was because of her mother's death. But now, given the way that Dani had been moping in and out of the agency, King wondered if there was something else going on. A lover's tiff, maybe.

Not my circus, not my monkeys, he reminded himself.

And he didn't have the time or energy to worry about it anyway.

He would call Piper, leave a voicemail for Lou—or hell, maybe even catch her—and give the update. Then, within twenty minutes, he'd be home, shoes off, pants undone in front of the TV with his leftover barbeque on his lap.

Better yet, he remembered the St. Louis Blues were playing at seven. Maybe he'd smoke a joint and watch the game.

With a significant uptick in his energy levels, King scrolled through his contacts, found Piper's number, and dialed. It went to voicemail, but that was fine. His aim could still be achieved.

"Hi, this is Piper! I can't come to the phone right now, but you know what to do!"

Beep.

"Hi, P, this message is for Lou, so just hand it over the next time she's around." He paused for the presumed handoff before saying, "Hey, Lou, I just got off the phone with the lab tech Konstantine referred us to. The bag is useless. Turns out it's a major brand found in just about every department store in France, so all they could tell us from the serial and batch numbers was that it had in fact been shipped to Paris, but they couldn't be sure which Monoprix it had ended up at, let alone where it was purchased or a time frame. As for the chemical the perp is using to dissolve the bodies, it's mostly lye. There's some other compound that they're not quite sure what it is yet, but it's the lye doing the work. This is no good for us because lye is in all kinds of things. Soap. Cleaning products, drain cleaner, food preservation, you name it. But in its liquid form, it's very toxic and harmful if you breathe it in, so if you come across someone with a breathing problem, that might be our guy, or, er, *gal*."

Smooth, he thought.

"I also spoke to the director again. I wanted to take a stab and see if maybe there was a connection between Delphine and Assia." Mel passed by the window and King waved. Lady, however, jumped up and ran to the door. King stood from his desk and opened the door to let Lady out. He watched as the dog trotted happily after Mel, following her up the street.

It occurred to him then that they could've asked Mel to help with the French interviews, since she knew more French than either Lou or himself, but he suspected that French and French Creole weren't a direct translation.

"I showed him photos of Assia and asked if he'd seen her around the museum, or if he could check the security footage for her. He freaked out about that, something about"—and here King tried to do a terrible French accent—"'Do you know how many girls her age wander through this museum each hour? Let alone days, weeks, months? And you can't even tell me when you think she was here?'" King dropped the accent. Doing it made his throat hurt. "He also said that they *do* have lye in their restoration department. Something about needing it to fix Roman pottery. I thought that was weird for a contemporary art museum, but then he went on about juxtaposing styles for adding meaning, and honestly, I missed all of that, but the point is, if Delphine and Assia were killed by the same person, there might be a connection to the art museum."

The light was fading through the large glass front windows. King needed to wrap this up.

"Anyway, I just thought you should know that there might be a—albeit thin—connection between Assia and Delphine. Maybe Delphine was an outlier, something happened and the attacker wasn't able to take the body away and dissolve it like they usually did, or maybe—"

The voicemail beeped. "If you're happy with your message, press two. If you'd like to re-record your message—"

King pressed two. Then called Piper again.

"Got cut off there. Anyway, if he attacked Delphine at home, I don't know why he'd run away unless she fought back and the attacker was injured. But good luck calling to see if anyone turned up in the hospital injured that night. A city the size of Paris must see wounds like that every hour of every day. Still, maybe we can check the hospital closest to her house on the night of the attack and see if anything hits. Otherwise, I don't know why he would take off without the body if dissolving them is his MO."

King wasn't even going to try to pronounce the name of Delphine's partner. Instead he said, "The boyfriend didn't come home for two more hours. Oh, and the footage did show him at the Grand Palais. He's on camera almost the entire time except for a three-minute bathroom break around nine. So he probably didn't kill her. Three minutes is a tight fit."

The door to the agency opened again and Dani crossed the threshold with her heels in her hands and her handbag thrown over her shoulder.

King said, "Hey. I'm leaving Piper a message. Want me to pass anything along?"

She gave him a small smile before bending over his desk and scrawling a note on his blank notepad.

He turned the yellow legal pad toward him so he could read it.

"Piper, Dani wanted me to tell you that she's looking for another apartment like you wanted."

King didn't bother to add that Dani had underlined the *you* three times.

He turned to Dani for confirmation, but she was already trudging up the stairs to the apartment above, the door closing behind her.

Definitely trouble in paradise, he thought.

"Well, that's all I've got. Lou, let me know what you want to do next. Piper, I hope that you're doing okay. I haven't heard back from the funeral home yet, so nothing to report there, but when I do, you'll be the first to know."

He terminated the call, pressing the phone into his chin thoughtfully.

This rift between Dani and Piper was putting a kink in King's plan.

He'd been planning to offer to host Thanksgiving dinner at his place for the five of them this year—Lou, Piper, Mel, Dani, and himself. He didn't think that Piper had had a good Thanksgiving with her mother in years, but more than that, he knew from experience that holidays after a loss were particularly hard. The lack of someone was keenly felt around a time where the national propaganda pushing *togetherness* and family cheer could drive a person mad. The Thanksgiving dinner was going to be the first of many efforts to make sure that Piper didn't feel alone this holiday season.

But now, maybe he should check with Piper before he invited Dani? It would feel weird to exclude the girl, given how she'd become as entrenched in their team as Piper and Lou. They were a set, the five of them—and as much as he hated the idea of being cozy with a crime boss, Konstantine was also becoming a permanent fixture.

But he needed more time with that idea.

Then again, Dani had family in the area, parents and

extended, from what he'd gathered, so maybe she already had plans.

One problem at a time, he chided himself.

Right now, dinner.

King tidied up his desk and shut down his computer for the day. He checked to make sure the coffee pot was clean, turned off, and gave the place one appraising look-over before stepping out into the sunny street and locking the door behind him.

"Robbie," a voice called.

King pulled his key from the lock and turned toward the voice.

It was Beth. Today she wore a deep purple pantsuit with golden hoop earrings. Her smile was bright as she looked over the rim of her glasses at him.

"Why, hello," King said reflexively, noting distantly how a dizzy sensation flooded his head. "What brings you down here?"

"I was three blocks away at the precinct for an interview and I thought, you know what I'd like? *A muffuletta*. And there was a sale, buy one get one free, and I thought, now who would I like to eat this with? Why, Robbie King, if he's available."

She smiled, and King's plans for leftover barbeque evaporated.

"How do you feel about hockey?" he asked.

"I love to watch sports as a general rule. Basketball is my favorite, particularly the WNBA, but there isn't a good game on tonight, so hockey will do."

"Come on then. Here, let me carry that."

King took the sandwich bag and watched Beth fall into step beside him. It wasn't lost on him, the way his stomach fluttered as they continued down Royal Street in the direction of the shop.

"Do you live far from here?" she asked. "I knew you walked so I assumed it was close."

They turned a corner to find a pack of unwashed hipsters with a set of pots and an accordion, remixing a song by The Strokes. He could smell the alcohol rolling off of them from here.

"Very close," King said, placing one hand on the horse-head post to inspect his shoes. "My apartment is above Melandra's shop."

Beth's eyebrows rose. "Oh. How interesting."

As they crossed the threshold into Madame Melandra's Fortunes and Fixes, the chandelier overhead moaned eerily, giving the impression that a ghost had swooped down from the ceiling and was circling over their heads. The air was saturated with incense, a deep, earthy sandalwood permeating everything. Mel was clearly close to closing up for the day, with all the candles restocked and figurines in order.

She was sweeping the floor when they entered, bending to scoop the dust into the white pan she held in one fist.

"Good evening," King called out.

"Good evening, Mr. King," she said without looking up.

When she did straighten up, she saw Beth.

Her eyebrows rose a little. "Why hello there, Ms. Miller. What brings you here? Candles? Fortune-telling, perhaps?"

Beth only smiled. The overhead light caught on the gold beads in her hair and sparked.

"I've come to watch hockey," Beth said. "But I must say, your shop is beautiful. Very well put together. I can tell you've worked hard on it."

Melandra's smile beamed a little brighter. "Thank you. I have."

"And I was so sorry to hear that your bastard of an ex-husband went missing in prison. I hope you don't mind me saying, but after what he put you through, I hope he turns up dead."

Mel and King exchanged a quick look.

Neither of them were worried about Terrence showing up unannounced and causing any more havoc in their lives. The man had earned a one-way trip to La Loon, and had left the prison in the company of Louie Thorne. They knew he wouldn't bother anyone ever again.

"Yes, well, let go and let God." Mel dumped the dust into the waste bin and tapped it against the rim for good measure. "Who's playing tonight?"

"The Blues," King said.

"Ah, your hometown. Well, you two enjoy yourselves then."

And if King didn't know better, Melandra's devilish wink was directed at Beth and not him. But Beth was giving Lady's ears a good scratch—whether she saw this wink or was hiding her face, King couldn't tell.

"Thanks, you too," he said cautiously, and crossed to the stairs.

As he approached his door, King ran a mental checklist of whether or not his apartment was fit for company. No dirty socks in the living room or dishes on the countertop. Had he made anything smelly to eat? No. He hadn't cooked in at least two days.

With a deep breath, he opened his door and motioned for Beth to step inside.

Over her shoulder, he made a quick, panicked appraisal. But the kitchen was clean and the living room tidy.

As he put the sandwich bag on the island counter, he peeked into his bedroom to make sure his bed was made and there was nothing embarrassing to be found, like his underwear on the floor.

He was in luck. All clear.

"Oh, this is nice! I wasn't sure what to expect. French Quarter apartments can go either way. They can be really nice, or really *not*," Beth said. "But this is very well done. And it's the perfect size for you."

"Yeah, I really like it," King said, and he did. The large living room with its red leather sofa and enormous coffee table. The checkered kitchen and gray countertops. The bedroom big enough for his king-sized bed. It was true that the bathroom was a tad small for a man of his size, but it was clean and had a shower, tub, and sink that all worked. What else did he need?

"It's the balcony I love," he told her.

Without waiting to be asked, Beth crossed the living room and opened the balcony door. She stepped outside and cooed her appreciation as King fished out two plates from the cabinet and arranged the sandwiches and chips onto them.

"Do you want to eat out here or inside?" she asked.

"It's a little chilly to eat outside. Let's eat in the living room if that's fine by you," he called. "Do you want water or a soda? I'm afraid I don't have much else in the house."

"I'll have whatever you're drinking."

She came back into the apartment and shut the door.

"Robert King." She sniffed. "Do I smell ganja in here?"

King froze, his hand on the handle of the refrigerator.

He considered lying to her, but he knew instantly that would never work.

She continued sniffing the air, reminding him for a horrible moment of Lady.

"I definitely smell—ah, yes." She bent down in front of his vinyl collection and began thumbing through them. It wasn't until she found the Bob Dylan record did she whistle.

She opened it up, and there was his small, very old, very stale stash of weed.

"Am I going to go to jail for that?" King sat the sandwich plates down on the coffee table.

She arched a brow. "For less than a gram? You've got one, maybe two joints here? Do you think I have time to prosecute someone for two joints?"

He was well aware of her case load. "No. No, I don't think you do."

She sniffed the plastic bag again. "And by the look of it, you've had this for a *very* long time. I'm guessing that you don't smoke often."

"No, I don't. But you're very knowledgeable about weed."

"I'm the DA," she said. "And I raised a teenage son."

She closed the vinyl and slid it back into the stack with the other records.

"Oh, you have Cooke's *Ain't That Good News* and *Portrait of a Legend*."

She slid *Portrait of a Legend* out of its sleeve and put it on the player. The music whined to life just after. She began to dance slowly to its rhythm, and King sank onto the sofa.

Watching her dance, one hand on her belly, the other held up as if in testament as she swayed slowly back and forth, he realized he'd missed having company. A woman's company.

More than that, he liked Beth very much.

"I like it when you look at me that way," she said, finally sitting down on the sofa beside him.

"I like to look," he admitted.

"Do you? That's nice to hear." Her braids clacked as she gathered them in her hand and slid them over one shoulder before leaning forward and grabbing her sandwich plate. "To be honest, I was worried I'd scared you off the other day. When you'd said, 'Thanks for the offer, let me think about it,' I thought that might be code for 'Get me the hell outta here.'"

King laughed. "I don't usually speak in codes."

"No, you don't." She smiled at him again, this time over her plate as she ate another chip. "I like that about you. You're direct but you're also kind. A lot of people call themselves blunt when really they're just jerks. You're no jerk."

His face was growing hot.

She wrinkled her nose. "And you're cute as can be when you blush."

"Thank you." King shoved half of the muffuletta in his mouth to prevent himself saying anything.

"Did you have a chance to consider my offer?" she asked, slipping another chip into her mouth.

King didn't know what to say. Should he tell her that yes, he had? It had crossed his mind, on and off again in the days since they'd last talked. And when he had let his mind run through its daydreams, its fantasies, he couldn't deny that Beth was a beautiful woman.

He respected the hell out of her, and he'd believed her when she'd said that should this sour in any way, it wouldn't affect his work.

"I can't promise anything," he said. "I'm not at my full... emotional capacity."

Her brow furrowed. "Yes. I remember you telling me about Lucy."

King started. "Did I tell you her name?"

"No," she said, and pointed at the urn on the edge of the coffee table. "She's right there."

Dear God. King hadn't even seen it. First he'd been concerned with not spilling their plates and then he'd been watching Beth dance slowly, sensually, in his living room.

I was watching her, while Lucy was right there.

Because in the far corner of the table was the silver urn with Lucy's name etched into the shining metal.

Lucy Catherine Thorne.

An invisible belt tightened around King's chest, and on its

heels, an undeniable wave of guilt. *How can I even think about this, about moving on, when she's—*

Don't be stupid, a voice said. *Lucy doesn't give a shit about that. And that's not even her. That's a pile of ash.*

He wasn't sure how long he'd been staring at the urn when he felt a warm hand on his knee and a gentle squeeze.

"I'm sorry," he said, tearing his eyes away. "I don't mean to kill the mood."

She shook her head. "Nothing to apologize for."

"This can't be what you had in mind when you came over with sandwiches."

She smiled. "If you think I'm put off because you have an actual real-life beating heart, Robbie, you're mistaken. I'm still interested, though not tonight. And not here because I suspect this was the last place the two of you were together, am I correct?"

She was.

She nodded, silently considering something. Finally, she said, "My place it is, then. Tomorrow night when you get off work. You bring the dinner this time."

She gave him her address.

"But—"

She held up her hand. "It's an open invitation. If you want to come, come. If you don't, I'll know perfectly well why. There'll be no hard feelings. I swear it."

King let this thought settle in.

"What about tonight?" he asked, as the first Sam Cooke song ended and the second began to play.

She reached for the remote and turned it to the sports channel. "Tonight, let's watch this hockey game."

20

———

Lou stood in the space beneath her kitchen island and surveyed her arsenal. The room smelled of sawdust and plywood. And it was warmer than the apartment above. The shelves held guns, ammo, grenades, blades. A machete the size of her arm was propped up in a corner. Hooks screwed into the wall held a flamethrower and two bulletproof vests.

As she looked over her options for the night ahead, she couldn't remember the last time she'd been *excited*. The promise of a fight, bloody violence, and even the possibility of death made her limbs itch.

She shrugged on a tactical vest with throat and bicep protectors. This would be her first time trying it in a fight, since usually she went with as little coverage as possible to keep her movements loose. When Melandra had accidentally shot her through the shoulder and Lou almost died, she'd quickly grown tired of listening to Piper, King, and even Konstantine complain about her need to upgrade her gear.

So she'd try the new guards tonight, but if it was too hard to move with them on, they were coming off. She added

Kevlar sleeves to her forearms and an extra layer of protection to rest across her quads. But she decided against anything for her lower legs. The thick leather boots that went halfway up her calves felt like enough.

After the armor was in place, she chose the Brownings from the shelf, loaded them, and slipped them into the holsters hugging her ribs. Twin Glocks went into her thigh holsters.

She thought about packing more guns, but the truth was, her targets would have guns, and if she needed to, she could take them off their corpses. What she couldn't materialize from thin air was ammo. So instead of adding another holster, she wrapped two ammo belts across her torso. On each hip, she added grenades and enough .40 S&W cartridges for the handguns.

Lastly, she pulled her new Benelli M3 Super 90 off the shelf. This was also a new gun that she'd gotten only because Konstantine thought she'd like it. She would've ignored this assumption if not for two facts. The first was that Konstantine was one of the few people who'd seen her fight and lived to tell the tale, so perhaps he did know something about her tastes. Second, he'd been right about the Brownings, which she'd been favoring over her Berettas since he'd given them to her.

So fine. She'd take the Benelli shotgun tonight and see how it did.

This is enough to get started, she thought. If she ran out of guns and ammo, she could always come back. That was one of the many advantages that she had. A quick sidestep through darkness and she could grab more guns or ammo. Though she admitted, if only to herself, that she hated leaving the heat of battle once she was in it.

With her arsenal locked away again, the hidden latch on her kitchen island secured, she stood fully armored and ready in her apartment. The orange-pink hues of sunset spilled across her wooden floors as she gave the St. Louis skyline one last lingering look. The high-rise buildings and metal arch looked golden in the last collected light of the day. The water shimmered, sparking white and blue as a small speed boat pushed north against the current.

Lou was happy. She felt steady. At peace.

Lucy sprang to mind. Aunt Lucy as she'd been on the Hawaiian beach just hours before she'd died, with her long hair spilling over one shoulder.

I just want you to be happy, Louie. At peace.

Probably not what you had in mind, Lou thought with a smile, knowing that Lucy was far beyond caring what she did now. *But I am happy.*

A crow flew past her window, calling out.

Lou took this as a good sign.

She took one more deep breath.

Her lungs found resistance from the body armor, but she liked the compression.

With a smile, she shut herself up in her empty linen closet, the shotgun pointing upward to fit in the space.

For a moment there was only the sound of her breath in the softening dark. The slow exhalation of moist air from between her lips.

Erjon Hysa, she thought. *Where are you?*

Because while Stefano had referred to them collectively— the Albanians—there were in fact more than twenty crime families that controlled organized crime throughout Europe, the Americas, and Asia. And even if Stefano hadn't used his name, Lou knew exactly which of the families were on friendly terms with Vittoria.

Lou had made it her business to know. The way that some grandmothers followed the lives of soap opera characters, Lou had made a study of the world's crime factions for years.

Erjon Hysa's clan, the largest and most dangerous family clan, had crossed Lou's radar before, when she'd been looking for Angelo. Lou had passed him by at the time because instead of trafficking drugs, Erjon's crew focused on humans and human organs.

Luckily for Erjon, until very recently, Lou'd had other interests.

Her plan for tonight was simple. She would destroy Erjon's clan and anyone that might take up his cause against Konstantine when he was gone.

Revenge killings, after all, were a given unless Lou made sure there was no one who could seek revenge.

Erjon was the most important target, given that he was kyre, their patriarchal leader, but Lou would kill the kryetars, the underbosses, too, if she had the chance.

Erjon Hysa. And anyone who poses a threat to Konstantine, she told her compass. "All of them."

The compass responded in kind, whirling, clicking, searching the other side of the ocean.

It snapped into place, a sharp tug, a certainty recoiling through her.

The shadows swelled, shifted, and with one step toward a closet wall she'd never reach, Lou found herself in an enormous house.

The ceiling was at least sixteen feet above her head. She looked up, noting the stained glass. The dark, silent staircases.

From an adjacent hall, a man in a bathrobe pattered slowly across the marble floor with half a sandwich—or something that looked like a sandwich—in his mouth.

She thought he would simply walk by without noticing her, but then he did.

He looked once, then again in shock, his eyes doubling and tripling in size. He opened his mouth to scream but choked on his own midnight snack.

Lou didn't wait.

She pumped the shotgun once and fired, blasting a hole through the man's side. He hit the floor, dropping hard and fast.

The food—Lou could see it was a fried pasty now, and it made her think of calzones—splattered across the marble floor.

Blood pumped out of him at an alarming rate, spreading in a rapidly growing pool. But the man wasn't dead.

Lou crossed the floor and bent over him, giving him a good once-over. It wasn't Erjon. An underling then, because Lou never questioned her compass.

She pumped the shotgun again.

"No—" he began, but she pulled the trigger, spraying his brains across the floor.

Where is he? Where is Erjon?

Someone was yelling upstairs. The voice carried down to Lou, words she didn't understand.

Lights in the house began to click on, bright and infuriating. The shotgun blast had been too loud. But if she was being honest with herself, she'd wanted to wake the house. She wanted to spur them all to action. The bigger, the better.

Sneaking through each room, quietly dispatching her targets, wouldn't have been fun at all.

Where's Erjon?

A sharp tug to the right, toward the staircase leading upstairs. A bullet whirred past her head, biting into the wooden door behind her. She looked up to find four men on the balcony above taking aim.

She pumped the shotgun and fired three times. Three men tumbled over the railing and crashed to the floor below.

She realized that if she really wanted to fight a large group at once, the Benelli's pump setting was too slow.

Let's speed things up.

She converted the gun to its semi-automatic setting and reloaded it with as many shells as she could fit into it.

Footsteps rushed toward her. *A lot* of feet.

She smiled. *Much better.*

She chambered a round.

She couldn't stay here, where she was exposed. She could be shot from all sides, even from above. Not to mention that now that the lights in the house were turning on one after another, she was losing precious ground.

Lou stepped into the shadow cast by the staircase and slipped. In place of the staircases and foyer, Lou was above now, looking down.

No sooner had she settled onto the landing above did six men run into the foyer from the right doorway and eight from the left. A few stepped into view from beneath the balcony's landing, but she couldn't see them clearly without stepping into the light. But there must be more footmen beneath her. She could hear them, if not see them.

Still, she had plenty of targets to be getting on with.

She pulled the trigger again and again and again, moving from right to left, her aim to kill fourteen new targets.

Her excitement grew as each new head split open, throats spurted, and men doubled over as if socked in the gut.

The semi-automatic setting was *definitely* better.

But her gun clicked, empty. She needed to reload.

Resting the shotgun against a shoulder, she pulled a Browning and fired. The first two bullets blasted through one man's cheek and out the back of his head, splattering the front door with brains. The next three bullets caught two men in the back, between the shoulder blades, as they began to flee. They hit the ground face first, unmoving.

She stepped away from the railing and reloaded the shotgun as a fresh shower of bullets blew apart the wooden bannister. Then the landing was assaulted, holes punching open in the floor at her feet and the wall by her head.

They were shooting through the floor from below, trying to use it as cover for her return fire.

A bullet blasted through the front of Lou's boot, tearing a hole in the leather, barely missing her toes.

She swore and stepped into the room behind her. A bathroom, dim and vacant.

She leaned across the bath and turned on the water, letting it run into the plugged tub.

Just in case, she thought, should she need an exit to La Loon. Perhaps with the infamous Erjon in tow. Though climbing into tubs with corpses wasn't her *favorite* thing.

She shut the bathroom door loudly, hoping to give them the impression that she'd retreated inside, cornered and helpless.

Yet in the thin patch of shadow behind the bathroom's door she asked again, *Erjon Hysa, come out, come out, wherever you are.*

She stepped forward.

When the world reformed again, she was in a closet. Albeit the largest closet Lou had ever seen, the size of her living room perhaps, with clothes running along two opposing walls. Lou's compass clicked, and it wasn't mistaken.

He was here.

She crept forward, looking for feet beneath the hanging garments. But many of these had shoes stacked neatly beneath them, and discerning an empty shoe from one containing a foot wasn't so easy.

Come on out.

You know you want to.

More gunfire spattered in the distance. After a short silence, feet pounded up the stairs, the shouting growing louder. Then there was banging on a closed door.

They hadn't realized she'd left the bathroom yet. Good. That gave her plenty of time to deal with Erjon. And it wasn't lost on her that he probably wanted to cry out, to tell them that she was here in his closet, not in the bathroom, but to do so would sign his death warrant.

Lou kept her eyes on the clothes, every item perfectly still, betraying no movement.

She passed silk shirts and pants hanging in plastic wrappings.

Her navel contracted suddenly, and at the same time, a metallic scraping screeched over her right shoulder.

She dropped, turned, and fired.

The shot missed, punching a hole in the back wall.

Erjon shouted and kicked out. She moved, and instead of a foot to the face, the hit landed hard on her left shoulder. Her weight folded on that side, the shotgun clattering to the floor. Without thinking, Lou kicked out her right leg and struck his charging body. His knee folded, bringing him down into a crouch.

Then she was on her feet again, thrusting the butt of the shotgun up, connecting with his chin.

He fell flat on his back, and Lou could've ended it right there. Just bent over and shot him in the face.

But she was enjoying herself. Relishing the way her whole body felt alive with adrenaline.

So she let Erjon sit up, only watched him with the shotgun propped against one shoulder as he touched his mouth tenderly and rolled his eyes up to meet hers.

He was shirtless, with his hair hanging in his face, his chest heaving.

"It's you. It's really you," he panted, blood running from the corner of his mouth. His eyes widened to the size of half-dollars. "I thought you were a bullshit rumor that he spread to protect himself."

"Nope." Lou repositioned the shotgun.

"No, please." Erjon came up onto his knees, holding his hands out in front of him in a defensive posture, as if this could hold her back. "Please. Tell Konstantine that I won't—"

Lou pulled the trigger and blasted a hole through Erjon's chest. The man was blown back onto the floor of the closet, crumpling against the far wall. His wide eyes rested open and unseeing on the closet's ceiling.

A door banged open and Lou turned in time to find two men crowd the doorway to the closet. Cries rang out as they saw Erjon's bloodied corpse spread out on the floor.

Lou shot each, knocking them back, before shoving aside a line of silk shirts and stepping through the dark.

When she found footing again the upper hallway was cleared. The door to the bathroom she'd used now stood open, water still spilling from the faucet into the tub, over-flowing onto the floor.

She listened. But apart from the running water, the house was quiet.

Almost quiet.

Somewhere, a child was crying.

Lou took the opposite hall, slowly checking corners and nooks as she passed. It wasn't until she found the bedroom at the far end of the hallway that the crying grew clear.

She pushed open the door and found a little girl's bedroom, all pinks and soft whites. A canopy bed drowned in stuffed animals.

Lou opened the closet and inside found a woman clutching a crying girl to her chest.

The woman took one look at Lou with the shotgun and began to plead.

"Please. Please, no."

Will they come after Konstantine? she asked her inner compass.

The compass remained still, quiet. Lou was more than a little relieved by that.

"I won't hurt you," she said, and disappeared without firing a single shot.

Lou found six more men on the estate and shot them dead. The two she'd left unharmed in the closet were the only survivors.

She considered going back for Erjon's body.

It seemed like a waste, not to use Erjon's big, beautiful tub to take at least one body to La Loon, but her whirling compass told her that her job wasn't done.

This house had been cleared, Erjon's immediate entourage extinguished. But there were others.

Extended members of the Hysa clan that would take up his work now that Erjon was gone.

Lou took a moment in the silent house to reload her guns and survey the carnage of the half-destroyed mansion.

Then she asked, *Who's next?*

The shadows swallowed her.

One man was halfway through a blow job when Lou stepped into his dark bedroom and pressed the shotgun into the side of his head. His eyes didn't even flutter fully open before she pulled the trigger and disappeared.

A second had been standing on his patio, smoking a cigarette and drinking coffee.

Lou's first bullet exploded the cup. The second split his skull in half, his bathrobe falling open to reveal his corpulent body as it hit the paving stones.

Who? Who? Who? she asked the compass inside her. And each time it delivered her.

One man was bent over his breakfast table, shoveling eggs into his mouth, a newspaper spread in front of him, when Lou stepped out of his pantry and pressed the gun to the back of his head.

Another had been out for a morning walk with his dog, spouting orders into his cell phone as a cigarette bobbed between his loose lips.

Lou stepped out from a hedge to meet him.

The moment he saw her, the cigarette fell from his lips.

She pulled the trigger and the shotgun clicked empty. No problem. The Browning worked fine.

The dog, scared by the shot, had taken off across the park, tail tucked between his legs, without looking back.

She caught two men in a car together, and here she began to feel *really* nostalgic. She'd finally caught Angelo in a car like this, blowing out his driver's brains as the car sank to the bottom of the bay.

So now a small laugh escaped her as she materialized in the front passenger seat and found a startled driver gripping the wheel.

The two men in the back sat up straighter, coming alive with the alarm ricocheting through their bodies. Lou's compass snagged as she turned the gun on each, so she put a bullet in each of their heads. The driver was trying to find a gun under his seat, but driving the vehicle and reaching for it wasn't proving possible. Lou ended his struggle with a quick *tap-tap* from her Browning, knocking his head against the window. It shattered, creating a spiderweb pattern on impact.

She was out of the car before it crossed the road's painted lines and slammed into a road sign.

One more, she thought as her compass snagged for a final time. *There's one more.* Her compass was sure of it.

But when she materialized this time, a spray of bullets hit her.

Four, five, six, seven.

Click. Click. Click.

Lou's chest hurt where the vest had absorbed the force of the bullets. When she opened her eyes she found an older man, perhaps King's age, reloading his pistol with shaking hands.

Lou aimed the shotgun, but another wild, panicked bullet cut through her forearm. Then one slammed into the bicep cover and a third clipped her hip as she moved to evade the shots.

When his gun clicked empty for a second time, he was screaming.

She didn't understand all the words falling rapid fire from his lips. Either he was begging, swearing, or cursing her name.

It didn't matter. Her bullet went through his brains just the same, knocking him back over a desk to the floor behind it.

When the room rang silent with the report from her shot, she waited.

But the compass was still. The urge to move fading within her. She went around the desk to check that the man was truly dead, and he was.

He lay on his stomach, his head turned to the left, the eyes open and unseeing. The gun had fallen from his hand and lay a few inches away.

Lou waited for the compass to whirl again, to tell her who the next target was.

It remained still. There was no pull, no longing.

The job was done.

21

"*S*ì, *sì. Grazie.*" Vittoria terminated the call with shaking fingers. Her hand clenched and relaxed around her cell phone compulsively.

What should I do? Cosa faccio adesso?

"What's happened?" Alessandra came to sit beside her on the sofa, the fireplace lighting up half of her face. "*Dimmi cos'è successo.*"

Vittoria forced herself to set the phone down. "The Hysa clan is dead."

"Erjon is dead?" Alessandra's eyes searched her face as she took Vittoria's hand.

Vittoria pulled away.

"Erjon. Dren. Guzim. Ilir. *Everyone.*" Even the bastards who were sixth and seventh down the line. *La Strega* did good work. She'd left no one. "Only Yeta and Afrodita survived."

Alessandra fell back as if struck. "Who would do such a thing?"

She grabbed a pillow from the sofa and pulled it against her hair.

"*Dio mio.* Do you think it was *La Strega?*"

"Of course it was *La Strega*." *You idiot.*

Vittoria usually loved Alessandra's eyes. For their warmth, for their bright innocence. But now, doubled in size, she looked like a cow-eyed moron.

No, she thought. *I'm the one who has been stupid. Very, very stupid.*

She'd miscalculated.

Why had she thought that she could use the woman as Konstantine had?

Why had she thought that Konstantine could simply ask her for help and that his refusal to do so was merely possessiveness? A reluctance to share his power.

He had an asset, an ally, and wanted to keep it to himself.

And all that bullshit about *I don't own her, I don't command her* was just some diplomatic way of telling Vittoria no. Or perhaps even that the rumors of Konstantine's style were true.

That he was kinder to women, more respectful than most of the men in their profession.

None of that mattered now.

What mattered was that Hysa's clan was dead and Yeta and Afrodita had clearly described a wraith of a woman with a shotgun and mirrors for eyes.

Erjon threatened Konstantine, and *La Strega* destroyed him completely.

Will she see me as a threat too? How will I convince her otherwise?

Vittoria threw her phone onto the table and it landed with a crack.

Alessandra gasped.

"Don't be dramatic," Vittoria said, pressing her fingers into her temples. She was getting a headache. "It didn't break."

But when Vittoria lifted her eyes, it wasn't Alessandra staring down at her.

It was her. *La Strega.*

She was already here, and she was pulling Alessandra over the back of the sofa by her hair.

"*Aspetta! Aspetta!*" Vittoria was on her feet, clearing the table and chairs to meet Lou where she stood. The living room was softly lit with morning light, but even as the shadows receded, there was still enough darkness to give *La Strega* the advantage.

Responding to her voice, both Giuseppe and Flavio rushed into the room.

She didn't release Alessandra as she turned and shot both men through the head before refocusing her attention on Vittoria.

More footsteps immediately pounded down the stairs. The cavalry was coming, rushing from the rooms above to Vittoria's rescue.

"Do you want anyone else to die?" *La Strega* asked in English. "I will kill everyone who comes into this room if you don't give me a choice."

And you and you and you. Vittoria's mind snagged on that phrase, repeating it again and again.

"*State tutti fuori!*" she screamed. *Everyone stay out!* "*State tutti fuori!*"

The footsteps faltered. Murmured concern rumbled in the hallway.

"Vittoria," Alessandra whimpered, her hands clasped over those pulling her hair.

"Hush," Vittoria said. To *La Strega*, "What do you want from me? Why are you here?"

Vittoria wished that the woman would lift her mirrored shades so that she didn't have to look at her own scared face. She looked too old in that reflection. Old and helpless.

"I came to give you a message," she said.

"I am listening," Vittoria said. She stood up straighter, trying to return some of the dignity she felt she'd lost.

"If you ever try to manipulate Konstantine again, ask too much of him or—"

"We're family," Vittoria said, raising her chin a little higher. "Our father—"

Lou shoved Alessandra away and grabbed Vittoria by the throat. She had her against the wall, choking, before she could even blink.

Vittoria kicked, clawing at the woman, but it seemed to do nothing. *How is she so strong? She can't be a woman. She can't be.*

Vittoria knew women.

"You look a little like your father, especially when I'm close to you like this. Do you know what I did to your father? Your brothers?"

How could Vittoria forget the reports of the Martinelli curse? As one by one her half-brothers were killed, their bodies never recovered except for Benito's, which had been thrown at her father's feet bloodied and battered.

And then her father, killed.

"Do you want me to show you what I do to a Martinelli when I find one?" the witch asked.

Vittoria wanted power, of course. But she wanted to live long enough to wield it.

"No," she spat out, even as her throat ached under the ruthless grip.

"If you try anything like this again, you won't be his family. You'll be *dead*."

Here the witch smiled, and it sent a sickening shiver through Vittoria. *Satana in persona. È venuta a mangiarmi viva.*

"Did he send you to tell me this?" Vittoria asked.

"He doesn't know I'm here."

"Then why come? You've killed the Hysa family. Why come here and—"

The fingers around her throat tightened. That was answer enough.

La Strega wanted to make it perfectly clear that Vittoria had overstepped. She'd crossed over into the witch's territory, and if she did it again, she would not survive.

Vittoria understood perfectly now. This woman didn't belong to Konstantine. She'd never belonged to Konstantine.

Konstantine belonged to *her*.

"Okay," Vittoria choked out. "I understand. I will not hurt him again. I'm not a threat to him, I promise."

For a moment she didn't move. Then, slowly, she loosened her grip and stepped back.

Alessandra remained on the floor, softly crying.

"Don't give me a reason to visit you again," she said quietly, but before Vittoria could muster a reply, Lou drew her fist back and slammed it across Vittoria's face.

Vittoria cried out and collapsed, catching herself on her hands and knees.

"That's for Matteo."

When Vittoria looked up, cradling her face, the witch was gone.

22

—————

Konstantine sat back in his chair, a frown on his face. It wasn't even noon and the day was shaping up to be *very* strange. The phone in his hand was warm from the back-to-back calls he'd been receiving for nearly an hour now.

Konstantine was still like this, considering the news, when a knock came at his door.

"*Entra.*"

Stefano pushed the door open with one hand, balancing a tray in the other.

He placed the tray on Konstantine's desk, twin espressos on white saucers and a bowl of red grapes between them.

"Why are you frowning?" Stefano slid one of the coffees toward him.

"I just received *three* very interesting phone calls," Konstantine said, lifting the little espresso cup to his lips.

Stefano took the other coffee and settled into the chair opposite the desk. "From whom?"

Konstantine took another drink before speaking. "The

first call was from the Peçi family. They wanted to know if I *needed* anything?"

Stefano arched a brow. "Was it a threat?"

"No," Konstantine said, returning the cup to its little saucer. "They were very adamant. They want us to know that we're not on bad terms and they look forward to working with us soon. The second call was from the Hoti family. They wanted to know what they could do to broker peace with us."

Stefano was unable to hide his smile behind his espresso cup.

Konstantine cocked his head. "What happened?"

"The Hysa family is dead."

"The *entire* Hysa family?" Konstantine rose up in his seat.

"She spared Erjon's daughter and the girl's mother. Otherwise, yes."

She. Konstantine didn't need to ask who *she* was. Lou.

"Why did she kill them?" *How did she know I had a problem?*

Stefano shrugged. "Maybe she was bored."

"Or maybe you told her our situation."

Stefano said nothing to this. Instead he asked, "Who was the third call from?"

"Vittoria."

Stefano snorted. "What did she want?"

"To tell me that she hopes Matteo is doing well and to apologize for hitting him."

Perhaps Konstantine had not been hallucinating as he'd crossed the palazzo that morning and called his usual hello to the boys playing soccer out front. For the briefest of moments he'd thought he'd seen Matteo, running and laughing amongst the group.

When he'd looked a second time, he had not been there. In fact, the whole pack of boys had run from Konstantine's sight.

He'd thought this was strange, but children were often

wild and erratic. He thought perhaps it was a new game, or maybe even they'd done something mischievous, and he would discover what petty offense they'd committed later. But he hadn't considered that the brief sight of Matteo had been anything other than melancholy for the missing boy.

"Also, that his things will be arriving this afternoon." Here Konstantine met Stefano's eyes. "Matteo is here."

"*Sì*," Stefano said, throwing back the rest of his espresso. With a smack of his lips, he leaned forward and put the empty cup on the tray.

"Did you bring him home?" Konstantine asked.

"No," Stefano said. "Your woman did."

The *snap-pop* of air resounded in Konstantine's ears. When he looked up, Louie was emerging from the dark corner of the office.

As soon as she stepped into the light, he knew exactly what had happened. Blood was splattered across her face and drying across her hands. She still wore her tactical gear, and all the holsters but one were empty. Whatever guns she'd used were either returned to her apartment or ditched in the heat of the moment.

"What's the emergency?" She looked to Stefano first. "I was about to take a shower."

Konstantine opened and closed his fist. "Did you really kill the entire Hysa family?"

Lou shrugged. "I was bored. The case in Paris is taking too long."

Konstantine couldn't hide his skepticism. "How convenient for me that you killed the ones most troublesome for me. I wonder where you got the idea?"

He cut his eyes to Stefano. The bastard didn't even have the decency to hide his smile.

A little head peeked into the office through the window in the door.

"Hey! *Vieni qui adesso!*" Konstantine called out.

The door handle turned slowly and Matteo stuck his head inside. "*Sì?*"

Konstantine motioned him forward. "*Vieni qui.*"

Matteo looked like he'd rather do anything else, but slowly he passed between where Stefano sat and Louie stood to arrive before Konstantine.

"Where did she hurt you?" he asked.

Matteo threw an accusing look at Stefano.

"*Stronzetto. Non ho detto niente.*"

"Liar," the boy said in English.

Stefano threw up his hands.

"He didn't tell me," Konstantine assured him, realizing not for the first time how big his hands were on the boy's arm. *He's still a child. A child.* "Vittoria called this morning to say she was sorry."

Matteo whirled to look at Lou. She returned his smile and Matteo laughed.

"Show me," Konstantine said again.

Slowly Matteo turned and lifted his shirt.

On his back were two long welts, red and angry. There were also tape marks. Someone had cleaned him up, and he was glad for that.

One welt had begun to scab. Clearly Vittoria had broken the skin. The other was puffy and turning purple with a forming bruise, but the skin was unbroken.

A quiet rage filled him as he pulled the shirt back down.

"Did she pay for this?" Konstantine asked, cutting his eyes up to Lou's.

"I killed a few of her people."

"How many?"

"Three, I think. And I punched her in the face."

Stefano snorted.

"It wasn't enough, in my opinion," Lou said.

Konstantine agreed, and yet he was glad that she hadn't killed Vittoria. Despite the problems between them, maintaining a unified front helped him to control the older, more powerful families in Italy, those who still respected the Martinelli name.

Konstantine turned Matteo around to face him.

"I'm sorry that—"

"*Questi sono per te. Guarda! Guarda!*" Matteo pointed frantically at the stack of comic books that Konstantine had pushed to the corner of his desk when arriving that morning. He hadn't had long to contemplate them before the first of those bewildering phone calls had come through.

"What is it?" Konstantine accepted the book Matteo thrust into his hand.

He watched as the boy flipped through the pages, looking for something. Then he was pointing at the cramped writing filling the white spaces between the comic panels.

"*Ho scritto tutto, tutti i suoi segreti,*" he said proudly.

Lou placed a hand on the boy's head. "You have a spy."

Matteo visibly preened at her touch.

"Is this what she whipped you for?"

"No, she whipped him because she wanted you to send me," Lou said.

Konstantine put the book down and pulled Matteo into his arms. He squeezed him, hard, before placing a kiss on his cheek. "Bravo il mio ragazzo. Sono così orgoglioso di te." *I'm proud of you.*

And Konstantine remembered the first time Padre Leo had held him up like this, squeezed him tightly and said he was proud. It was a different office, many years past, but he hoped it comforted Matteo as much as Padre's kind words had comforted him.

Then he released him and patted his cheeks.

"Now both of you, get out of here." Konstantine pointed at the door. Stefano rose and motioned for Matteo.

Before the office door closed, Stefano turned to Lou.

And bowed.

Shock vibrated through Konstantine's mind. *What the hell—*

Then the door closed and they were alone.

"I—" he began, and didn't get far.

A blade pressed against his throat. He stopped breathing.

Louie Thorne stood over him, a knife in her right hand, her gaze bare and cold.

"The next time you send a child instead of me, it will be the last thing you do." She tilted her head. "*Capisci?*"

When he didn't respond immediately, the blade cut the skin under his jaw. It burned, warm blood welling up to meet the steel.

"*Ho capito,*" he said.

She took the blade and stabbed it into the desktop.

Then her lips were on his throat, licking, kissing the wound.

He slid his hands into her hair, pulling her face up to his.

"I'm sorry," he said, and fell into the kissing, a collision of lips and hunger. His fingers couldn't work at the armor fast enough. All that Velcro ripping apart as he removed layer after layer from her body, until he finally found her bare skin beneath.

It excited him to taste his blood on her tongue, electricity sparking along his skin.

Then she was leaning her weight against his, forcing the chair farther and farther back.

He resisted, rising up instead and seizing her. One shove and he sent the coffee tray skittering off the desk and onto the floor. The comic books followed.

Then her legs were hooking around him where he stood,

pinning him against her.

"Why did you do it?" he asked. He kissed her throat, her neck.

"Why do you do it for me?" she asked, pulling off the holsters, the Kevlar sleeves.

"Because I—" He searched her face. *I love you.* "I always want to help you."

Down to her t-shirt and pants, she looked up at him. "I only did what you would've done for me."

A swell of relief washed over him.

"They're really dead? All of them."

She smiled. "Very, *very* dead."

No war. At least not today.

And Matteo was home with him.

He was glad that Lou had disciplined Vittoria in his place. He wasn't sure he'd have had the restraint to stop from really hurting her.

He was furious, and yet...*yet* he couldn't hold on to it.

Not with Lou kissing him, pulling his shirt over his head, running her hands down his bare chest. Not when she was pulling at the belt around his hips.

He pulled her shirt off and pushed her back onto the desk so that he could remove her boots.

"I'm covered in blood," she said.

"I don't care."

"And probably brains."

"I. Really. Don't. *Care*," he said. "And I took off my shirt."

This made her laugh.

"What?"

"As long as your clothes are clean."

He seized her mouth with his, swallowing her laugh.

Then he was inside her. She contracted, then relaxed, her legs wrapping around him, pulling him deeper inside and holding him there.

He was suddenly very glad this desk was large and sturdy, given the abuse it was now withstanding.

Her nails raked up his back and she pressed her face into the side of his throat.

She moaned into his ear, causing his rhythm to falter.

"Don't you fucking *dare*," she whispered.

Konstantine flicked his eyes up, remembering for a moment the window in the office door. Blessedly, Stefano had pulled the shade on his way out.

Good friend.

Lou's rhythm changed suddenly. She grew very still, her hold on him tightening and the breathing in his ear closer to a pant.

He felt her contract a moment before a flood of heat and wetness washed over him.

Then she bit him, hard. That was enough to send him over the edge.

But she didn't let him go immediately. He was forced to stand there, still inside her, supported only by his unsteady legs.

"You can always ask me," she whispered against his neck.

He kissed her forehead, resting his weight against her for support.

"You don't owe me anything," he said.

It might be true that he had stepped in to assist her several times over the years. That when it came to protecting her friends in New Orleans, or protecting her anonymity, he'd done all he could without question. But how could that compare to what she'd given him?

Even now, just to be with her, to look on her face, into those golden eyes full of mischief and slaked lust. To kiss her flushed, warm cheeks.

"Maybe I like it when you owe me," she said. And began to gently rock against him again.

23

Piper woke to the sound of Lou singing in the shower.

Lou.

Singing.

"What is happening?" she murmured to the pillows as she squinted through the light—*God, why is there so much light in this room?* Had Lou never heard of curtains?

Lou kept humming the happy tune that Piper couldn't quite place, even after she'd dressed and had come into the living room to dry and brush her hair.

Piper sat up on her elbows in the bed. "Seriously, what is going on?"

Lou paused with the towel in her hair. "What?"

"Are...are you in a *good mood?*"

Lou smiled.

"Did you just get laid or did you catch the Paris killer?"

"No to the Paris killer."

Piper didn't miss that she'd avoided the sex question altogether. "Okay, if you didn't catch the killer, who did you kill?"

"Some mafia."

"Ah, okay." Piper stretched her hands over her head. "Big

firefight, lots of bodies. No wonder you're cheerful. I'm going to need coffee before I join this revelry."

Lou pointed at the Styrofoam cups on the countertop.

Piper practically purred as she leapt out of the bed and seized one. Since one was black and the other the color of caramel, Piper didn't even have to ask which was hers.

"Oh yes. Yes, *very* nice." She took a big drink, and that pleasant tingling sensation washed over her body, warming her from the inside out. "Mmmm."

She took another sip, closing her eyes to fully enjoy it.

"Do you want to look for bones with me?"

Piper peeked one eye open to find that Lou had abandoned the comb in favor of two pairs of night-vision googles. She was examining the lenses and adjusting the head straps.

"Of all the weird things you say to me, man." Piper rolled her neck, and it cracked up each side. "But yes, I'd like to dig up dead people with you. Why not? I have nothing else planned today."

Piper had been filling the quiet hours in Lou's apartment with her homework and was nearly caught up. She just had one paper left for her psychology course, and that one wasn't even technically late. It was due tomorrow.

"Not dead *people*," Lou corrected. With the goggles tightened around her face she looked alien and insectile. "There are only bones left."

Piper chose to continue sipping her coffee rather than split hairs with her over what constitutes a dead *person*. "What are we going to do with the bones once we find them?"

"Drop them in public places so they can be found. I've already done this twice, and that went well. At least, the police were notified. The story hasn't broken publicly yet though, so I need to bring more up to the surface."

"How many?"

"As many as it takes to get them moving on the case."

"Wait." Piper choked on her coffee. "Aren't there like thousands of CCTV cameras in Paris?"

"Konstantine is going to hack the system at certain times so we can dump them without being recorded. Our first drop is in an hour, so we need to get moving."

Piper arched a brow. "And *when* did you guys work out this plan?"

"This morning."

Piper snorted. "I bet you did."

Lou's face might've been impossible to read, but Piper definitely thought she saw a hint of a smile before Lou had fully turned away.

She definitely got laid. And probably after her killing spree. No wonder she's singing showtunes.

"Of course I'll go with you," Piper said, finally satisfied enough to pry her fingers off of the coffee and set it down. "But it's cold in Paris, right? And we'll be underground?"

"You'll need a coat."

"And I'll layer up." Piper began pulling a t-shirt and sweater out of her clothes pile. "What about breakfast? Oh, can we get crepes first? Pretty, *pretty* please?"

Because Piper seriously doubted that she was going to be able to eat after digging up *not*-bodies all morning. Or at least, she'd definitely lost her appetite the last time she'd helped Lou dig up one of Jeffrey Fish's corpses. Then again, that had been gooey and decomposing.

These would be just bones. That might still be freaky though.

"If we make it quick and go *now*. Otherwise, we'll miss our drop-off times."

"I'm going to get a dessert crepe and a savory one. What about you?"

"Ham and cheese." Lou pulled the goggles off her head.

"And for dessert?"

"I don't need dessert."

"God, come on. Your gift is totally wasted on you if you aren't using it to eat fancy French desserts."

"Fine. I'll get an éclair."

When Piper had first arrived, Lou ate maybe once or twice a day. Now she was getting her into dessert. She'd come so far.

Piper sighed with pride. "That's my girl."

LOU'S FINGER WORKED THROUGH THE DIRT, TRYING TO GET a good grip on the bone buried there and pull it out. The killer really liked to pack them in. Most of them. Perhaps when the fear of discovery was still alive in their mind, they hoped to make the bones look like the others—ancient relics that had become one with the earth around them.

By the time they'd dumped their latest kills here, as with Assia's bones, their confidence had grown significantly. The newest ones were barely covered with dirt. They were just tucked into the wall, piled as one might pile stones, relying on their natural shape and compression to hold them in place.

Lou grabbed the exposed end of the bone she'd been working on and pulled. It was a sternum, she thought, knocking some of the caked mud off. She put it in her black garbage bag.

The garbage bag wasn't as nice as the canvas bag the killer had been using. But though it was far from the most attractive option, it allowed her to carry several bodies' worth of bones to the surface at once.

And it went with her idea of placing these bone-filled bags near garbage bins around town. It was probably the least conspicuous drop-off she could manage.

They'd filled two bags already, and made those drops in

the two-minute window that Konstantine had given her. Now they were working on the third round, both Lou and Piper filling their own bags as efficiently as they could.

"There is an uncomfortable number of spiders down here," Piper said. "I mean, I *like* spiders, but there are *a lot* of them. Do you get what I'm saying? And why are they so big?"

"Just concentrate on filling the bag."

"With spiders? Because I'm absolutely sure there are going to be spiders in this bag."

"Don't fill them heavier than you can carry."

Piper's throat made a sound like a swallowed scream. It was the fifth or sixth time Lou had heard it. "Okay, I'm done with this one. Maybe we should go up now, yeah?"

"You're done?"

"I think these other bones are older. Actually, I might've grabbed one of the old bones by mistake. Should I put it back?"

"No," Lou said. "It won't hurt if they know these bones are coming from the catacombs."

Dirt, old bones—King had said that any of it could lead them down here, and that's what Lou wanted.

Lou turned to find Piper in her night-vision goggles, gathering up her bag and hobbling toward her. She dropped the bag halfway and swatted at her hair, swearing.

The night-vision goggles had been a good idea. Lou felt a little stupid for not having thought of them sooner. It gave her vision in the pitch black, but didn't rob her of her advantage in the dark.

"One more each," she said. "And we'll go up."

Lou dug the last bone she wanted from this part of the wall and watched the dirt cave, filling in the gap she'd made.

It trickled out onto her hands and shoes as she shook the bone clean and put it into her bag.

Then she moved on.

They'd been at it all morning. This was their third round, their next drop-off with Konstantine was scheduled in twenty minutes, in a dumpster between a pharmacy and coffeehouse in the eighth arrondissement.

By Lou's count, they'd already carried the remains of at least seventeen victims to the surface, and they probably had at least five more already bagged.

"I need another victim then," Piper said.

Lou set her sack down and began trailing her hand over the packed earth. Her fingers snagged on small rocks, bone fragments, or the ends of bones themselves as she passed. She followed the bend in the path, Piper now in view with half of her face hidden behind the oversized goggles. She was standing between her filled bag and a mostly filled one, one long bone protruding from the top of the second.

Someone recent, she told her compass. *A victim who—*

About ten steps from where she'd been, the compass in her gut snagged. She froze, inspecting the area where her hand hovered.

These were clean, fresh, not packed into the dirt at all.

"Here," Lou said. "You can get this one."

Piper saw it and pumped her fist. "Yes. I love it when they're just sitting here like this. They're easier to pull out."

A sound caught Lou's ear, something as slight as a shifting of rocks, and she slammed a hand over Piper's mouth. Turning, slowly, she looked up the path.

"Grab your bag," Lou whispered.

Lou would be able to grab one of hers as it was within reach of Piper, but the other would have to stay where she'd left it.

Piper, to her credit, bent down and grabbed the tops of each of her bags as quietly as she could, her hand slowly wrapping around the plastic so as to not make any sound.

Lou's eyes remained fixed on the path, trained at the part where it bent, listening to the footsteps as they approached.

The footsteps echoing through the catacombs had been quick, certain, at first. Now they slowed. Lou's half-filled sack of bones was just two feet in front of the spot where the path bent. Could they see the bones?

Lou wished she had a gun. She hadn't bothered to wear her guns given the purpose of this trip, but if she'd brought one, she could've put a bullet in this guy's head and been done with it.

No more murders.

But without a gun, she had only one course of action. Get out of there without being seen.

Lou kept one hand on Piper's upper arm, ready.

She saw the shoes first.

The black boots inched into view. In the night-vision goggles, the person was little more than a shape, a shadow born of the tunnel walls themselves.

But he bent down to inspect Lou's half-filled garbage bag of bones—and Lou was almost certain it was a *he* now, from the slope of his shoulders and the angular build of his body. Those large hands concealed in leather gloves.

The only problem was that Lou couldn't see his face.

Not only was he covered head to toe in black, not only did he have a ski mask over the features of his face, but half of it was hidden away behind night-vision goggles, as large and cumbersome as the ones she wore on her own head.

He can see us. If he looks this way, he will see us.

Piper must've realized this the second after Lou did, as the sharp intake of breath behind Lou's hand told her so.

Then he was looking up, his head pivoting in their direction.

Lou slipped without waiting.

But in her reactivity, she hadn't thought of a destination,

hadn't decided where she would rather be, only *away, away from him*.

So when the world opened again, they were tumbling into Konstantine's living room. Piper was pitched forward, the untied sack falling open and bones spilling out onto the stone floor.

Konstantine was behind his desk, his laptop open in front of him, an espresso halfway to his mouth. He started, frowned at the dirty bones now littering his living room.

After a beat of silence he asked, "Was there a problem?"

"No, we're just here to decorate for the party." Piper rose and dusted herself off. "Hell yeah, there's a problem."

Konstantine's eyes were on Lou, his frown deepening. "*Amore mio?*"

"Yes," Lou admitted. "We have a problem."

Konstantine listened to their story for the second time before speaking. "He had night-vision goggles as well?"

"Right," Piper said.

"If he was wearing them when I ran into him the last time," Lou explained, "then he's seen my face."

Konstantine settled back into his chair. His eyes trailed to the CCTV Paris footage rolling on his screen. He noted that they'd missed their last timed drop-off, but no matter. They could catch the one after, and Lou would be able to dispose of the remaining bags.

After they cleaned them up off his floor, that was.

But that still left the problem of one sack in the catacomb and a man he did not know aware that Lou was hunting him.

"It's dangerous that he knows who you are but you don't know who he is," Konstantine said, scratching at his jaw.

"And you shouldn't just pop up and be like, 'Hey!'" Piper

added. "Because if he saw you before, then he also knows you can do the shifty thing. He saw you do it, right?"

"Slip," Lou corrected. "I call it slipping."

"Whatever. He'll be waiting for you. He might just shoot you in the gut if you pop up or something."

On his laptop a woman walked her dog past an alley, pausing long enough for it to piss on the side of a garbage can.

"This problem may take care of itself," Konstantine said. "It may not be necessary for you to confront him."

Lou turned toward him.

"Once the bones are discovered, and they will be *quite* soon"—his contacts in Paris would see to that—"then the authorities will begin hunting for this man. This may force him out into the open."

"What about the bag in the catacombs?" Lou leaned her weight against his desk, and it brought back delicious memories of that morning. "I have to get it. My fingerprints are on it."

She must've known what he was thinking because a hint of a smile played across her lips.

He would've suggested they christen this desk as well, if not for the blond girl stuffing bones into a garbage bag.

"Move it to the surface if you want. I wipe your prints whenever they're stored, so don't worry about that."

"Is that why you asked to ink my fingers?" she said.

"We're going to need a vacuum for the dirt," Piper said from the floor. "You have one, right?"

"It's in there." Konstantine pointed at the closet behind his front door. "How many people do you think he killed in all?"

"High forties," Lou said. "Maybe the fifties or even sixties."

"Then he has been at this for quite some time. And Paris must've been quite the feeding ground."

"Found it. Whoa, what kind of plug is this?"

He reached out and took Lou's hand. He thought she might refuse him with the girl here, but she let him take it and run a thumb over her scabbing knuckles.

Had she split these knuckles on Erjon's men or Vittoria's face?

"The next drop is in six minutes. That will be our last for today, don't you think?"

"Yeah," she said. "Hopefully it'll be enough."

24

King spent the morning calling his clients, informing them that he would be out of the office for the next few days. Most of them didn't care, since he wasn't a doctor's office with strict appointment schedules and what they needed from him could be provided by an email or phone call. But also because none of the cases in his current workload were approaching their deadlines. A simple stroke of luck, that was. Otherwise, none of this might have worked out.

He'd chosen to do his calls on his cell phone while walking instead of in the office. Part of it was the crying. He'd heard soft crying coming from the upstairs apartment on and off since Dani had left that cryptic note on his legal pad about moving out. King found it nearly impossible to do even the simplest of tasks—such as fill his electronic calendar with important dates—with a soundtrack of pitiful tears in the background.

It broke his heart to hear her like that. He liked Dani. In fact, after she pulled through Dmitri Petrov's torture and Diana Dennard's mind games, he'd come to respect the hell out of her. She was tough, but still kind. He only wished he could help her. More than once he'd considered knocking on the door and asking her if she needed anything.

But he also didn't want to embarrass the girl by letting her know that he'd heard her.

So instead, he'd locked up the agency and completed his morning calls while walking the lazy streets of the French Quarter. No one was really out at this hour, and because they were easing into the pre-holiday slump, he found the streets cozier, friendly, despite the chilly morning air.

He'd just gotten his coffee from Café du Monde and had stepped off the sidewalk to watch a young Asian woman juggle three blazing batons when his cell phone rang.

"Mr. King, this is Randall from the Greenfield Funeral Home."

"Good morning. Thanks for getting back to me."

"My pleasure, sir. I just wanted to let you know that the cemetery finally got back to me with a time for the excavation. They can get that grave open at ten for you, and give you an hour for your niece to say her goodbyes."

Okay, so King had lied and said that Piper was his niece and that he would be making all the funeral arrangements on her behalf. Randall hadn't questioned this, since the plot was already paid for and they'd collected Nadine's body from the hospital directly.

"We've got the remains in a little wooden box that Miss Genereux can place directly into the grave, by way of a little ceremony, if that's all right with you? The box is completely compostable, of course."

"That should be fine," King said. "So we'll meet you at the cemetery at ten?"

"Yes, sir," he said. "The priest will say a short prayer for Ms. Crenshaw's soul, as you requested, and read Psalm 23. No other scripture shall be read."

King thought he detected a slight hint of judgment in the man's voice when he said *no other scripture*, but since King was the one writing the check, he didn't say anything else.

"All in all, I think it shouldn't be more than ten minutes, and then you'll have the rest of the hour to yourselves."

"That's perfect. Thank you."

King ended the call as the girl with twin braids caught all three of her batons and bowed. King clapped with the other few spectators and threw a twenty-dollar bill into her upturned hat.

Then he was walking again. As he did, he sent Piper a text.

Funeral at ten in the morning tomorrow.

Then we have a reservation at The Praline Connection at eleven.

He watched his screen but didn't get a reply. This was strange because Piper was usually so prompt when it came to texting.

Then he had an idea.

Lifting his coffee to his lips, he opened his news app on his phone and searched for Paris. Sure enough, the headline read, *Paris Panic! Bones Found All Over City*.

They've been busy, he thought as he read the details of the case. How bones from nearly twenty corpses had been discovered sprinkled—their word, not his—in various dumpsters and trash bins around the city. No suspects had been named, so Lou's face wasn't splashed all over the news with menacing *wanted for questioning* subtitles beneath.

Konstantine must've taken care of the surveillance. Good on him.

King was almost done with the article when Piper replied.

Thank you sooooo so much. Thank you for everything. I'll make it up to you, I promise.

He sighed and made a silent prayer that one day this kid was going to realize that just because someone was kind to her, it didn't mean she owed them. There was no score to keep. At least not when friendship was the currency.

King placed his hand on the horse-head post and wiped his feet on the mat outside Melandra's shop.

When he entered, he found her lifting glass candles from a box, stickering the bottoms with her sticker gun and then placing the candles in an opposite pile.

"Good morning," he said.

"Good morning," she returned.

Lady rose to greet him, her tail thumping against Mel's long skirt as he scratched her head.

"Funeral's at ten tomorrow. Do you have someone who can watch the shop for you?"

He stopped short of suggesting Dani.

"No need. We haven't had five customers today. I can stand to close it for a few hours."

King waited, expecting to see the usual tension and worry that Mel radiated when the dip in sales came. When the uncertainty of her income and business were brought into stark view.

But her face remained relaxed, the muscles at ease.

"Are you worried about the dip in traffic?" he asked cautiously, taking up a sticker gun and mimicking her movement.

"No," she said with a small shrug. "Lou's got a ghost night coming up. Things will pick up after that. And we're always a little slow before Thanksgiving. It doesn't mean we won't have a good holiday shopping season."

What a difference a year makes.

Back when Mel's husband had been threatening her, harassing her, extorting her for money, her financial concerns had eaten up a great deal of her energy and peace of mind. Now it seemed that Mel felt more than confident that whatever happened, she would be just fine.

He'd always believed that, of course. But he was glad to see that she saw it now too.

"So you and Ms. Miller?" Melandra asked with a sly smile as she lit another St. Jude candle embellished with the saint's face from the open cardboard box.

"What about her?" he asked, his eyebrows raising.

Mel smirked. "Don't play dumb with me. Are you dating or not?"

"Where'd you get the idea she even wants to date me?"

"Do you think I'm blind? That I don't have two working eyes in my head?"

King snorted. "I didn't say that."

"Well? Answer my question."

"I don't know," he said. "It feels a little strange after Lucy."

Mel nodded, watching his face while her hands did the work. "I can imagine."

"But I don't think Lucy would care," he said, scratching his jaw.

"Of course she don't care. Why would she care?"

"I don't know. In case she can see me."

Mel rolled her eyes. "She's got better things to do than watch us all the time. I'm sure of that much."

King looked at the candle in his hand, at the hallowed saint with its halo of light.

When he didn't speak for a long time, Mel said, "As far as women go, I think Ms. Miller is a good match for you."

"Yeah? How so?" King placed the candle on the glass counter and grabbed another from the box.

"She's as smart as you. Takes no shit like you. And that means that she also won't let you play any games."

King was offended. "I don't play games with women. I'm very honest."

"I'm not talking about cheating or anything like that. I'm talking about head games, emotional games."

King's scowl deepened. "I don't play those either."

"Maybe not on purpose. But this whole 'I like you, you're an amazing woman, but I'm not going to entertain the idea of dating you because I'm worried what my dead wife will think' thing—I doubt Ms. Miller will stick around for that. She'll probably give you time, but if it turns out that you aren't ready, she'll move on. She's not going to lose any sleep at night over it, if you get what I'm saying."

"I'm too old for someone to be losing sleep over anyway," King said. But he was more than a little happy to hear this assessment. Something about it eased the worry in his chest. It was good to know that Mel thought Beth could—and would—take care of herself first, unlike some of the other women he'd dated in the past.

"Mmhmm. Keep on thinking about it," Melandra said, her smile deepening.

Lady's tail began to thump against King's shoe. Mel scratched her ears.

"She's a wonderful woman." *Who made me an offer.* "Of course I'm thinking about it."

"Don't think *too* long," Melandra said, pulling the emptied cardboard box from the glass case. "That's all I'm saying."

Piper's apartment was empty when she showed up to get ready for the funeral. She was grateful for this, because she didn't think she could handle the sight of Dani right now without falling apart. But alone, she managed to find a black dress and white sweater in the back of her closet, put them on, and clean herself up.

She noticed little things about the apartment, too.

The viola, for example, was gone. And while Dani's

clothes and toiletries were still visible, other belongings had gone into cardboard boxes, stacked up neatly in an unused corner of the living room, close to the front door.

It hurt Piper to see them. It hurt her more than she'd expected, her chest compressing.

But this is for the best, she thought. *Dani will be so much happier when she's living the life she deserves.*

In the full-length mirror in her bedroom, she took one more look at herself, and sighed. "This is as good as it gets."

Someone knocked on her apartment door. She opened it to find Lou in black dress pants, a black buttoned-up shirt, and a new leather jacket. The mirrored shades were pushed up onto her head.

"When did you start using doors, you freak?" Piper asked, stepping back as she adjusted one of the hoops in her ears.

"I wasn't sure if you were ready."

"I am." Piper threw up her hands. "How do I look?"

"Good."

"So do you. Is that a new jacket?"

"And boots," she said, coming into the room. "Mel and King are downstairs. They want to ride over together."

"First you knock on doors and now you're going to ride in a car? For *me*?" Piper put a hand over her chest. "Who died? Oh right."

She did finger guns at Lou.

But then Lou's arms were around her, hugging her tight, and tears flooded Piper's eyes.

"I'm sorry this happened," Lou whispered.

For a moment, Piper couldn't speak. She was too choked up by the hug. Then she said, "Yeah, I got that when you killed Willy."

Lou stepped back and pulled a tissue from her pocket.

"And you have tissues? Who *are* you?"

The corner of Lou's lips tilted up in a smile. "I carry

tissues when I interview women about their dealer boyfriends. Sometimes they cry."

Piper dabbed at her eyes. "You're just full of surprises today."

"Everything okay up there?" Mel called from downstairs. "We're going to be late."

"We're coming!" Piper said, and grabbed her wallet off the counter and her jacket off its hook.

One more glance at the packed boxes in the corner made her heart clench.

Not now, she thought. *Deal with that later.*

It took them about fifteen minutes to get everyone into the car and over to the Greenfield cemetery. It was already five after ten, so the priest was standing over the exposed earth. The concrete grave cover that usually kept her father's bones from rising with the water table had been pulled back to expose only churned earth. Fortunately, Piper didn't see her father's bones. Maybe they'd already disintegrated, or someone had thought to carefully tuck them out of sight.

Either way, now there was a small box-shaped hole for Piper to put her mother's remains in.

"I'm sorry I'm late!" Henry called, rushing toward them in a long black coat, his hair slicked back away from his face, an enormous bouquet of red roses in his arms. He was about to hand Piper the flowers when he saw that she was holding the wooden box.

Instead, he threw his arm around her and squeezed her so hard she thought she might pop.

"Fuck." He placed a kiss on the top of her head and said, "I mean, *fuck*."

"I know," Piper said, trying not to look at the frowning priest. "I know."

Then he looped his arm through hers as King motioned for the priest to begin.

While the priest prayed for her mother's soul, Piper held the box between her hands, surprised by its weight. How could all of her mother be reduced down to this five or so pounds?

She thought of how many nights she came home and found her mother passed out on the sofa, her drugs strewn across the coffee table. How she would pull a thin blanket off the arm of the chair and cover her mother's frail body with it, tucking it in tight and placing a kiss on her cheek.

Good night, Momma, she'd thought then. And now.

She began to cry.

As the tears ran down her face, King, Mel, and Henry all moved in closer, surrounding her, placing their hands on her. And despite her best efforts, the tears flowed harder, until she could no longer hear the priest's prayers over her soft whimpering.

Then she was asked to come forward, put the box into the ground, and push the dirt over it. The caretaker or funeral director—really Piper had no idea who the bone-thin man with the frizzy gray hair was—offered her a shovel.

Piper didn't take it. She pushed the dirt over her mother's grave with her bare hands until she couldn't see the box at all.

Then arms were around her. Holding her, telling her she would be okay.

And somehow, she knew it was true. She *would* be okay. Her mother wouldn't be. But she would be fine.

And this terrible truth broke her heart a little more.

She wasn't sure how long she stayed like this, crying in the circle of her friends. But when it began to rain, she looked up. Found that it was mostly Henry who held her, while King and Mel in their black clothes and somber faces remained close. Lou had stepped back a bit, watching the machinery roll into the cemetery to close the grave again.

What she was thinking behind those mirrored shades,

Piper couldn't guess. But she seemed nonplussed as soft raindrops splattered onto the shoulder of her new leather jacket.

Piper caught sight of someone over her shoulder. Dani, her hair pulled up in a bun off her slender neck. Her black dress and black pumps were wet with rain. In her arms was a full white bouquet, interspersed with soft pink blossoms.

"I just wanted to leave this," Dani said. She was offering the bouquet to Lou, as if the very idea of approaching Piper was out of the question.

Lou just looked at the flowers. Piper almost laughed.

"Stay," Piper said, pulling herself up to standing as the rain began to fall harder. "At least for the lunch."

The relief on Dani's face was visible.

"Okay," she said. "Where are we eating?"

Thunder rolled overhead.

THE LUNCH WAS GOING BETTER THAN KING HAD HOPED, though it was far from a party. Dani and Piper hadn't sat together, and Lou was between them. All the faces around the table had a depressed and dour look about them. Even Henry, who could usually be counted on to carry the conversation with his high energy.

Now, no one seemed to manage more than one-word responses.

Yet they got through, despite the rain pouring down outside and the thunder rolling overhead. Each took their turn distracting Piper. They talked about everything except her mom, the funeral, about what might happen next. King knew that conversation was coming. There was the matter of her mother's estate, after all, but that could hold for a few days.

Piper needed a break. She'd needed one for a long time.

"I can come back to work tomorrow," Piper said. "After

this I'm going to finish my paper and get it in tonight. Then I'll be all caught up."

"Too bad," King said, "because I've closed the agency until Monday."

"What? Why?"

"Nothing pressing to be done and I thought we could all use a few days off."

Piper turned on Mel. "I guess it's just me and you then."

"Not really," Mel said. "It's been slow. You know how it is the week before Thanksgiving. I'd say we're fine until the Black Friday rush." Mel slid her gold bangles down onto her wrists.

"That's right. It's Thanksgiving next week," Piper said. "I totally forgot."

"Ugh, don't remind me." Henry rolled his eyes. "I have to drive to Pensacola to see my sister and her kids."

Piper frowned. "You love your sister."

"I do. Yes," Henry conceded, tapping his long nails on the printed tablecloth. "But she invited our shithead of a father, so, say the word. If you need me to stay in town and eat turkey with you, I'm here for it."

"No." Piper scowled. "Go see your nephews, dude. They need a fabulous man in their life. Especially if your dad is coming to dinner."

Henry sighed, running a finger across his eyebrow. "You're right. I know you're right. But I'm going to need a drink or five when I get back, so pencil me in for that Saturday night."

"Done."

"Speaking of Thanksgiving," King added, glad to see the flow of conversation picking up, "I wondered if you'd join me and Mel for dinner that Thursday. And Lou's going to be there too."

Lou arched a brow, a clear *that's news to me*.

"Really?" Piper asked. "Last year and the year before you were busy."

King gave Louie a look that he hoped she could interpret as *This is important, you better show up for this.*

"I love turkey," Lou said in a flat monotone.

"Do you? It's the sides for me. Mashed potatoes, macaroni and cheese, stuffing," Piper said. "Oh god, could we have waited until the food came to talk about this?"

King couldn't pretend like Dani wasn't at the table, he'd decided. He'd invite her, and if something happened between now and Thursday, he'd just have to rely on the girls to work it out.

"What about you, Dani? You going to join us? Mel's table seats six."

"There's a green mole that my mom's cook makes for the turkey." Dani tucked her hair behind her ears. "And she uses piquant cornbread for the stuffing. It's really good. I could get the recipes if you guys want to try it."

King encouraged her with a nod. Piper, he noticed, remained silent.

"All of that sounds *amazing.* You better save me some leftovers." Henry craned his neck over his shoulder at the kitchen door. "Where the hell is our food?"

King looked out the rainy window and spotted Beth walking slowly past with a black umbrella open above her head. When he turned back, Mel was watching him with a smug look on her face.

"Excuse me," King said, rising from his seat.

"Sure," Melandra said, her smugness deepening.

King rushed out into the rain, trying to stick close to the building, where he remained mostly protected by the balconies extended above him.

"Beth," he called out, but his words were swallowed by thunder. "Beth!"

She stopped walking, turning slowly to survey the street. When she saw him, her face lit up.

"Can I help you, Robbie?" she asked.

This close he could see the rain splotches on her shoulders and the moisture droplets forming on her glasses.

"You're wet," he said by way of introduction.

"Don't worry about it. I'm not made of sugar," she assured him. And when his voice failed him, she added, "*Yes?*"

"I just wanted to let you know that I'll be by tonight. If your offer still stands."

Her smile broke open and King's heart kicked to see it. Why in God's name was he so nervous?

"Of course it stands. You have my address, don't you?"

He did, but confirmed it to be sure.

"That's the one," she said.

He ran a hand through his hair. "Okay. Then I'll see you tonight. Five o'clock. And I'll bring the dinner as promised."

She laughed. "Yes, you will."

Through the window, Melandra smiled over the rim of her glass.

25

———————

Lou sat up in bed, feeling as though she were half in, half out of a dream. She'd been in the strange room again. The black glass on all four walls. The sense that she could see something if she got close enough to the glass, but also a terror that if she did, something bad would happen.

She clasped a hand to the back of her neck and squeezed the tight muscles there.

Beside her, Piper slept, her breath rolling in and out in an easy rhythm.

When Lou had shown up with dinner, hot dogs from a stand in Chicago, she'd caught her crying. But at least the tears had quickly dried once she'd started in on her hot dog.

She'd tried to remember what it was like when her parents had died. The murders themselves were crystal clear. That first *flash-bang* of the gun going off in her parents' bedroom as she stood in the backyard with her father. The sound of her mother's wineglass breaking.

That horrible moment when Angelo had burst through

the back gate and her father had lifted her, throwing her into the pool. All of that, she remembered.

But the months that followed. The crying, the grief, the nighttime searching for and not being able to find her father. It hadn't mattered how hard she longed for him, missed him.

He was gone.

Those months were a blur. Bits shone through. Flashes. Of Lucy begging her to eat. To take a shower. To go outside and get some air.

But mostly, what Lou remembered was the atmosphere of her grief. How it was like the air she breathed. Everywhere. All around her and inside her.

It was endless. Until it wasn't.

If Piper was in the same place now, she wasn't showing it. She was sad. Lou could see that. The dark circles under her eyes were pronounced, and Piper hadn't made the effort to hide them.

She's going to be okay, Lou thought. That protective, possessive feeling that first urged her to bring Piper here, to keep her close, relaxed. *She's going to get through this.*

Lou's compass whirled and clicked to life, responding to some silent call she couldn't hear. Paris, she knew, once her navel snagged on those invisible coordinates.

Lou slipped from the bed quietly, careful not to touch or uncover Piper too much. She watched her sleep while she pulled on her boots, but the girl didn't stir.

All that crying seemed to have worn her out.

Grabbing her new leather jacket off the sofa arm and her Browning off the kitchen island, Lou glanced at the pre-dawn river before stepping into her empty linen closet.

The shadows thinned, enveloped her, and when she'd returned to the physical plane again, she was back in the cemetery. Père Lachaise, with its old tombs and enormous trees, an older, grander version of the cemetery where they'd buried Piper's mother that morning.

In moments like this, it was almost possible to believe that Paris was the mother of New Orleans.

Etienne had his back against Delphine's tomb, the weeping angel draped dramatically above his head. One of his hands rested on a bent knee, the other kicked out into the grass.

"I knew you'd come," he said.

Lou said nothing to this. Though if she were being honest with herself, it bothered her how quickly they were figuring it out, how to call her. Piper and even little Matteo knowing how to call her was fine. She wanted them to reach out when they needed help. King, Melandra, and Dani too. She supposed even Stefano, if he had reason enough.

But now Etienne?

It was getting a little ridiculous. Perhaps when she felt sure it wasn't an emergency, she should ignore these calls in the future, just to keep everyone guessing. Keep them from being too reliant on her. She could make mistakes, after all. She wasn't a replacement for self-reliance.

Soft crying caught Lou's ear and she turned. A young woman, perhaps eighteen, nineteen, was on her knees in front of a grave marker. She had one hand on the stone as if praying to it.

Lou didn't understand the French she murmured to herself, not only because of the distance or language barrier but because mostly the girl was sobbing into her hand-kerchief.

When Lou turned back, Etienne was watching the girl too. Something had changed in his eyes.

Lou couldn't be sure what. Had they always been that dark? Or the pupils that large?

"Are you an angel or a demon?" he asked her.

"Depends on who you ask," Lou said, grateful that he was using English for her.

"You said that you wanted to help me. For Delphine."

"I am helping," Lou said, her hands loose in her jacket. "I'm looking for the one who killed her."

He nodded. "Yes, I thought so."

She expected more questions, something along the lines of *What have you learned so far?* or *How is the investigation going?*

But he seemed to be weighing something in his mind.

"My Delphine was an artist. Her work, her beautiful works, were magnificent."

"I saw them at the museum." Lou shifted and the Browning pressed into her ribs reassuringly.

Etienne's lips pursed. "No, not those. The ones she has at home, her private collection. *Those* were the real art. The little creations she made before were only practice. She had to learn, my Delphine, like all great artists. It takes time to perfect one's art."

Etienne's eyes slid away, tracking something over Lou's shoulder. It wasn't until the girl passed, her face hidden in her handkerchief, that Lou knew what he'd been watching.

"I want to show you Delphine's art. Her passion. I think if you saw them, you would understand my Delphine. My talented, beautiful, *lost* Delphine."

The eyes which had been so dark and hungry the moment before were now soft and sorrowful again.

Did he kill her? Has he killed anyone?

Her compass remained silent, unmoving.

"Where's her art?" Lou asked.

"At our home. Will you come? It must be very soon, I'm afraid. Her creations don't last long. And there are only two left. Please come. Come tonight."

"I'll come," Lou agreed, the Browning again brushing her ribs.

"Will you? Thank you. *Thank you.*" Etienne brightened at this, his eyes lighting up for the first time. "Perhaps once you see it, you will understand her. I just want someone who will understand what I've lost. Such a terrible, *terrible* loss."

"What time?" Lou asked.

"Eleven," he said. "They are best viewed at night. When it is darkest. Sort of like you."

He smiled then, and it was ice cold, his words frozen cubes trailing down Lou's spine.

There were only a few hours between then and eleven that night.

He turned his eyes up to meet hers. "Please don't be late."

KING CHANGED HIS SHIRT THREE TIMES. THEN HE SPENT several minutes in his bathroom debating whether or not cologne was in order. Some women loved it. Others found it irritating to their nose and throat. If he put it on and it was too much, it would be difficult to wash it off. He could go into the bathroom and splash water on his throat, he guessed, but only if he didn't get any on his clothes.

Finally he decided he would get ready as he did every day. That's the way he'd been when Beth had seen him and had decided she was interested. So he'd just pretend he was going to work.

Yes to the cologne then.

Mel, blessedly, had been in her apartment with Lady when he'd stepped out onto the landing and locked the door behind him. The dog barked once, and Mel shushed her. He stood frozen in the hall, half expecting Mel to poke her head out and comment on his appearance, but she only called out, "Heading to dinner, Mr. King?"

"Yeah," he said, feeling like a high schooler at the top of

the stairs, on the brink of lying to his parents about where he intended to spend the night.

"Take care then," she said. And that was it.

The worse part, by far, was the condoms.

When King went to the convenience store across the street and found the condoms comically opposite the diapers, he grabbed two boxes. No big deal. The embarrassment came when he slipped the packages across the counter to Zeke, the cashier he saw nearly every day.

Zeke only arched a brow at the boxes before running them across the scanner.

Stupid, King thought. He should've picked a gas station or pharmacy he never went to.

"You know," Zeke began, "we have wine in the back, where the beer is, if you want to—"

"No, thank you," King said. But as soon as he'd refused, he reconsidered. "Actually, one second."

"Sure, dude, it's just me and you in here."

King wandered back to the cold cases and found the wine. Quickly, he realized he had no idea what Beth liked. Sweet white wine? A super-dry red?

He decided to skip the alcohol.

"No luck?" Zeke called out as King was walking back to the register.

"Not tonight."

Zeke handed him the bag with his condoms in it as King handed over a twenty-dollar bill. "Well I'm sure you'll still have a good time."

King's Oldsmobile was parked in the alley behind the shop. He tucked the condoms into the inner pocket of his duster, turned the key, and eased out onto St. Peter.

It only took him about ten minutes to find parking outside of Beth's townhouse on Prytania Street. The pretty pink-and-white-brick exterior was beautiful in the orange glow of sunset. He checked the address against the numbers above each door and realized she was in the one on the far left.

Hope her bed is against that outside wall, he thought. Otherwise, he'd be sending an apology letter to the neighbors in the morning.

King didn't even make it all the way up the walk before Beth opened the front door.

"I wasn't sure you were coming in," she said, her smile wide. "You were looking at my door for a long time."

He wasn't sure what to say as he crossed the threshold and stood in her living room. The colors were bright and adventurous. A yellow sofa with turquoise throw pillows. Two red armchairs opposite a glass coffee table. The rug was some sort of cream-colored Indian print with multi-colored elephants repeating for the full length of it. The hard floor stopped at the kitchen, where it gave over to white ceramic tile.

"Don't be shy," she said, offering to take his coat. "I won't bite you unless you ask me to."

"I forgot all about the dinner until I rolled up," he said. "But you can pick the takeout and I'll pay the bill."

"All right," she said. "That's fine with me. There isn't much in this city that I won't eat, let me tell you."

King laughed, shrugging out of his duster and handing it over.

But as soon as he handed over the jacket, he remembered the condoms in the pocket. He reached for the coat.

Beth must've seen something in his face.

"What is it?" she asked. "What's wrong?"

"I just, uh—" His face grew warm. "There's something I need in the pocket."

Frantically he wondered what he should do. Ask to take it

into the bathroom? She might think he was a cokehead or something.

And it was too late anyway. Beth's hands were searching the pockets until she found the first, then the second box of condoms and pulled them out.

"Oh," she said. "Oh, I see."

King didn't want to seem like the sort of man who forgot to pick up dinner but showed up with *two* boxes of condoms.

"I'm sorry," he said.

"For what?"

"I..." What was he going to say? *I don't want to seem presumptuous. Or single-minded.* She was the one who'd said she wanted to have sex.

"*Two* boxes," she continued, pushing her glasses up onto the bridge of her nose. "And Comfort XL."

King clasped the back of his neck.

"Well," she said over the rim of her glasses. "I *do* like a man who comes prepared."

26

———————

Piper felt strange being back in her apartment. Lou had told her that she could stay longer if she wanted, but Piper missed her bed, her living room, having her clothes in an actual dresser instead of being piled onto a couch. She could never fully relax when she was a guest at someone else's place, and after everything, Piper was ready to relax.

However, this hadn't prepared her for the awkwardness of coming home to Dani sitting in the living room, arms-deep in a cardboard box.

Piper turned back, reconsidering her decision to come home now, only to find Lou had already gone. *Probably on purpose*, she thought. *She wants me to talk to Dani.*

"Hey," Dani said.

"Hey," Piper countered, knowing her smile was forced and awkward.

Dani looked away first. "I'm sorry I'm still here. I'm just waiting for my parents to show up. They're late."

"That's okay," Piper said. "It looks like you need more time to pack anyway."

Thank God she didn't live here longer, Piper thought. Because the few things that Dani had to pack up were only items that she'd accumulated since losing her apartment in the explosion. That meant that the majority of the things in the apartment—the cookware, furniture, and décor—all belonged to Piper.

And yet, even in their short time together, Dani had accumulated enough to fill five whole cardboard boxes.

Dani's phone pinged. After she read the text, she said, "It's my mom. They're here. They just need to find parking."

"Okay," Piper said. "Do you want me to help you carry anything?"

"No, but is it okay that my parents come up and get boxes? I swear they won't be rude or—"

"It's fine," Piper assured her. Even if Piper felt like a dirty orphan in front of the polished Allendales, it wasn't like they'd be here for long. They could think whatever they wanted about her or her one-bedroom apartment as long as they kept it to themselves.

Dani stood and brushed invisible dirt off the front of her jeans. After a long, mournful look, she said, "I'm just going to go down and open up the agency for them."

"Sure," Piper said, suddenly unsure what to do with her hands. She slid them into her pockets. "I'll be here."

Dani disappeared into the hall, her footsteps echoing as she descended the staircase into the office below. And Piper was left to stand there and look at the boxes, thinking, not for the first time, that maybe she was making a mistake.

Sure, she didn't care for Dani's mother, and no way in hell could she ever go back to that freaking mansion in Mandeville, but Piper didn't have to in order to keep dating Dani, did she?

Dani could get her big, beautiful apartment, and they

could just go back to having sex and spending time together like they had before the explosion, right?

She's not going to want to have sex with you after you threw her out, asshole! a voice chided.

And you'd only be delaying the inevitable, said another.

What if they fell in love, got married, and had babies? She was just supposed to never return to the Allendales' house again? What about Christmases? What if Dani wanted to buy herself a nice car or go to Europe or something? Was Piper going to stop her because she couldn't afford to go and she didn't want Dani to pay?

No, I'd tell Lou to drop my ass off there, she thought. No airfare.

Shut up, she argued against herself. *It'll never work. Better to end it now while everything else is already shit. Get it all done in one go.*

A clean break.

"It's up here?" a voice called. Beverly Allendale had arrived. "*Really?*"

Piper took a deep breath and straightened her back.

Beverly ducked into the apartment the way one ducks spiderwebs in a haunted house.

"Hi," Piper said. She made a show of forced cheerfulness. "Come on in."

With her brown hair coiled in a tight bun on top of her head and her hand at her throat, Beverly looked like she'd rather do anything else. She inched into the room, careful to keep her cream-colored suit from touching anything, as if the walls—*hell*, maybe the air itself—were coated in filth and grime.

"The boxes are there," Piper said, pointing to the corner. "And I think Dani has just one suitcase in the bedroom. I can carry that."

"Where is Tavi?" Beverly asked as Dani reappeared,

pushing the door open as wide as it would go for the ensuing move.

"I told you, Mom, Piper is allergic. Tavi is staying with a friend of mine."

"God, who *wouldn't* be allergic in this tiny place. You can barely breathe in here."

"Mom!" Dani cried. "This is a beautiful apartment. One of the nicest in the French Quarter that I've ever seen."

Beverly frowned. "Well, honey, that's hardly saying anything. The French Quarter is like one giant bar."

"Can we please just get these boxes down to the street?" Dani asked, giving Piper an *I'm so sorry this will all be over soon* face.

"All I'm saying is that if this place wasn't so small, it would be easier to keep it clean."

"This apartment is *clean*!" Dani cried, promptly dropping the box she'd been lifting from the top of the pile. "I just cleaned it this morning!"

And she had. It was one of the first things Piper had commented on when Lou had dropped her off in the living room. She'd thanked Dani for cleaning straight away.

"You *cleaned*? Why?" Beverly asked. "This isn't even your apartment."

"Because I live here, Mother. That's what people do. They clean their houses."

Beverly snorted, touching her bun as if a hair might be out of place. "I can't believe you lived like this. Next thing I know you'll be renting a room in a drug den. This is hardly a step above."

Piper's stomach clenched. She pinched her eyes shut against the wave of pain crashing over her. The image of her mother, unconscious, unresponsive on the couch. Of Willy shoving her out of the car onto the curb as she lay dying, his taillights fading into the night.

"Piper, oh my god, Piper. I'm so sorry." Dani's hands were on her shoulders, then on her face. "Mother, apologize to her right now!"

"For *what?*"

"For being such a *bitch*! Apologize to her! *Now.*"

"Daniella Allendale, what language! How dare you talk to me like that? Is this the kind of people you're running around with now? Where this sort of language is acceptable?"

Piper didn't understand what happened next. Their heated English had given way to a torrent of Spanish. Somehow, in Spanish they sounded even angrier, the exchange growing louder and more heated until Piper felt like she was going to be sick.

She needed air. She needed to get out of here.

"Excuse me." Piper slipped away out of the apartment and down the stairwell.

Dani called after her, but Piper couldn't stop. She needed fresh air or her head was going to explode. She crossed the sunny office, her sneakers squeaking across the polished floor, and stepped out into the early evening, taking a big deep breath as soon as the agency door closed behind her.

"Yes, yes, I *know,*" a man said. "It is *very* difficult to listen to, isn't it?"

Piper turned and found Dani's father standing on the curb.

He wore a Hawaiian shirt and khaki pants. Over the shirt was a thick blue cardigan. He drew deeply on his pipe before exhaling up toward the sky.

"Are you cold?" she asked.

He shook his head. "No, I'm fine. Thank you."

Piper wasn't sure what to do with herself. She could go for a walk. But then who would help them get the boxes out of the house? This guy looked like he was ready to catch a flight to the tropics, not do some heavy lifting.

Mr. Allendale pulled a sleek silver cigarette case out of his pants pocket and opened it. Beside the wrapped tobacco for his pipe were ten dark cigarettes, fragrant even from where Piper stood.

"Oh, no, thank you." Piper only smoked when she was drunk, as a rule, and for that reason, didn't even buy cigarettes or carry them on her.

But given her current predicament, and the miniature war waging in her apartment upstairs—which she could still hear despite *two* closed doors—a cigarette didn't sound half bad.

Mr. Allendale still held the case open for her.

"I don't usually smoke."

"Nor do I," he said. "But sometimes, it's nice, isn't it?"

She couldn't argue, so she plucked the offering from the case and slipped it between her lips. "Thanks."

As he lit Piper's cigarette with a sleek lighter, silver to match the case, Mr. Allendale said, "When Daniella told us she was moving again, I was sorry to hear it."

Piper wasn't sure what to say to this, so she took her first long, deep drag on the cigarette. It was smooth.

Very smooth. They must cost a fortune, she thought.

"You know, I visited her, when she was in the psychologist hospital," he said, exhaling his own thin blue smoke toward the sky.

That wasn't what it was called, the psych ward at New Orleans General, but Piper didn't dare correct him. No one appreciated that crap.

"Really? She didn't tell me that," Piper said between drags.

"I don't think she knows I came. I'd gotten a call from a nurse who works there. Emmanuelle Perez. Good girl. Good family. Anyway, she told me Daniella had come in, and so I came to see how she was."

"What did Beverly think of that?"

Mr. Allendale laughed. "You think I told her? No, no, no. I enjoy my peace, you know."

Piper smiled, and exhaled blue smoke toward the sky.

"Daniella was sleeping when I arrived. She looked—" He stared at his pipe. "She looked small. Very tired. Like she did when she was a little girl. Always tired, my Daniella."

Piper wasn't sure where this was going, so she took another drag on the cigarette—and *damn* these were good cigarettes. They didn't even burn her throat on the inhale.

"My wife has always been very hard on our girl. Lessons, lessons, *lessons*, you know. All of Daniella's life is full of these lessons. Riding lessons. Italian lessons. Music lessons. Leadership lessons. I tell her, '*Beverly*. She is a child! Let her play. Let her *rest*.' But no, my wife is a very attentive mother. She wants her to succeed, of course. Me? I want her to be happy. And I know that success and happiness are not the same thing."

Our mothers couldn't be more different, Piper thought, putting Beverly Allendale and Nadine Crenshaw together side by side in her mind. An over-attentive mother who planned every minute of her daughter's day, her life, and a neglectful mother who didn't even notice when her daughter came or went.

He sucked on his pipe, the embers glowing red. "That was why I was so glad when she met you."

Piper choked. "Me?"

Mr. Allendale smiled. "Yes, *you*. With you, Daniella is always smiling. She is laughing. She is having a good time, always, when I see her. So I'm sad that she's leaving now. Will you still be friends?"

Piper's heart clenched. "I want to. I just..." *God, am I really going to say it?* "I care about her a lot."

"I know," he said, and reached out to pat Piper's cheek affectionately. "I know. I see it in your eyes. You are both good girls, but sometimes it doesn't work. García women are *very* passionate. She gets it from her mother."

Piper laughed, flicking her ash onto the street.

"Yes," he said with a heavy smile. "But hey, you never know. Things have a way of working out."

A door slammed, and Piper turned in time to dodge the agency door swinging open.

As Beverly spilled out onto the street, she took one look at the pair of them smoking and huffed. "I'll be in the car!"

She marched away from them down Royal Street toward St. Peter.

Mr. Allendale opened his silver cigarette case. "Take another."

"No, really, I wasn't lying. I don't smoke unless—"

"Take it for the next bad day," he said with a wink. "Go on."

"Thanks." Piper slid the cigarette behind her ear.

Mr. Allendale extinguished his pipe and slid it into his pocket. Then he offered Piper his hand. She shook it.

After a gentle pat on the top of her hand, he pulled open the agency door and went inside.

For a moment, Piper just stood on the street, watching the people pass and thinking about nothing in particular. She could still feel the warmth of Mr. Allendale's hand clasping hers. That fatherly pat on her cheek. She didn't think anyone had patted her cheek like that since her dad had died. And that had been a long time ago.

She considered going in and offering to carry boxes, but her phone buzzed.

Are you around? Henry asked.

Yeah, why?

Can you come down to The Wild Cat? I need extra hands.

Piper took one last drag off her cigarette before stamping it out with a twist of her sneaker. Then, with her hands in her pockets, she made her way toward Bourbon Street.

27

———————

Konstantine wondered if this counted as a date. He had never eaten in a restaurant with Lou before. In fact, he was painfully aware of how rarely they were in public together. He had never taken her to a movie, or to a party. He'd never taken her shopping or for a long, slow drive through the country.

Sitting down to a meal with her now seemed almost absurd.

Yet there she was, across from him at the table, a wine glass within reach. Her head was turned, offering him a delicious view of her profile, her pale neck as she looked out over the Piazza della Signoria.

It was full tonight, crowded with people of all ages, despite the encroaching night. They lounged on steps, the fountain's lip, or at dinner tables like theirs arranged at the edges of restaurant terraces. The central fountain lit from within burbled and the street vendors tried to entice both children and parents with lit-up trinkets that could fly, bounce, and dance in the dark.

Cheap plastic things that would be broken before bedtime, or soon forgotten at the bottom of a drawer.

Despite the perfection of the moment, he wanted to tell her something—what he'd learned that day over a brief but intense phone call. The last test had come back, offering insight into her strange, hellish world. That place she called La Loon.

But there was something in her demeanor tonight that made him hesitate. It didn't feel like the time or place.

"What is it, *amore mio*?" Konstantine asked. He met Lou's eyes over the dinner table, the wine glass sparkling in the candlelight. "Is this too much?"

Lou's lips twitched. "I have eaten at a dinner table before."

He shrugged. "Of course, but when I asked you to dinner, perhaps you were imagining something less formal?"

"This is nice," she said.

Perhaps it was the darkness that suited her, or the open space surrounding them. But she'd seemed comfortable letting him order for her, insisting only that he get her something with steak.

Now she was looking at him.

"What?"

"I like what you're wearing," she said with a suggestive smile.

Muscles in Konstantine's guts tightened. He was only wearing a black turtleneck, soft black pants, and leather shoes. The shirt was pushed up past his elbows to expose his forearms. Had he gone any higher, it would have shown his gang tattoos. So he'd been careful to keep it just beyond the bend in his elbow.

"Thank you," he said with a tilt of his head. "Are you in a hurry?"

"No, why?"

"I am aware that the American notion of dinner is thirty minutes, usually consumed standing or in front of a television. Italians take their time. It might be two hours before all of our courses are served."

"I don't have a TV," she said.

He smirked at her. "Will you be spending the night with Piper again?"

"She went home."

He wondered if his eyes reflected the candlelight as hers did.

He thought again of telling her what he'd learned about that strange world of hers, what, if any, implications it might have for her. But he decided against it. It was such a beautiful moment. Why ruin it with serious talk?

"But I have a date in Paris at eleven," she added.

His jaw clenched involuntarily. *It's only an expression*, he reminded himself. "A date?"

She smiled. "Yes, with a handsome French widower."

He set his wine glass down. "You're taunting me, aren't you?"

She shrugged a shoulder. "Etienne wants to show me Delphine's art."

"I'm sure," he said coolly. "Are you going alone?"

"Why? Should I bring you?"

Yes, he thought. But knew that was more than impractical. "Perhaps not me. I'm not as good at putting people at ease as your detective is. Why did you agree to go?"

Lou eyed him over her own candlelit glass. She took a deep drink before saying, "I don't seem like an art aficionado to you?"

There was a shift in her tone. Had he said something wrong?

"Forgive me. I only meant that you must have another reason for going."

"I want to see where Delphine died."

He lifted the glass again, swirling the wine inside. "King would know what to look for at a crime scene, wouldn't he?"

"He'd probably tell me that there'd be no clues at this point. He'd be right, but I'd still want to see it. If I can see the space, maybe I'll get a sense of how big the person who killed her was." When he said nothing, she added, "If it's a high tub, or if the walls are narrow. Low ceiling. All of it gives me an idea of what size the killer is. I doubt she was stabbed then climbed into the tub while dying, so whoever it was probably put her in there. And I want to compare the space to the size of the guy we saw in the catacombs."

The man who saw you, he corrected in his mind. He didn't like that the killer knew Lou's face. Perhaps he was already hunting for her, planning how to trap and kill her. And what could Konstantine do for her if she got hurt in Paris?

Very little.

He had people there, of course. They could reach her far faster than Konstantine could, but that hardly made her safe.

Don't think of that, he scolded himself. *Focus instead on this gorgeous evening.*

"You're very beautiful," Konstantine said after a beat of silence. "Will you permit me to be a bit...romantic right now?"

It was her turn to tilt her head. "I didn't realize I'd forbidden it."

She hadn't, but he'd seen the way she would tense, turn away, whenever he became too expressive with his affections. When she'd been shot and had almost died, she'd told him, *Don't fall in love with me.* To which he'd admitted, *I already have.*

When she'd heard this, she'd pinched her eyes shut as if to block him out.

But this was a special occasion. Their first normal outing

together. He didn't want the moment to pass by unacknowledged.

"It means a lot to me, to have you here. At dinner," he said. He took the wine bottle off the table and bent forward, refilling her glass.

She seemed to consider this.

It was true they almost always kept to his apartment. There were the times when she'd found him in his church, in his office, or in the main sanctuary, but ninety percent of the time, they were in his bedroom. And he'd been to her place only twice.

"Given the prices of the place, it's going to cost you a lot, too."

He smiled, having expected a joke, knowing she would deflect the seriousness of his tone.

"All I'm trying to say," he said, "is that it is very nice to sit and look at you like this." He gestured at the table, the piazza. "I hope we will do it more often."

"Keep dressing like that," she said, "and we will."

He laughed. "So I am not the only one who cares about my clothes."

"After dinner, do you want to get gelato?" he asked.

"Is that what we're calling it now?" She smiled over the rim of her wine glass. "Sure. I wouldn't mind some gelato."

AFTER DINNER THEY ENDED UP IN BED. THOSE CLOTHES IN which Konstantine had looked so handsome were on the floor, his body now slick with sweat. She was glad she'd pulled her hair up before they'd begun. She didn't have time for yet another shower before going to Paris.

She ran a hand down his chest. Then she kissed it, licking the salt off his skin.

He purred affectionately.

"Who is the cat here?" she teased. "You or Octavia?"

With one hand on his hip, she moved down his torso. He slid a hand into her hair and fisted it.

"Please," he said. "I beg you."

She rolled her eyes up to meet his. "What?"

"*Sono esausto.* And you'll be late if you begin again."

He had a point. According to her watch, she had only twenty minutes to get to Paris. But she didn't want to go. She wanted to stay in his bed and see how long she could torture Konstantine before he fell asleep.

Octavia chose this moment to jump onto the bed. Perhaps she'd recognized her name.

"*Ciao, bellezza,*" Konstantine said.

The cat bypassed Lou entirely and went for Konstantine's face, bumping her head against the bottom of his chin.

"She's in love with you," Lou said.

"No," he said. "She's affectionate."

Lou wouldn't have used the word *affectionate*. The cat seemed indifferent at best to Lou, except for mealtimes. At mealtimes, the little beast did come alive, and might even reward Lou with a nice headbutt into her cupped palm. Otherwise, she wanted to be left alone to enjoy the sunlight.

"When Dani gets her own place she's probably going to want her cat back."

Konstantine cupped his hands over Octavia's ears. "Don't say such things to her. She will be with me forever. I've already promised her."

The genuinely sad expression on his face made Lou smile.

"Besides," he said, "she makes the apartment so cozy. It won't be the same without her."

"You better hope that Dani and Piper make up then," Lou said.

She glanced at her watch. Fifteen minutes.

Konstantine was watching her when she looked up. "Leaving, then?"

"Why are you jealous?" She stood and crossed to Konstantine's bathroom. "He hasn't even flirted with me."

"You underestimate me, *amore mio*. I am jealous of everyone and everything that occupies your time."

"Maybe you do need a pet then," she said over a shoulder before stepping into the hot stream.

Just a quick rinse, she thought.

When Lou got out of the shower, she found Octavia sleeping in the crook of Konstantine's arm as he read a book. It was hard to deny that the pair were in love with each other. It was an odd complement to what Lou shared with Jabbers, the six-armed beast from the shores of La Loon, with her reptilian black skin and rows of shark teeth.

Lou smiled to herself, thinking of Jabbers curled up and sleeping beside her like that.

"Can I borrow a shirt?" she asked. She could wear her pants and underwear, but her shirt had stayed on the longest and she'd already been sweating before Konstantine had removed it.

"*Sì.*" He pointed at the top dresser drawer.

He watched her pull a black t-shirt from his drawer and pull it down over her naked torso. Then he sat his book open, face down on his lap. "How do you feel about leaving some of your clothes here?"

"If you don't want me to wear your shirt, just say so."

"No," he said. "No, I like to see you in my clothes. But I'm thinking of your convenience."

Lou could step into a shadow and then into her apartment. It was hardly inconvenient to get her own clothes. She'd only asked for a shirt now because—and she'd never admit this aloud—she wanted his scent to linger on her. Wearing his clothes would accomplish that.

"First dinner in a restaurant, now my own drawer?" she teased.

"Is it too much too quickly?" he asked.

This guy.

"Yes, it's all moving so fast, I don't think I can bear to have my underwear in a drawer beside your underwear."

"That is sarcasm."

"Yes," she said, shutting the drawer. "Yes, it is."

Lou slipped her arms through her shoulder holster, putting one of the Brownings in place before shrugging on her leather jacket. She wanted to check the fit before adding the other. This new jacket wasn't quite as loose as Lou wanted, but it would get there. It just needed to be broken in a bit.

"Be careful tonight," he said, clearly deciding to drop the topic of the drawer. He returned to his book.

"Konstantine," she said.

He looked up. "*Amore mio?*"

She tapped one of the top drawers, the smallest one, with the barrel of her gun. "I want this one."

He was still smiling when she left.

28

K ing lay in Beth's bedroom staring at the unmoving brown ceiling fan with its golden pull strings. Again, for the second time since Paris, he had the urge to smoke. He couldn't remember the last time he'd smoked, having officially quit years ago. But now, as he listened to Beth clean up in the adjacent bathroom, humming some slow, jazzy tune as she did, he definitely wished for a cigarette.

King was pleased with how the night had started. True, they'd gone straight to bed, even before ordering dinner, but he hoped that was a mark of eagerness and mutual attraction more than a lack of anything.

In Beth's bed, she'd been confident, comfortable in her own skin. She'd also been vocal, which King liked very much, and she hadn't been afraid to give directions, which King liked even more. He hated when he had to guess whether a woman was enjoying herself or pretending to.

And she'd been just as interested and invested in exploring his body as well.

She'd discovered early on that he liked his neck to be kissed, bitten, especially just above his collarbone.

King was recalling this, warming to the memory, when Beth's closet door began to slide slowly open.

The happy feelings evaporated as King searched for a weapon in the tangle of sheets.

Attacker? Ex-boyfriend? Secret husband? He didn't know what was coming out of the closet, but he wanted to be ready to meet it, whatever it was.

It was Louie Thorne.

"Christ," he swore, gathering the covers up to hide his bare chest.

"What's that, honey? You say something?" Beth called from the bathroom.

"Uh, nothing. I've just got a work call coming in," he said. "I'll take it outside."

He jabbed a finger at the window, hoping Lou would interpret this properly.

Lou stepped back into the closet and disappeared. King clambered out of bed, pulled on his pants and shirt, and padded barefoot downstairs. Lou was sitting on Beth's stoop when he opened the front door.

"Isn't this more suspicious?" she asked. "You talking to a woman outside."

She was right. "Take me to my apartment then."

She snorted. "Yes, a complete disappearance. Not strange at all."

But her hand was on his arm and she was pulling him through the dark. That drop-sick feeling washed over him—God, he hated that—before his apartment reformed around him.

"Thank you," he said, feeling less than grateful.

"What are you going to do if she looks for you and you're gone?"

"My Olds is still parked outside her place. I'll just tell her I decided to walk around a bit."

Lou slipped her hands into the pockets of her leather jacket.

"So what happened? What's going on?" King put his cell phone away.

"I'm going to Etienne and Delphine's place. I want to check out where she died. I was going to ask if you wanted to come with me."

King thought of Beth's face when he'd shown up with no dinner and two boxes of condoms. And now he'd jumped out of the bed almost as soon as they'd finished having sex. Leaving now would be more than a little insensitive.

"I should stay," he said, rubbing the back of his head. "There's not going to be anything at the house to find anyway."

"You could interview Etienne again," she said. "Or distract him while I search the house. I want to see where her body was found."

Already I'm disappointing her, King thought.

"When you see him tonight, ask him if we can do a formal interview. Tomorrow or the next day. Anytime," he said.

"Anything I should look for while I'm there?" she asked.

King considered this. "Lye. Oh, and hemlock."

"Hemlock?"

"It's a flowering plant that's poisonous. Turns out that the other chemical they got from the bones is hemlock."

"Basically, keep an eye out for weird chemicals," she said. "Anything else?"

He couldn't think of anything, and yet he also didn't want her to go. Looking at her standing there made him uneasy. Was it really about Paris though? Or was he simply embarrassed that Lou had found him in another woman's bed—a first since Lucy's passing.

"I can't think of anything else," he said finally.

"I'll take you back then."

When her hand fixed on his arm, his apartment dropped away. In its place was a cold sidewalk beside a copse of trees.

"Where the hell is this? Oh, wait." After a moment he oriented himself, recognizing the Garden District, and there, Prytania Street.

"To keep up with your 'I took a walk' lie," Lou said, staying close to the shadows. "You better put your phone up to your ear if you're going to sell this."

King pulled his phone from his pocket and did just that.

Lou snorted. "Her place is that way."

"Hey," King said, feeling more than a little silly with the phone against his ear. "Be careful tonight, okay?"

Lou's lips quirked. "You too."

Then she was gone.

King began padding down the sidewalk barefoot. When the townhome came into view, his heart sank at the sight of Beth standing on her porch.

"There you are!" she said. "Out there barefoot! Let me get a towel for your feet."

She had one ready before he reached the step.

"I'm sorry," he said. "It was one of my clients. He can be longwinded so I thought I'd take a stroll. It's so nice out."

It was, in fact, getting very cold.

"I decided on Caribbean for dinner," she said. "I'm in the mood for fried plantains. Do you like Caribbean?"

She held out two towels. One wet, one dry.

He took the wet rag in one hand, cleaned his feet, and then towel-dried them with the other.

"Who doesn't like jerked pineapple chicken?" he said. And hoped that by the time he'd finished eating, this terrible, uneasy feeling would go away.

29

It took Piper and Henry only fifteen minutes to erect the castle backdrop on The Wild Cat stage. Henry really only needed someone to steady the painted wooden set while he snapped the stabilizers into place. It also needed to be just the right height so that Henry could stick his head through the cut square serving as the tower's window to sing the first half of his rendition of "When Will My (Queer) Life Begin?," a satire of the song from the Rapunzel movie.

Once the job was done, Piper wished him luck with the show and headed back toward the apartment to see if Dani or Mr. Allendale still needed help.

She'd just turned off of Bourbon Street onto St. Peter, moving deftly through the thickening crowd, when someone yelled her name. She looked up both sides of the street, but no one caught her eye. No one she knew, anyway.

"Piper!"

She looked again and found a flushed Dani jumping up and down, waving at her.

Piper closed the distance, meeting her on the corner.

"What's wrong?" she asked as the girl came to a gasping stop in front of her. "What happened?"

Dani held her side as if it were cramping. "I...was just...looking...for you...everywhere."

"Sorry, I went to The Wild Cat. Henry needed help setting up his stage set for tonight. Do you need to sit down?" Because she sure as hell looked like she needed to sit down. "If you need someone to move those boxes, I can get them. Just let—"

"No," Dani said firmly. "No, I want to talk to you. I *need* to talk to you."

Piper's heart began knocking in her chest. What was it about a girl saying "I need to talk to you" that dumped adrenaline into her veins?

She rubbed her forehead with her fist. "Okay. Then let's go to the garden."

The garden was only a block away, and there would be plenty of places to sit down. There were steps and benches, and the stone ledges lining the fountain, or even the grass beneath the trees, would be suitable enough, assuming it wasn't still damp from the rain earlier.

As they walked together, Piper watched Dani struggle to get her breath.

"Seriously, how far did you run?"

"I thought you went to Café du Monde or something, so I went that way. Then I circled the square. I ran into one of those girls you know. Black, curly hair. She said she thought she saw you in the French Market."

Scarlet, Piper's ex, could be a bitch when she wanted to.

"I didn't go to the market, sorry. I was at The Wild Cat the whole time."

"I thought you might be. I was heading there next."

"Why didn't you just call me?" Piper asked.

Dani's jaw worked. "I threw my phone when I was

fighting with my mother and then I couldn't find it. I think it went into one of the boxes. It was stupid. Anyway, you're here now."

Piper stepped aside so Dani could pick wherever she wanted to sit. She chose a stone bench beneath the statue of Jesus, collapsing onto it with one hand still holding her hip.

"I think I was panicking more than actually out of breath," she said, rubbing the back of her neck. "I was scared I wouldn't find you."

It had been a while since Dani's PTSD had flared up. Piper squeezed her hand reassuringly. "You found me. But seriously, if it's about the boxes, I can—"

"Shut up about the freaking boxes," she said, pulling her hand away.

"Okay." Piper rubbed her palms on her knees. "Then tell me what's up."

"First of all, I'm so sorry about my mom."

"Oh, it's okay—"

Dani threw her hand up. "*Don't*. Don't you dare apologize for her. What she said was terrible and I can't even believe it came out of her mouth. I mean, I've always known that she was a snob, but that was *so* disrespectful. I'm embarrassed for her."

"We don't pick our parents," Piper said, thinking, not for the first time, of her mom. On and off she'd flickered through Piper's mind as she'd moved throughout the day. Sometimes the tears would come, making her throat thick and uncomfortable. Other times, it was only the cool wave of sadness that made her heart heavy. "Your dad seems pretty cool though. We talked before Henry texted me."

Dani placed her hand over her heart. "Oh god, he didn't say anything, did he?"

"No, no! He was super sweet. I like him."

Dani exhaled toward the sky, visibly relieved. "Oh thank

God. I mean, he's way better than my mother, but just nothing has gone to plan today so I was prepared to find out he stabbed you or something."

"He gave me cigarettes."

Dani snorted, surprised. "He only shares those with people he really likes. You must've made an impression."

Or I must've looked really sad, Piper thought.

How many times had Henry asked her if she was okay as they were setting up the stage? Too many.

Dani was looking into Piper's eyes, *really* looking.

"What is it?" Piper asked.

"What do I have to do, Piper? Just tell me what I have to do."

Piper's heart kicked. "What do you mean?"

"Do I have to get rid of the viola? My car? Do you want me to give away all of my money or never talk to my parents again—"

Piper drew back. "What? No."

"Whatever it is, please just tell me what I have to do to keep you."

Piper's stomach dropped.

Dani leaned toward her, searching her eyes as if the answers were written there. "I don't care about any of that other stuff. It's just...it's just shit. And if I have to get rid of it for you to be comfortable, I'll do it. I'll make a freaking Craigslist ad for my car tonight."

"I don't want you to do that," Piper said.

"Then tell me what I have to do. I know you think I don't like that apartment because it's smaller than my old one, but I swear, Piper, I *swear* to *God*, I have never been happier in my life. I could live in a freaking cardboard box with you and be happy."

So happy now. Always smiling, Mr. Allendale had said.

"Liar," Piper said. "Where would you put all your fancy

skin-care products if we lived in a box? You need electricity for the mini fridge you keep them in."

"Do you really want me to go?" Dani asked. "Look me in the eyes and tell me you really want me to move out."

Piper looked into those warm brown eyes, but found her throat wouldn't cooperate.

Her mind kept saying, *No. No, I want you to stay.*

Dani took her hands and squeezed. "I sent my parents away. I know you *said* you want me out of your apartment, but I'm not leaving. I'm not letting you break up with me when you're not even my official girlfriend. If you want to break up with me and throw me out of your life, you're going to have to ask me out first."

Piper laughed. "You're being serious right now?"

"Yes," Dani said, and squeezed her hands again. "You have to be my girlfriend for at least a whole day before you can get rid of me."

Piper didn't know what to say to this. It was true that she had never officially asked Dani to be with her. Things between them had simply evolved somewhat organically. First when Dani had been in the hospital after Petrov's attack. Then as Dani tried to process her PTSD. When Diana blew up her apartment, it had just seemed really natural that Dani would come stay with her.

And now...

"Piper." Dani gave her a pleading look. "Please tell me what I have to do to keep you."

"Keep me?"

"Keep you. In my life, as my girlfriend. I'll move out if you insist, but before I do that, I want you to look me in the eyes and tell me that you don't like me living with you. That you don't like waking up to this unwashed face, having coffee with me in the mornings, taking showers with me, watching TV at the end of the day, all snuggled up on the sofa. Look me in the *freaking* eye and tell me you want your space, and I'll leave."

Piper looked her in the eyes, but she couldn't say it. Because she loved all those things. And more.

"I mean, I definitely like taking showers with you," she said.

Dani nudged her. "Be serious."

"I do like it. All of it. I like living with you," Piper said. "But we come from really different worlds. You know that, right? I can't live like your parents. I wouldn't know how to act and I'd be stressed out all the time wondering if I was embarrassing you or—"

"Are you kidding me? You could *never* embarrass me. This afternoon you showed ten times more class than my mother did."

"But I won't ever be able to give you those things. I can't buy you a house like that. I can't even afford the insurance on your SUV. You'll always have less with me and it's going to hurt. I'm going to feel terrible about it *all the time*."

"First of all, you're making a lot of assumptions about our not-even-official-yet relationship. Who said you need to provide for me? Are you saying I can't be the breadwinner in our relationship?"

Oh god. Was Piper walking into some sort of feminist trap?

Dani must've seen the panic blooming on her face. "Listen, before we get into all that, let me just say something."

Piper swallowed. "Okay."

Dani looked out over the garden, at the bare trees and swaying grass. Finally, she said, "Do you remember the night I watched you do card readings in the square for the first time?"

"When you were undercover in all that goth makeup, shivering half to death? Yeah, I remember."

Piper missed the black eyeliner, truth be told, but Dani had kept the black nails, which was a nice touch.

"I knew right then that there was something special about you. It isn't just how smart you are, or how hard you work to make other people smile. And it wasn't just that you're a great listener. I mean, you're a *really* great listener. Hell, it's not even our amazing chemistry."

God, yeah, we have amazing chemistry. Piper's stomach muscles tightened just at the thought.

If Dani saw the blush spreading across her face, she ignored it.

"It's that you are so *genuine*. You are the most genuine person I've ever met. You're not artificial, or elitist like my parents. You're *real*. You're a hundred percent real with me and there isn't a single person in my life who has treated me with as much kindness and love and respect as you have. Okay, maybe my dad, but a lot of the time he goes along with my mom, so you're even doing better than him."

Piper's throat was so tight she could choke. Her gaze had slid down to their clasped hands while Dani spoke, but now Dani tilted her chin up and forced her to look her in the eyes.

"I don't need another freaking car or a fifty-room house, Piper Lynn Genereux. I need you because of how you make me feel. Loved. Safe. Happy. And because..."

She searched the park.

"Because what I feel for you is the realest, truest thing I've ever had. Please don't take that away from me."

Tears spilled from Piper's eyes, and Dani wiped them with the cuffs of her sweater.

"I know this is rich coming from the woman who literally lied to you and deceived you just to get to know you, but I mean it. I want to be with you, Piper. And not for anything you can buy me. I want to be with you because I love you."

Piper thought of her mom, dead in her forties, a whole

stream of ruined partnerships in her wake. Had her mother ever been happy with anyone? Had she ever felt loved and cared for the way Piper did with Dani? And was Piper really going to throw it away because she felt like she couldn't give Dani diamonds or sports cars or whatever the hell she was supposed to give a rich girl?

Here was the most amazing girl she'd *ever* met, saying that she wanted to be with her. *Her.* Not for the money or security she could provide but just to be with her.

It was impossible for Piper to believe that anyone could ever like her so much, but even with that aside, there was a simple truth:

Piper loved her. She loved seeing her and kissing her and talking to her. She loved sleeping with her—both literally and metaphorically. She loved spending time with her, and whenever she heard something funny, Dani was the first person she wanted to share it with. She liked having Dani in her orbit, as an integral part of each day. She loved her smile. Her laugh.

And she wanted Dani to stay.

Piper didn't believe she deserved her, but she wanted her to stay. Always.

"Did you hear me?" Dani said. "I love you."

"I heard you."

"If you don't—"

"I love you," Piper spat out. Her face flushed with heat. "I love you too."

Dani's face erupted in the biggest grin as she flung her arms around Piper's neck.

"Then please don't make me leave," she whispered into Piper's hair. She pulled back and cupped her face. "Let me stay and we'll just be together and happy, and argue over who is going to pay for what, *whatever*, but mostly we'll just be happy. Really, *really* happy."

Piper laughed, dabbing at her eyes with her sleeves.

"Please," Dani said. "Please be with me. Be my girlfriend."

It was terrifying, the idea that Piper might have a decent future. Piper wasn't sure she could ever believe it possible, not with all the terrible things that had happened in her life so far. But she also couldn't forgive herself if she didn't try. Her mother hadn't tried, and look where it had gotten her.

At the very least, Piper had to be brave enough to try.

"Okay," she said, and wrapped her arms around Dani too. "Stay and be my girlfriend."

Dani squealed and squeezed her hard again. And when Piper began to laugh, Dani finally let her go, but only so they could kiss.

30

———

The path leading up to the large house in the fifteenth arrondissement was thick with brush. Shrubs taller than Lou herself crowded the stone path at a black door. For this reason, it was easy to materialize in the shadowed space between two shrubs and step onto the path. But Lou wondered if this was a mistake once she saw the cameras above the doorway.

She pressed the doorbell and felt a sharp prick in her finger.

She yanked it back. A large droplet of blood was forming on the tip of her right index finger.

What the hell?

She bent and inspected the doorbell but didn't see anything. There was a thorny plant growing along the door, but Lou didn't think she'd touched that.

Had something bitten her? Some angry insect who'd felt she'd invaded their home? Lou didn't see any bugs, and besides, it was late in the season.

She sucked the blood off her finger.

Footsteps sounded, and she touched her jacket once to make sure her guns were concealed.

At the last moment, she wondered if she should turn back and get her Kevlar sleeves and her knives.

She decided against it. This would be quick. Only long enough to see where Delphine had been attacked, and then she would leave. Even if Etienne had nefarious plans, he could hardly take her on. He was just one grief-stricken man.

The door opened and Etienne appeared with a wine glass in hand, wearing a black turtleneck that instantly made her think of Konstantine. Except that Konstantine looked very handsome with the candlelight in his eyes and his muscular forearms resting on the tabletop. Etienne, while far from ugly, still didn't wear the ensemble quite as well.

"You came," he said with a breathy sigh of relief. He stepped aside so she could enter. "Please."

Lou crossed the threshold, turning as he moved behind her to close the door. This maneuver prevented her from having to expose her back.

"I am glad you came," he said, his excitement visible. "I wasn't sure if you would."

"I wanted to see where Delphine died," she said. Was this too gruesome or direct? King thought she lacked tact when it came to certain conversations, but she'd always preferred to be blunt with the people she helped. The worst had already happened to them. There was no need to protect their feelings now.

And Lou had had plenty of success before King came along, so no need to doubt her methods now.

Etienne motioned her forward. "Don't worry, it is part of the tour. But first, a glass of wine."

What is it with European men and their wine? she thought.

She trailed behind him as he led the way to the kitchen. As they walked, she took note of where the shadows pooled.

Doorways and closets. Large pieces of furniture. Unfortunately, the house was well lit. Dramatic sky lighting from above seemed to cover most rooms from corner to corner. If she needed to make a quick escape, she would definitely need to find a dark room.

There was always the option to shoot out the lights, too. But Lou thought that was rather dramatic. She'd only resort to that if necessary.

For this reason she began to take note of all the closed doors. The pantry, the bathroom, anywhere she could duck inside and turn off a light should she need a quick escape.

There was already a wine glass sitting on the wooden countertop when they entered the kitchen. Beside it, an opaque bottle. Etienne lifted it and filled her glass halfway with red wine.

"Here you go." He lifted the glass from the top, his hand cupped over it as he held it out to her.

"No, thank you," she said. She had no intention of drinking this wine, in case it was spiked.

"Oh, please. Drink with me. I can—"

"I'm fine," Lou said, trying to keep a cap on her irritation. "I don't have a lot of time."

"*D'accord*." Etienne arched his brows but at least stopped trying to give her the glass of wine.

With his own glass now full, he led the way out of the kitchen and into a large living room featuring many of the same design details. High ceilings and dramatic lighting. Etienne babbled about the interior design and the style of the paintings on the walls as they passed. While the walls were white, the paintings themselves were somber and dramatic. Two in particular highlighted slit throats, and a third showed a man in the throes of dying, his naked torso bent in agony.

Lou regarded these, noticing that the warmth in her hand

was spreading through her, transforming into a weight that was settling on her shoulders and upper arms.

After a moment of silence Etienne said, "She kept the real art upstairs. Come."

At the top of the stairs, three of the doors were shut, one was open.

"This is where I found her," Etienne said, gesturing at the luminescent bathroom. "My Delphine."

Lou stepped in, trying to ignore the growing ache in her hand.

The tub was the centerpiece. Deep and set in the center of the room, light seemed to hit it from every angle. Because the walls, tub, and floor were all white, Lou could imagine how it must've looked with the bloody water overflowing from the tub, sloshing onto the floor.

As dramatic as everything else in this house.

Also, because of the width of the bathroom, it would have been more than possible for a man to lift Delphine and throw her into the tub. The man in the catacombs, though on the tall side, would have definitely been able to maneuver in this bathroom.

Delphine, given her shorter stature, would've found it difficult to climb over the high lip of the tub as she was bleed-ing. Perhaps she'd already been stabbed, then lifted into the tub before the water was turned on.

Or she just fell back into it. Lou imagined a scene in which Delphine, stabbed and dying, turned on the water, let the tub fill, and simply opened her arms, falling into the water.

What a weird idea, she thought, noticing that the weight in her arms was somehow invading her brain as well.

Etienne was watching her out of the corner of his eye. Lou could feel his gaze on her.

"Let me show you her work," he said.

He turned away from the bathroom and crossed to one of the closed doors.

He did not turn on a light when he entered. In the dark, he said, "Come in. Don't be afraid."

Lou wasn't afraid.

While most women wouldn't want to walk into a dark room with a stranger, in the dark, Lou felt the safest. If he tried something, if he so much as put a hand on her, she could slip.

And after wandering these over-lit rooms, the dark space was more than a little welcome.

Then Lou stepped into the room. And her heart began to hammer.

It was the room.

The room.

Four walls of strange black glass. She reached out to touch one to be sure it was real. It was. The glass was cool to the touch, giving the slight impression that her reflection moved like a shadow beneath the glossy surface.

"Let me turn on the light," Etienne said, his voice nearly in her ear.

Lou almost said no, but it was too late.

Light burst into being, the room filling with it.

Not from a fixture overhead, no. The lights were *inside* the walls.

Lou's pulse raged in her ear.

In the glass display before her were two bodies. Two women cut open and arranged like the vivisections from the museum. But these were not insects or plants.

These were human. Human *women*.

One's chest had been opened, the flesh pinned to each side in flamboyant ribbons and the soft tissues removed. The heart somehow remained suspended inside the emptied and cleaned rib cage. Her breasts had also been removed, placed instead in her delicately cupped hands as if the woman had taken them off and were offering them to the viewer.

One of her legs, particularly her inner thigh, had been cut open, revealing the long lean muscle beneath.

But the face. The face was a mask of agony, the features frozen in permanent horror as she stared right at Lou, unseeing.

The second body was not so neatly preserved. Her flesh was turning gray, shriveling up. This face was contorted as well, the head bent back in a silent scream, the jaws gaping to release the force of the sound. Because it was slowly decomposing, Lou realized, the face didn't look as fresh as the other. The graying skin had begun to sag, slide away from the bones, revealing barely contained eyeballs in their opening sockets.

With the lights on, Lou could now see how many squares there were. Twelve in total, including the two the dead women occupied. Had every one of these squares been full of girls? Could Delphine really have displayed as many as twelve mutilated bodies at a time?

"Delphine did this?" Lou asked.

"*Bah, oui*," Etienne said. "I do not have her gifts or talent."

"Delphine killed them all."

"Of course," he said.

Delphine killed them all. Delphine. That was why Lou's compass could never find the killer. *Take me to the killer*—but the killer was dead. And Assia—was that the same?

Lou struggled to rerun the details through her mind, piecing together the truth. It was far harder than it should've been.

She didn't feel well.

Etienne sipped his wine and said, "Delphine discovered a tree resin which, when heated correctly, can preserve the body for longer, but as you can see, they still do not last. So disappointing. I want to gaze at them forever, each beautiful little creation. *But*, Delphine argued the temporality added to the beauty of the work."

That was why I couldn't find anyone, she thought. Those walls were filled with resin, and thin enough only for the bodies that filled them. The light source seemed to come somewhere from the ground, below their suspended feet, shining up through the gelatinous material. Or were the lights above? Lou couldn't be sure.

Etienne cupped one elbow, wagging a finger at her. "See, you aren't horrified. You are made of different stuff, no? I could tell from the moment I saw you. I can feel the darkness inside you. It speaks to me."

A wave of nausea washed over Lou and she staggered. The lighted images of the women's bodies doubled, tripled, created layers upon layers until she couldn't see.

"What's wrong with my eyes?"

Lou reached out for the wall but missed it. Nothing was there.

"It's the hemlock," he said. "It's affecting you more slowly than the others, which is interesting. But it *will* paralyze you. We used it on all the specimens. It immobilizes the body, so that Delphine could begin before the heart stopped. She liked to feel the heart beating in her hands. She said it was her favorite part."

How had she come into contact with poison? She hadn't drunk anything. She'd been so careful.

"The doorbell was a bit sharp, wasn't it?" Etienne laughed. "We kidnapped a delivery girl the same way."

Lou lunged for him, intending to wrap her hands around his throat, but her palms connected only with the lit glass.

She considered pulling her gun, but shooting blindly was stupid. The shot would ricochet in a room of this size, possibly hitting her instead.

"Who killed Delphine? Was it one of these women?

Assia?"

Etienne sighed. "I told her never to work on the art alone. Without me, it isn't safe. Even da Vinci had his assistants, you see. But Delphine was very particular. She listened to no one. *Artists.*" He laughed at his own joke. "But the girl must have woken up while I was away at Le Grand Palais. Delphine hadn't even given her the hemlock when she began. It was careless."

Was that what happened? Had Delphine, in her excitement, begun something she couldn't finish?

Assia fought back, managed to wound Delphine fatally, but it hadn't saved her.

"You killed Assia?" Lou asked.

"*Non.* They were both dead when I arrived. There was blood all over this room. The bathroom. I cannot be sure, but I think Assia attacked. But Delphine finished her."

So maybe Lou's vision of Delphine turning on the tub and falling back into it to die with all the pomp of one of her subjects hadn't been too far from the mark.

"But you helped her?"

"Oh yes. I would find the beautiful girls for her. Perhaps in a park or when they crossed the street. Sometimes I would invite them in for a glass of wine and they would accept."

"What about Assia? She was a student—she went missing a few days before Delphine died."

"Yes, the last one. Delphine saw her walking by through a window. 'She's so beautiful, look at her bone structure,' she cried out.

"So I went outside, tried to talk to her, but she was resistant. Sometimes they are."

Lou tried to quell the nausea building in her guts.

"I had to strike her here." He touched the back of his neck. "Then I carried her. She was only twelve meters from the front door. But I couldn't stay. I was expected at Le

Grand Palais within the hour. I asked Delphine to wait until I got home, but she didn't listen. Oh, *pourquoi, Delphine?* Why didn't you wait for me?"

Delphine killed Assia. Assia killed Delphine.

There was no killer at large. Only Etienne, the dutiful, if deeply deranged, accomplice.

"I had to put the girl's body straight into the wash," Etienne said. "Delphine didn't even get to..." His voice cracked. The grief Lou had seen before reappeared. "I *told* her. I *told* her to wait until I got home and we could do it together. But she didn't. She *didn't* wait."

He threw his wine glass against the floor. It shattered, warm spray wetting Lou's legs.

Lou tried to find the light switch on the wall, the trigger, anything that would allow her to make it dark again, but it was smooth. And because the light streaked in all directions, making details impossible to pick out, she would never find it.

The door, she thought. *I need to get to that other closed room.*

"First I thought you were my Delphine, her ghost. You came to the park that night when I was watching that woman. I almost took her, but you appeared. And again when I dreamt of Delphine you came. 'You are not alone,' she told me. 'You are not alone,' and then you arrived. It was like a gift."

"I'm not your fucking gift," Lou said.

Etienne ignored this. "Then in the catacombs, I was so full of despair, and *again* you came. Whenever I was lonely, whenever I hungered, you came for me. I thought this was all coincidence until tonight. Tonight, I was going to do it. I was going to take the girl in the cemetery, and what happened?"

Lou didn't need to answer this rhetorical question. She knew what had happened. She'd come to the cemetery and had found Etienne sprawled beneath the weeping angel.

What she'd seen in his eyes hadn't been a mistake. She should've never doubted that he was a monster just because he also grieved.

I won't make that mistake again.

Lou's legs were shaking. The heartbeat in her ears sounded strained, erratic.

Fingers brushed her arms, and she tried to grab them but they were already gone.

"Perhaps you are the manifestation of my desire, my thirst."

"Stop talking," she said. *Shut up, just shut up.*

He did not, in fact, shut up.

"Tell me what you are, my strange apparition. You come, you go. You are drawn to me the way I am drawn to you, aren't you? Why have you chosen me? Is it because the catacombs run under this house? Do you haunt me or this place?"

Lou ran her hand along the wall until it broke open. There. The hallway. And beyond that, the closed door.

Her escape.

She just had to make it there.

"Tell me," he begged again. "Are you to be my new artist, or the art?"

When the hand wrapped around her arm this time, she threw her elbow back, felt it connect hard. Etienne cried and fell back. The loss of his body weight staggered her.

She stumbled out into the hall, willing herself to stay upright on her feet, though her legs were going numb. Her arms were too heavy.

"Where are you going? This house locks from the inside," he called after her. "You cannot open a door or window without my keys."

Something musical tinkled behind her. Was he shaking a key ring at her? *That bastard.*

He laughed, but the sound was thick. Lou hoped she'd

broken his nose and that was blood clogging his throat. That was the least he had coming to him.

"If you scream, the walls will only swallow it. We sound-proofed everything. The walls. The windows."

Lou didn't need a door or a window. She needed the dark.

She grabbed the handle of the closed door and pushed, but it didn't open. It was locked.

"Stay with me," he begged. "I am not done with you."

Lou stumbled a few feet forward and tried the second closed door, but this handle too didn't budge. The room was shut tight.

"I only want to open you up." His voice was closer now. "I want to see that darkness inside you."

Lou threw her shoulder against the door. It bounced, but it didn't open. She was growing too weak. It was getting harder to breathe.

Definitely hemlock, she thought, believing now more than ever that there must have been the thinnest needle protruding from the wood beside that doorbell.

She was running out of time.

"I cannot turn you into one of Delphine's beautiful creations," he said. "My work will be crude, but I will try my best. I will open you up as...as *gently* as I possibly can."

His voice was close, too close. She thought that was his warm breath on the back of her neck.

With a rally cry, she slammed her shoulder into the door again, and this time, it busted inward. She fell forward into the blessed dark.

There had been a brief sensation of fabric brushing her face, perhaps coats or shirts. It didn't matter. It was enough. If the room had walls or a floor, Lou would never know.

She was swallowed by the shadows before she ever hit the ground.

31

"I suspect we will only need to be there two days, four including travel," Konstantine said, lacing his hands in front of him and steepling the fingers. "Just long enough for me to speak to Antonio, tour the warehouse facility, and perhaps give my regards to the Merrito family. We should think about what gift we are going to present them."

"Am I going with you or do you need me here?" Stefano asked. The man was staring down at his phone, only periodically glancing up to regard Konstantine over the mountain of documents on his desk.

It was late, too late. Konstantine's eyes burned and he longed for his bed. But it had been impossible to fall asleep after Lou had left him. It hadn't helped that he'd found Stefano burning the midnight oil too.

I should just go back to bed, he thought. *She will be fine.*

But first, I will finish what I started.

Konstantine rubbed his jaw. "I think it would be better if you—"

A crash cut his sentence in half.

Stefano swore, his eyes opening wide as he stood, his legs knocking the chair back.

"Konstantine."

Konstantine rose and came around the desk. There on his stone floor was Louie. She was face down and looked as if she was trying to push herself up but couldn't.

"Louie!" he cried, falling to his knees beside her. "Louie, what's happened?"

Stefano helped him turn her over.

Konstantine searched her arms, her throat, chest, legs, looking for bullet wounds or a cut. But there was nothing. She tried to open her hand and Konstantine took it, unclenching her fist carefully to inspect it. There was a dark spot on her index finger, but that couldn't be it. It was tiny. Insignificant. As if she'd merely pulled a splinter from her finger.

"What happened?" he begged her. He pushed her hair off her face and found her burning up.

"P-p—" Her teeth chattered. "*P-poison.*"

Her legs began to spasm.

"Poison?" he asked. "You were poisoned?"

Lou tried to answer him, but her eyes pinched shut.

There were countless poisons in the world, and without knowing what was coursing through her veins, there was no way for Konstantine to know what antidote may help her.

"H-hemlock," she ground out, spitting the word between gritted teeth.

Hemlock. There was no antidote for hemlock.

What will I do? What will I do? What will I—

"What do you want me to do?" Stefano asked, his eyes wide.

Konstantine couldn't answer.

"Paolo," Stefano said, using Konstantine's first name. He

was the *only* one who'd ever gotten away with doing that. "Tell me what to do."

Konstantine looked at Lou, shivering—no, *convulsing* in his lap. She was going to die if he didn't do something.

She was going to die.

"Water," Konstantine said. "I need water."

Stefano went into the bathroom and turned on the tap.

"No, I need to put her in water."

"Cos' è? Una fottuta pianta?" he cried, turning on the tub's faucet.

It would take too long to fill the tub, and it was too small for him to fit in with her.

In her condition, she would need someone to help her get to the surface. What if her muscles gave completely? Didn't hemlock cause paralysis? He couldn't remember.

"Non importa. Aiutami!" Konstantine said, and stood, laying Louie gently on the floor. "I have to put her in the fountain. Help me carry her."

"Help you? She's a *girl. Non pesa niente.*"

"She's much heavier than she looks."

Stefano opened the door to the office and then lifted Lou's legs as Konstantine slipped his arms under hers.

They lifted her together on three and Stefano swore. "Are there bricks in her pockets?"

"Hurry up."

They carried her into the courtyard, and blessedly, none of the children were there. No one had to be sent away. It was only the three of them as they lifted Lou over the lip of the stone fountain and into the flowing water.

It was only three feet deep. Konstantine prayed it was enough.

He climbed in after her, trying to keep her head above water.

Stefano threw up his hands. *"Cosa fai?"*

"This is the only way I know to help her."

"Drown her? And then yourself? *Dio mio.*"

"I can't explain now," he said, hoping that Stefano wouldn't try to do anything reckless, like dragging him out of the fountain.

Konstantine *had* to go. He had to.

There were a hundred things that could go wrong. Lou could die in La Loon, trapping Konstantine forever in that nightmarish place, without the ability to return home. Or that monster of hers, upon seeing him, might devour him whole as she had his brothers, one by one.

Don't think about that, he scolded himself. His fears wouldn't help her.

Konstantine lay down in the water beside her and spoke directly into her ear.

"Louie. We have to go to La Loon. Do you hear me? I am going to dunk us under and you have to take us."

Her eyes fluttered open, and for a moment he thought he saw a flash of recognition.

"Okay. One...two..." He dunked them both beneath the water.

They cleared the surface, their backs resting against the bottom of the rippling pool.

He waited.

And waited.

But the water didn't change from dark blue to red. It didn't warm.

Nothing happened. He waited for a heartbeat longer until he was afraid he might drown her.

He came up choking.

"Louie. You know I can't do it! You have to! You have to take us across."

He shook her a little, hoping to bring her closer to consciousness. He was losing her.

He was losing her fast.

"Perhaps it's the light," Stefano said, his hands gripping the side of the fountain.

"What?"

"The light, in the fountain. Perhaps it's too bright."

Konstantine regarded the light beneath the cherub's face. "*Sì*. Turn it off."

Stefano's feet pounded the courtyard. There was a beat of silence and then the light cut off. The gurgling water fell still.

"Please try," he told her, gathering her into his arms once more, trying to get a good grip on her. "I'll explain everything later, but you have to take us through those waters. *Now*. On three. One...two..."

He dunked them again, their backs hitting the stone floor for a second time.

Then they lay there in the dark.

A terrible panic began to rise up in him, his heart beating faster than it ever had before.

She was going to die.

She was going to die here in his arms and he could do nothing to stop it.

No, please. No, please, not now. Not after everything.

But then the water began to warm, a subtle shift in temperature. Konstantine dared to open his eyes, to find they were much deeper now—the bottom of the fountain had fallen away and its blue waters had shifted to a deep blood red.

Wrapping one arm tighter around her waist, Konstantine kicked for the surface, pushing harder and harder, as fast as he could toward salvation.

32

———

An eternal purple twilight and hazy yellow mountains formed in the distance as Konstantine burst through the surface of the lake. Twin moons serene in the sky above the blood-colored water stretching off into the distance. And that familiar scent of sulfur, what he'd come to think of as the scent of hell, hit his nose with full force.

But they'd made it. They'd crossed over.

"Come on," he said. "Hang in there."

Konstantine dragged Lou to the shore, only so far as to rest her head on the embankment, safe from the threat of drowning but keeping the rest of her in the water.

He pulled off her coat, stripped her down to only her shirt and pants. He tossed the leather jacket and gun onto the land for safekeeping. Then he inspected the pricked finger again, trying to see the shape of the wound. Had it been a needle? A glass shard?

It was too small to see clearly, especially in this low light.

It didn't matter. It only mattered that he hold it beneath the surface of the water.

He lifted the hand but it looked the same. Maybe the water needed to get into her veins?

Konstantine reached into his soaked boot and found the blade. Sliding it out of its sheath, he adjusted its wet handle in his grip.

He didn't want to cut her hand, something so well used, but he also hated the idea of cutting her.

Would making her drink it work? he wondered.

That's when the monster screeched, and Konstantine's stomach knotted, his bowels threatening to empty themselves right here at the water's edge.

Quickly he slashed Lou's arm. A second, third, and fourth cut followed. All shallow, but enough to introduce the water to her bloodstream. He was about to do a fifth and final cut when the beast burst through the black forest and into view.

As soon as she saw him she shrieked, coming up onto her hind legs, the other four claws in a crooked position beside her pale, scaly stomach. The black muscles of her body contracted as she came forward, her head bent, her eyes on him.

"Would you believe," he told her, "that I'm trying to help her?"

She screamed again, showing him her puffy white maw opened wide and the row upon row of sharp teeth contained within.

"Please don't eat me. *Per favore,*" he said, even as his grip on the blade tightened. His voice sounded calm to his ears but inside he knew better. His mind was filled with a single panicked mantra: *please please please please please—*

He tried to keep the air moving in and out of his lungs.

The beast nudged the side of his head with hers, and for an awful moment he thought she was going to open up and snap her jaws shut over his throat.

But then she backed up and turned a circle, coming

around to Lou's other side. She did the same headbutting motion, but this time, when Lou's head only lolled, she let out a soft, cooing sound. Almost like a dog's whine.

She did it again.

"I don't know what else to do for her," Konstantine admitted. He didn't put down the knife, but at least the creature seemed more interested in Lou's well-being than severing his spine.

"I thought the water would help," he added.

The beast's long white tongue rolled from its mouth and licked up Lou's arm. The blood left on the surface—or perhaps it wasn't blood but water from the lake—began to dry as pink droplets on her skin.

Lou's eyes fluttered opened.

"Don't give up," he told her. "*Don't*."

A heartbeat later, she was unconscious again.

The beast lay down beside them, its great yellow eyes fixed on Lou.

It was right. There was nothing else for him to do but wait.

Konstantine began to pray.

Lou woke to a thick, slick tongue dragging across her face. She groaned and tried to sit up.

She felt like *shit*.

Her whole body ached. Either she'd clenched every muscle for the last few hours or someone had run her body through a pulverizer.

"How do you feel?"

Lou turned and found Konstantine sitting beside her. His hair was wet and stuck to his face, no doubt from the trip through the water. But the relief collected in his features shone through.

"Like hell," she said. "What happened?"

La Loon loomed before her, bizarre and sulfuric with its blood-red waters. And this was a fitting setting, considering how she felt. But she had no memory of how she got here, or why it was Konstantine sitting beside her.

Was she dead? Was this a dream?

Konstantine ran his hands through his wet hair. "You don't remember?"

Remember...

She thought of the dinner with Konstantine first. Then the sex. Then...she'd gone to Etienne's. That large house, those macabre paintings. The doorbell that had pricked her.

"He poisoned me," Lou said. "I'm going to kill him."

"The Frenchman?"

"It was Delphine." Lou pressed her fingers into her temples. Her head hurt so bad. "Delphine killed all those girls. She cut them up and displayed them. Assia was the one who stabbed her in the gut."

"That's why you couldn't find your killer," he said. "Your killer was dead."

After a beat he asked, "Did he really use hemlock? That's what you said."

"That's what he told me. And King said they found traces of it on the bones. I should've never rang the doorbell. I'd been so careful about that stupid wine glass and—"

Here Konstantine's concern drained a little. "You were drinking with him?"

Lou was too miserable to give him the look he deserved. "No, I *didn't* drink with him in case he spiked the wine. But it was the doorbell. There must've been a needle too thin to see."

Jabbers pushed her head against Lou's.

Lou reached out and patted her. "I'm not ignoring you. I'm just working out what the hell just happened."

Jabbers began to purr.

"You collapsed in my office. Good thing, because I don't have a bathtub in my apartment," Konstantine said. "I don't know how I would've helped you if you'd followed me there. Perhaps someone is looking out for us."

Lou didn't have it in her to debate the existence of God at the moment. She simply kept her mouth shut and let Konstantine recount her surprise arrival in his office, her condition, ending with, "So, I put you in the fountain."

"You put me in a public fountain? I hope you charged admission for that show."

"No," he said. "We used the one outside my office. I wasn't sure it would work, but I had to try."

"Maybe my head is broken, but I still don't understand why you thought bringing me here was the answer." She frowned. Because if she'd found Konstantine poisoned, the idea of dunking him underwater wouldn't be *her* first instinct.

He bit his lower lip. "I have something to tell you."

"You have herpes?"

He scowled. "What? *No.*"

"You killed one of my friends?"

He huffed. "*No.* I would never."

"You slept with someone else?"

Konstantine pinched the bridge of his nose. "I will never. Do you have any more guesses?"

"No. So spit it out." She sounded more than a little irritated to herself. "What did you do?"

"Do you remember when we came here together the first time and I collected all of the samples? From the soil, from the air, the plants. The rocks."

She did. But not so much for the entertainment value of Konstantine meeting Jabbers for the first time and relishing his barely contained horror as they'd traversed this nightmare landscape together. She remembered it because it was the first night they'd had sex, in the cave hidden amongst the cliffs.

"What about it?" she asked, and wondered if he was thinking about that night too.

"One of the test results was very strange. Very, *very* strange. So I had my lab run more tests."

"Of course you did. *And?*"

"There is something different about this water."

Lou frowned. "What's wrong with the water?"

"It's not exactly water."

"What the hell do you mean, it's not *exactly* water?"

"And it heals you."

She only blinked at him.

"It has the ability to heal wounds. It is full of these strange little microbes that speed up healing."

"Microbes? What kind of microbes?"

"We don't know. We don't have them on earth."

Lou stared out over the red waters. "And you learned this from the sample you took?"

"*Sì*," he said. "And these microbes are everywhere. They're in the plants, the soil, Jabbers. The air. The water. I want to take a blood sample from you to see if they are in your system, and if they are, how long they live there before they die."

"Are you a mob boss or a scientist?" Lou asked.

He ignored this. "Have you tried drinking it?"

The idea disgusted her. "Do you know what's *in* this water?"

"Didn't you ever wonder why you healed so quickly after a fight? Why you could be nearly *dead* one night and simply sore the next?"

Lou had wondered, but like most things, she hadn't thought about it for too long. She'd assumed it was part of the very weird special ability package that she'd inherited.

But now that she thought of it, why wouldn't Lucy have healed? Cancer or no cancer, she would've healed too, since they had the same gift.

Except Lucy only traveled by shadows. Never water.

"It took forever to heal my shoulder," Lou said, trying to force images of her dying aunt from her mind.

Konstantine held up a finger. "But do you remember what you were *not* doing then?"

"I didn't cross over."

"No, after the shopkeeper—"

"Melandra."

"Yes, after she shot you, you didn't hunt for many months."

That was true. And her healing had taken forever.

Come to think of it, it wasn't until she crossed over after her long hiatus that her shoulder pain began to actually disappear.

Lou pointed at the lake. "So you're saying this water heals me every time I cross over and these microbes get into my bloodstream?"

"Yes. That is what I'm saying."

"Do these microbes do anything else? Make me stronger? Faster?"

"That is the interesting part. We can't be sure what all it can do without more tests. It heals wounds, slows the effects of poisons, but does it also slow aging? Cure cancers?"

Lou's heart sputtered at that, the idea that maybe her aunt Lucy could've been saved if only she'd agreed to come here.

Konstantine put a hand on her leg. "I'm sorry. I shouldn't have said that. I only meant that I would like to know more. Wouldn't you?"

"If you're looking to get out of drugs and start selling this fountain of youth water instead—"

"No, no." He shook his head. "I don't want to exploit it. This is why I was worried about telling you. I thought you would be upset."

"I'm not upset," she said. Because no one could come to La Loon without her. It wasn't like they were going to show up and drain the lake when she wasn't looking. She could protect this place from everyone, even Konstantine, if it came to that.

There was only one way in and out of this place, and that was her.

He squeezed her hand. "I'm simply curious. Aren't you?"

"A little," she admitted.

Lou thought of the time she'd almost bled to death on the shores of La Loon. At the last minute, Jabbers had pushed her into the water. One nudge of her huge head had knocked Lou back in.

At the time, Lou had thought it was because the creature understood that Lou came from another world, and that maybe if she went back, she could get help.

Now she wondered if the creature simply understood that the water could heal her.

"You knew all along, didn't you?" she asked, placing one hand on the creature's head.

Jabbers only blinked one yellow eye, then the other.

Finally, Lou said, "I'll let you have my blood. For your tests."

Konstantine brightened at this. "Thank you."

Then his hands were on her face, pulling her to him until their foreheads touched. After a shaky breath, he said, "You scared me."

She pulled back and smiled. "I told you I would."

33

———

Someone was knocking on the door. King rose, placing his soda on the coaster, and crossed the kitchen. When he opened the door, he found Piper on the other side with a bowl of popcorn tucked under her arm.

"Turn it to Channel Four," she said with her mouth full. "You're missing it."

He stepped aside to let her in. "Missing what?"

The girl marched into his apartment like she owned it, and seized his remote from his oversized coffee table.

"The fact you still have cable is wacko," she said. "How do you—Ah, never mind."

The picture stopped flicking.

"Tonight we have a gruesome story of murder," the news anchor said. "The remains of over sixty victims have been uncovered from the Paris catacombs, nearly all of them women between the ages of fourteen and seventy-three.

"Fourteen?" Piper cried. "Assholes."

She fed Lady a few kernels of popcorn.

"Hey, stop that!" King hissed. "She's a working dog. You'll ruin her."

Piper grumbled, but tipped the bowl away.

Etienne Martin moved across the television in handcuffs, his head down as he was put into the back of a police car. To King it looked like someone had broken the man's nose. It was twice the normal size, swollen and purple.

Piper shoved another handful of popcorn in her mouth. "He looks like Steve Jobs except for the nose. That's the guy we saw in the catacombs, right?"

"Yeah."

King looked away from the television long enough to see Lou stepping from his shadowed bedroom into the living room, her eyes fixed on the screen. He hadn't even seen her arrive, looking as she always did in her leather jacket, mirrored shades, hands resting loosely in her pockets.

King jabbed a thumb over his shoulder. "Why didn't you use the door?"

"Ghost night," Piper said around another mouthful of popcorn. "She can't be seen until she does her spooky thing."

King returned to his place on the sofa, Piper taking up the other end. Lou chose to stand.

Piper offered him the popcorn, but he declined. "Dani's bummed out that she wasn't the one who broke the story."

"Where is she tonight?" King asked. For the last two days he'd heard quite a bit of laughter coming from the apartment above his head while he'd tried to work. He was guessing by Dani's acceptance to Thanksgiving dinner and Piper's general perkiness that the girls had made up.

King was glad to see it.

"Her parents went to Houston for the holidays, so she drove home to steal some stuff. I told her to bring whatever she wants. I don't know where we're going to put it all, but whatever. That's a problem for another day. By the way, if you didn't know, she's rich. So if you want to raise the rent on the place, have at it."

King didn't need the money, and he liked having the girls close so he could keep an eye on them. "I'll keep that in mind, but I've no plans to raise the rent on you."

Piper shrugged. "Just letting you know in case your retirement funds are running low."

The fact that King seemed incapable of quitting made *low retirement funds* seem improbable.

The news anchor continued on. "The bodies of the women were brutally tortured before their remains were interred in the catacombs below their home. Officers found that a wall in the basement of the residence had been partially excavated, connecting it to an unused part of the catacombs. This particular portion of the catacombs had been initially excavated in the seventeenth century, but was never fully restored or integrated with the rest of the city's museum. It appears the homicidal couple were using this underground passageway to hide the victims' remains."

"There must've been a false wall," Lou said. "Something they put up to hide the opening between his house and the tunnels."

"Probably," Piper agreed. "They haven't said anything about the dissections."

"They won't put that on TV," King said.

Piper snorted. "Yeah, they'll wait to put that in the book."

King recalled the delicate little creatures splayed open in Delphine's light boxes. Based on what Lou had told him she'd found that night in the couple's home, he could only imagine what it had looked like, those two young women, cut open and wing-pinned like that delicate blue butterfly.

He was more than a little grateful he hadn't been the one to see it.

"The motives for these killings are unclear at this time. More as this story develops." Etienne and wide shots of his

Paris home were replaced by a feel-good story of a veteran reuniting with his dog after a year apart.

"I'm surprised you let him live," Piper said, her eyes on Lou now. "If someone poisoned me, I would've had a hard time letting that go."

"I'm not going to let him go. I'm going to kill him."

"Nice. When?" Piper asked, and flicked a popcorn kernel in Lou's direction. It hit Lou's jacket and fell to the floor.

"It'll take them a few months to fully excavate the tunnels. Once they have what they need, he might just..." Lou snapped her fingers. "Disappear."

"Going to take him to La Loon?" Piper asked.

"I'm going to slide a knife between his ribs."

Piper groaned. "*Damn.* Remind me to never poison you."

"You have to stop taking them from their cells," King said, plucking his soda from the coffee table. "It looks like they escape."

"Fine," Lou said. "When I'm done with him, I'll dump him back in his cell."

"Thatta girl," Piper said, and flicked more popcorn. This one went wide, and Lady gave King a longing look.

"All right," he said.

Lady leapt forward, snapping up the two fallen pieces.

"Who is ruining *who* here?" Piper scoffed. "Hey, are we all set for Thursday? Need me and Lou to do any shopping?"

"No, I've got the shopping and cooking covered." King's heart swelled. They'd all accepted his Thanksgiving invitation, even Dani. He was determined that it be a good day for all of them.

Even if that meant not sleeping and doing everything himself.

"Don't be a hog," Piper said. "Let us help you. We know how to pick up groceries."

"What if they don't have something? You won't know what to substitute."

Piper jabbed her hand at Lou. "Uh, *hello*. She can go to any grocery in the whole world, man. You'll get your cream of mushroom soup or whatever."

"Fine," he said. "You two do the shopping."

"And you should designate the sides. Just ask everyone to make something and you can focus on the meats." Piper smacked her lips. "It's the meats that matter."

"Don't ask me to make something," Lou said. "I'd rather clean."

Piper did finger guns at her. "Even better. I hate cleaning."

"I'm bringing Konstantine," Lou said.

King hoped his face remained neutral. "Okay. Mel's table seats six."

"Yeah, you said that." Piper looked down at her watch. "Oh shit, you better get down there and do your thing."

"Be right back." Lou pushed her mirrored sunglasses down over her eyes and stepped into King's dark bedroom.

There was a stiff *pop* between his ears, followed by an ache.

"I know," Piper said, sticking her pinkie in her ear and turning it. She scratched Lady's head with the other hand as the dog rested it on Piper's leg.

A sudden intense screaming came from downstairs. Seven or eight high-pitched wails were joined by a deeper, more terrified one.

Piper snickered. "I freaking *love* ghost night."

LOU SURVEYED THE CHAOS OF THE APARTMENT AND WAS quietly pleased. Piper was adjusting the chairs around Mel's kitchen table while Dani smoothed the white tablecloth with her hand. Konstantine was putting a dinner plate in front of each chair as Mel had instructed him to. And Lou remained on guard by the counter, standing between the foil-wrapped dishes that everyone had brought and a very hungry-looking Belgian Malinois.

"Don't try it," Lou said to her, and instead of cowering at such a tone, the dog's tail began to slap the kitchen tile hopefully.

"Does everyone have a wine glass?" Dani asked, placing a handful of silverware on the table. "If not, I can go get some from our apartment?"

Lou didn't miss the look shared between Dani and Piper at *our apartment*, the words punctuated by smiles.

"I think we have enough." Mel put the macaroni and cheese casserole in the center of the table. "But I miscounted the water glasses. Louie, can you grab me one more? It's in the cabinet behind your head."

Lou turned, opened the cabinet, and retrieved the glass.

"Thank you," Mel said, setting it beside one of the empty plates.

Piper was rubbing her hands together in front of the dishes lining the cabinet. "Oh my god, I'm so hungry I could eat the foil. When are we getting started? Everything's ready, isn't it?"

Lou counted heads. Five. Six, if she included the dog. "Where is King?"

"He went across the hall to get tongs for the meat."

"I thought I heard him go down the stairs." Konstantine came to stand beside her, his hip bumping hers as he bent to scratch the dog between her ears.

King burst into the apartment a moment later, and Piper jumped up to widen the door for him. "About time, man. I'm starving. Jesus, that smells good."

King put the turkey on the table and laid a large set of tongs and a carving knife beside it.

"I'm sorry, I got a text from Beth and I had to go down to talk to her."

"I thought she was heading out to have Thanksgiving with her son," Melandra said. "Everything all right?"

"Yes, she just wanted to say goodbye before she caught her flight."

Piper was nudging King with an elbow.

King's face was turning red. "She's just a very polite woman."

Konstantine leaned toward Lou and whispered in her ear, "What is going on?"

"King has a girlfriend." She made no effort to lower her voice.

"I do not," King said, coming to the sink to wash his hands. "We're just—"

"Having sex?" Lou offered.

"Does nothing embarrass you?" King said.

Lou couldn't recall the last time she'd been embarrassed. When she'd screwed up a kill, maybe.

"Man, I wish nothing embarrassed me." Piper moved up to the sink as soon as King was out of the way. Konstantine lined up behind her.

"Yes, everybody should wash their hands," Mel said, her bangles tinkling as she pushed her hair back from her face. She looked warm from the morning's efforts to get the meal on the table.

Dani must've seen what Lou saw. "Everything looks amazing, Mel. Thanks so much for having us."

Everyone said thank you.

"It was Mr. King's idea. I just supplied the dinner table."

No one was fooled by this, given they'd been in her apartment for the last hour, watching her try to get everything in place.

"Let's eat," King said, taking a seat. "It smells so good and

I'm starving. I want some of that spicy cornbread Dani brought."

Dani passed the breadbasket over.

Everyone took turns passing the dishes, filling up their plates. Lou almost laughed when she saw the tiny portions Konstantine had put on his.

"Americans do all the courses at once," she told him. "Just pile it on."

"But how will you know what you have and when you're full?"

"This is why he's so fit," Piper said. "Me? I intend to eat like a whale until my metabolism goes bust. And today is not that day!"

She punctuated this statement by plopping an extra spoonful of mashed potatoes onto her plate.

"Now before y'all eat," Melandra began, giving King a look as he shoved a slice of cut turkey into his mouth, "I want to hear what you're grateful for. I'll go first. I'm grateful for this meal and that I can share it with all of you." Then, after a pause, she added, "Also that my ex-husband is dead."

Piper snorted into her drink. "Good one."

Mel looked to King, who was sitting on her left.

King put his fork and knife down. "I'm also grateful for all of you."

"Copycat," Mel said. "Say something unique."

"And for new friends," he said, daring anyone to comment on this.

"Mmhmm." Mel looked to Piper, who sat on the other side of King.

Dani clasped her hands together as if in prayer. "I'm grateful that Konstantine and Octavia love each other so much, so that I can live with Piper."

"*Sì*," Konstantine said. He placed a hand over his heart

dramatically. "I adore her. She is so beautiful and soft, and her little face with those whiskers and—"

Lou nudged him, but Dani and Piper were laughing.

"I am grateful for Lady too," Piper said, and her hand went under the table.

"Don't give dogs turkey," King said. "It's bad for them."

"There's no turkey in my hand. It was a macaroni noodle."

"What are you really grateful for?" Melandra asked Piper.

"My new living arrangement? Have you seen her?" Piper leaned over and pinched Dani's cheeks, affecting a terrible Italian accent. "I adore her. She is so beautiful and soft and her little face with these whiskers!"

"Hey!" Dani cried. "I do not have whiskers. I waxed yesterday, thank you very much."

"Lou?"

Lou thought of Lucy, her bright blue eyes flashing across the screen of her mind. And the newfound knowledge of what La Loon's waters did to her every time she crossed. "My health. And that no one here is sick."

"Good one," King said. "Me too."

"Me three," Mel said.

"What about you, Konstantine?" Dani asked, tucking her hair behind her ears. "You're the only one who hasn't said what you're grateful for."

Konstantine looked at Lou.

Don't you dare, she thought.

With a smile and his arm stretched across the back of her chair, he said, "Gelato. I am very grateful for *gelato*."

Did you enjoy this book? Louie Thorne's story continues in *Overkill*, book 7 in the Shadows in the Water series.

GET YOUR THREE FREE STORIES TODAY

Thank you so much for reading *What Comes Around*. I hope you're enjoying Louie's story. If you'd like more, I have a free, exclusive Lou Thorne story for you. Meet Louie early in her hunting days, when she pursues Benito Martinelli, the son of her enemy. This was the man her father arrested—and the reason her parents were killed months later.

You can only read this story by signing up for my free newsletter. If you would like this story, you can get your copy by visiting ➜ www.korymshrum.com/lounewsletteroffer

I will also send you free stories from the other series that I write. If you've signed up for my newsletter already, no need to sign up again. You should have already received this story from me. Check your email and make sure it wasn't marked as spam! Can't find it? Email me at ➜ kory@korymshrum.com and I'll take care of it.

As to the newsletter itself, I send out 2-3 a month and host a monthly giveaway exclusive to my subscribers. The prizes are usually signed books or other freebies that I think you'll enjoy. I also share information about my current projects, and personal anecdotes (like pictures of my dog). If you want these free stories and access to the exclusive give-aways, you can sign up for the newsletter at ➜ www.korymshrum.com/lounewsletteroffer

If this is not your cup of tea (I love tea), you can follow me on Facebook at ➜ www.facebook.com/korymshrum in order to be notified of my new releases.

ACKNOWLEDGMENTS

We are here! Again. Seriously, why am I surprised every time a book is done? As you may have gathered, the writing life is not as solitary as one might think—or at least, certainly not the publishing part of it. I have many people to thank for turning my book into a real world creation, and if you've been reading the acknowledgments page of my other novels, you'll see the usual suspects.

Special thanks to my first readers: Kimberly Benedicto, Kathrine Pendleton, Angela Roquet, and Monica La Porta. They're always my first line of defense for all grammar and story issues. *Extra* special thanks to Monica in particular for her help with the Italian translations. *Grazie!*

Professional assistance included the always charming Toby Selwyn from across the pond. Thank you for sharing your keen editorial style with me. Another amazing cover from Christian Bentulan who has been with us since the series started, and of course, a shout-out to the lovely Alexandra Amor, my wonderful assistant, who formats all my books and also helps keep the business machine running so I can keep writing.

Last but not least, there's my amazing street team. You guys are always spotting those last minute typos and leaving the first reviews—two critical tasks required for each book's launch and subsequent success. You continue to show your love, support, and infectious enthusiasm for Lou and the team. To top it off, you tell your family and friends about my work and send loads of encouraging emails. All of this means more than you know!

So thank *you*!

ALSO BY KORY M. SHRUM

Fiction

Dying for a Living series

Dying for a Living

Dying by the Hour

Dying for Her: A Companion Novel

Dying Light

Worth Dying For

Dying Breath

Dying Day

Shadows in the Water: Lou Thorne Thrillers

Shadows in the Water

Under the Bones

Danse Macabre

Carnival

Devil's Luck

What Comes Around

Overkill

Castle Cove series

Welcome to Castle Cove

Night Tide

The City / 2603 novels

The City Below

The City Within

The City Outside

Jack and the Fire Eater

Poetry (as K.B. Marie)

Birds and Other Dreamers

Questions for the Dead

You Can't Keep It

Non-Fiction

Who Killed My Mother?

You can also support her on Patreon or visit her website to learn more about her work.